SAVAGE RAGE

BRENT PILKEY

ECW Press

Published by ECW Press
2120 Queen Street East, Suite 200, Toronto, Ontario, Canada M4E 1E2
416-694-3348 / info@ecwpress.com

This is a work of fiction. Names, characters, places, and incidents either are the product of
the author's imagination or are used fictitiously, and any resemblance to actual persons,
living or dead, business establishments, events, or locales is entirely coincidental.

LIBRARY AND ARCHIVES CANADA CATALOGUING IN PUBLICATION

Pilkey, Brent
      Savage rage / Brent Pilkey.

ISBN 978-1-77041-120-3
Also issued as:
978-1-77090-089-9 (PDF)
978-1-77090-088-2 (ePUB)

I. Title.

PS8631.I479S28 2012   C813'.6   C2012-902703-0

Cover and text design: Tania Craan
Cover images: ©Nuno Silva/iStock (man in hoodie); Marcus Lindström/iStock (blood)
Printing: Trigraphik   1   2   3   4   5

The publication of Savage Rage has been generously supported by the Canada Council
for the Arts which last year invested $20.1 million in writing and publishing throughout
Canada, and by the Ontario Arts Council, an agency of the Government of Ontario. We
also acknowledge the financial support of the Government of Canada through the Canada
Book Fund for our publishing activities. The marketing of this book was made possible
with the support of the Ontario Media Development Corporation.

Printed and bound in Canada

For Pegi and Dennis,
Mom and Dad

Thank you for everything
I love you both

A heartfelt thank you

When I wrote *Lethal Rage* there were times I couldn't type fast enough to keep up with my thoughts and I had the first draft done in three months. It was a selfish, joyful pleasure every time I sat down at the computer.

Then came time to write the second novel and that selfish, joyful pleasure became private, agonizing torture as, more times than not, I stared at a damned empty screen. I had the story in my head and knew where I wanted it to go but there were many times I just didn't know how to get there. *Savage Rage* took six months to write and would have taken a lot longer had it not been for the help of one special, amazing woman.

When the story ground to a halt or hit a brick wall, Mary was there to talk me through, over or around the impasse. If not for her help and input, *Savage Rage* would not be the book that it is.

So, thank you, Mary, with all my heart. In you I have found my Jenny.

Whoever fights the monsters should see to it that in the process he does not become a monster.
— Friedrich Nietzsche

Monday, 12 March
0230 hours

The wind had teeth.

Icy fangs tore at his exposed flesh, yet he smiled. The skin on his bare arms bristled at the wind's hostile caress, yet he stayed his ground, wrapped within the doorway's cold shadows. The hood of his sleeveless sweatshirt was pulled low over his brow, concealing his hunter's eyes beneath a second layer of darkness. The shirt's deep blue hue merged with the shadows, enveloping him in stillness.

He had learned the value of patience over the past four years. Confined and surrounded by enemies, those jealous or fearful of his status, he had learned to hunt. When to wait and when to strike. When to kill.

Now he was free and the city was his to hunt. So now he waited. And watched.

His prey, oblivious to the danger poised across the street, huddled against the wall of the community centre, seeking what refuge he could from the bitter wind. The building's south end and small parking lot were brushed by the yellow-orange hue cast from old and failing lights, and skeletal trees laid down sickly shadows in the flickering illumination. Beyond the community centre and its frozen playfields, a park lay encased in icy darkness.

His prey had been busy tonight despite the cold, busy selling. But now as the hour reached the heart of night, business was slowing. Only the most desperate of crackheads would be out at this time, in this cold. And a desperate crackhead was a money-less crackhead. His prey would soon be heading home.

The hunter's lips pulled back in a grinning snarl. The wait was almost over.

Marvin Gaye was cold. Fucking cold. Every time that bitching wind blew across the soccer field behind the community centre it cut through his jacket, shrivelling up his nuts as if he was standing balls naked. He couldn't stop shivering and when he stomped his feet they felt like clumps of ice shoved inside his Nikes. And his fingers burned. How could they be burning when it was so fucking cold?

He reluctantly freed his hands from what little comfort there was in his pockets to check his watch. Three o'clock. Fuck this, it was time to go home. Six hours standing out here was enough. Cold or not, it had been a good night. He had started the night with pockets empty of cash but filled with an eight-ball of crack to sell. He was down to the last of his crack — so little that he had it all stuffed down his crotch instead of hidden nearby — and had hundreds of dollars, mostly tens and twenties, squirrelled away in pockets, socks and underwear.

Marvin glanced at his watch again. Definitely time to go. Even the cops had stopped cruising by and scaring off his customers. Fucking pigs. But the cold had also worked in his favour, keeping the pigs inside their warm cars and off his back. The last thing he needed was another trip to the cells on a trafficking charge.

Marvin was a small-time dealer, just a step or two above a crackhead himself. He had been on the streets of downtown Toronto since he was fourteen, selling rock since he was seventeen and using since he was nineteen. At twenty-four, he was a burned-out old man, a wasted scarecrow of the boy named after his mother's favourite singer. If Marvin had ever known who his namesake was, the knowledge had long ago been burned away in the acrid smoke of his crack pipe.

Marvin was about to pack it in when he spotted a final sale coming his way. How did he know? With some, it was a familiar face. Others, a deep-set need in the eyes. But this one. . . .

"He must be hurting for a fix bad," Marvin laughed to

himself, watching the fool cross Queen Street, his arms startlingly bare. "Or he's one crazy-ass mother."

He waited impatiently, shivering inside his parka. How this fool could be out like that. . . . Marvin wrapped his hand around the knife tucked inside his coat pocket. If this fucker was crazy enough to let himself freeze to death, there was no telling what he would do.

"Hey, man, you looking?" he called out when the crackhead drew close, raising his voice to be heard over a gust of wind. The wind grabbed the crackhead's hood and snapped it off his head, revealing a scalp shaved clean on the sides, leaving only a band of short dark hair.

The man raised his head. Marvin saw eyes as cold as the wind and realized two things simultaneously: this was no crackhead and he was in deep shit.

Marvin tried to pull out his knife and that's when things got very bad. Very quickly. Very painfully.

The hunter waited until he saw the realization bloom in the dealer's face, then he smashed his fist into his prey's nose. Bone broke with a satisfying crunch. The dealer staggered back into the wall of the community centre, his left hand flying to his nose while his right swung a knife blindly in great, looping arcs.

The hunter swatted the knife away contemptuously, then drove his knee into the dealer's groin. The dealer was lifted onto his toes from the force of the blow before crumpling to his knees. Both hands clutched at his balls, the pain from his broken and bloodied nose forgotten, overwhelmed by the sheer agony ripping through his guts.

The hunter gripped the front of the dealer's coat and slammed him against the wall, then let the dealer slide down to an almost upright sitting position. He was crying now, openly bawling, and the hunter's guts rolled with distaste.

Fucking weak black bastard.

He jumped at the dealer, a vicious knee strike that smacked the dealer's skull against the bricks. This time the dealer didn't crumple so much as deflate, a balloon released with its tail untied. His eyes fluttered, then rolled back into his head as if he was trying to inspect the inside of his head for damage.

The hunter squatted down and casually looted the dealer's pockets. He did not rush; he had no fear of witnesses. Let them see. For soon his name would be known and feared by all the weak.

He transferred the dealer's profits to his own pockets, then rudely shoved his hand down the front of the man's pants. His hand groped among balls already swelling — had the dealer been conscious, the screams from his wounded testicles would have been enough to knock him out — and fished out the remaining half-dozen pieces of crack. They followed the money into his pocket. A treat for later.

The hunter wiped his hands on the guy's coat, then reached into the belly pocket of his sweatshirt, reaching for *it*. Erratic snowflakes sailed on the wind, flickering past his eyes in the sallow light. Its weight felt good in his hand. Solid. He ran his thumb over its dark, fierce edge carefully; it may be his, but it didn't care whose blood it drank.

That old fool Jeremiah had been right about one thing. *Turn to the good book, he had said and you will find your guide, your talisman.*

Well, he had found his talisman. How it had ended up in the prison yard was a mystery but as soon as he had seen it he knew it was meant to be his, his to use first behind bars and then on the streets he called home. Soon everyone would know those streets were his. Would know his name.

Not a full day after leaving captivity, it was time to take his first step into history.

The dealer's head hung limply. A line of bloodied drool dripped from his busted lip, dancing erratically before the wind snatched it away. He seized the dealer's jaw and shook his head till his eyes opened, focused. It would not do if he was unconscious for what was coming next. Not at all.

Still gripping the dealer's jaw, the hunter straddled his chest, pinning the dealer against the bricks with his weight. He raised his talisman slowly, reverently. Wide, frightened eyes clutched at the talisman but they were impotent to stay the hunter's hand. The talisman's edge lay on the dealer's forehead and the man flinched at its icy touch.

"Tell everyone who did this to you. Tell them and let them see."

The hunter bore down with the talisman, ripping flesh, digging for the hidden bone.

For Marvin Gaye, the pain went on forever.

Tuesday, 13 March
0017 hours

"5106, in your area. 339 George Street, the Seaton House. Male going berserk, attacking staff with a chair. Units to back up 5106? Time, 0017."

Jack's hands twitched on the steering wheel as the dispatcher voiced the hotshot. The urge to hit the lights and turn the scout car around was almost too strong to ignore. He took a deep breath and forced his hands to relax.

"Doesn't get any easier, does it?"

Jack glanced at the officer in the passenger seat and shook his head. "You'd think after three months up here I'd be used to it. Guess in my heart I'm still a 51 copper." He snorted. "Might be easier to forget I'm no longer down there if there was more going on up here."

His escort laughed but not without sympathy. "Welcome to 53 Division, Jack: the Sleepy Hollow of Toronto. Give it time, you'll get used to it." Brett Douglas spoke from experience, having transferred to the mid-city division after spending fourteen years in the shithole that was 14 Division. The two divisions, 51 and 14, were similar in nature: drugs and violence, and they bracketed 52 Division, the business and entertainment core of Toronto. As such, they were frequently referred to as the city's armpits.

Jack eased the car to a stop at the red light at Yonge Street and Eglinton Avenue. "How long did it take you to get used to the pace up here?"

"'Bout a year."

Jack groaned.

The light changed and Jack continued their slow crawl up Yonge Street. It was the first mild day after a cold winter and despite the hour, the streets and sidewalks were busy with people relishing the much-needed touch of spring. The snow still piled everywhere and the warmth had dropped from the air with the setting sun. The city could be dumped back into a deep-freeze tomorrow, but for tonight winter was in retreat and every club and pub was in full celebration mode. Jack even saw the odd open patio; he thought that was taking positive thinking to a new level of drunkenness.

Jack Warren, originally of 32 Division, lately of 51 and Officer of the Year, was bored out of his bloody mind. After spending the first six years of his career in the north-central part of the city writing traffic tickets and dealing with shoplifters, he had transferred to 51, affectionately known as the toilet, armpit and asshole of the city. In three brief months he had learned, painfully at times, the immense difference between being a police officer and being a street cop. And tragedy had scarred his life. His partner murdered, his wife taken hostage, himself seriously wounded at the hands of his partner's killer. But Jack had triumphed, avenging his partner and saving his wife. 51 had forged him in blood and fire and laid claim to his soul.

Now, half a year later, he was on his way to break up a house party. Oh . . . bloody . . . joy.

"Actually, Jack, I've never understood how you ended up here. After all the shit you went through, I'd've thought you would have had your pick of the squads. If you don't mind me asking, why *are* you here?"

Jack laughed and even to his ears it sounded bitter. Why, indeed. "It was a compromise. I wanted to stay in 51 and my wife, Karen, wanted me to quit policing altogether. When I told her 53 had no housing projects and was pretty much a dead spot, she agreed to let me work here."

"Agreed to let you?" Brett's voice held an amused note.

"It was either that or a divorce," Jack snapped.

"Hey, no offence meant," Brett pleaded, his hands held up in appeasement. "I'm all too familiar with an unpleasant home life."

"Sorry, Brett, I'm just so fucking bored here."

"That explains why you keep sliding down into 51 to help out with calls. Let me guess: your wife doesn't know that 53 borders the top end of 51 or that the divisions share the same radio band."

Jack smiled impishly. "I may have forgotten to mention that."

"But it was an honest mistake," Brett suggested.

"Absolutely," Jack agreed and they both laughed.

"Well," Brett proclaimed, "while 51 fights the good fight, we are on our way to rescue a poor teenager from his own stupidity."

"Speaking of that: it's gotta be a typo, right? *One hundred* unwanted guests? I can see one, or ten, but a hundred?"

"Nope, it happens a lot up here but more often at the end of the school year. Some kid's parents plan to go away for the weekend and Junior decides to invite a few friends over. By the time the weekend rolls around, word of the party has spread through the whole school and that little get-together becomes one big-ass party. By the time the house is getting trashed and there's an orgy on the parents' bed, Junior panics and calls us."

"Better call the ETF," Jack said dryly.

"Hey, you never know. We might get lucky and there could be some — dare I say it? — marijuana."

"Marijuana and drunk teenagers? I don't know if I can take the excitement."

"Hey, you have to take what excitement you can find in 53."

Jack goosed the car through a yellow light at Blythwood Road. "Why did you leave 14? It's like 51, isn't it? But with a different cultural makeup?"

"Oh, yeah," Brett agreed. "Drugs and all the shit that goes with them." He was silent for a moment, reflecting. "I guess I left because I didn't like the person I was turning into."

Jack looked at him. Brett didn't elaborate. "Meaning?"

"It's a story for another day." Brett sighed. "Let's just say that, after spending fourteen years among the shit of humanity, it starts to wear off on you." He was quiet again, then perked up. "But it's always nice to have that 14 or 51 copper inside you 'cause every once in a while he gets to come out and play and it scares the shit out of the pukes who have only dealt with spineless 53 coppers."

"Don't I know it." In the two and a half months Jack had spent on the road in his new division, he had actually seen cops back down or walk away from a confrontation. Not often and definitely not every cop, but even once was too many. "I still think you're right and they should go back to training divisions. Everyone should start in a shithole."

Brett nodded. "Certainly can learn a lot more than in a quiet place like this."

Jack enjoyed working with Brett. They were kindred spirits and had very similar views about policing. In particular, they weren't in favour of the touchy-feely style of community policing some of the brass were flaunting as the new direction for the Toronto Police Service. Hell, it wasn't all that long ago that it had been a force, not a service. But, of course, force had sounded too military, so the Toronto Police Service had been born.

Not that Jack and Brett were Neanderthals with badges, opting for brawn over brains. Not likely. Working in a shithole hammered home one lesson perfectly, and frequently: in a fight, anyone could get hurt. And lesson number two: whenever a cop got into a fight, there was at least one gun present. Why risk tangling with some guy and letting him get within reach of your gun if you could talk him into cuffs?

But, given the nature of the job, there were times when some knob just wouldn't listen to reason and it was off with the kid gloves and on with the leather ones lined with Kevlar. Sometimes brute force has a style all its own.

Jack turned onto Lawrence Crescent. The streets between Yonge Street and Mount Pleasant Avenue were lined with older, expensive homes and the neighbourhood oozed money. The division had too many neighbourhoods that oozed that way.

It wasn't hard to find the house. On a street where most people had already settled in for the night, one home was ablaze with lights. Cars crammed the driveway and overflowed onto the street. One ingenious driver had opted to park on the front lawn but had only made it halfway over the snowbank lining one side of the driveway.

Wonder if he was pissed before or after parking?

Jack stopped on the street in front of the house, clogging the last bit of clear roadway. It was either that, or park more than two blocks away and Jack wanted the scout car close by; he had a feeling someone could be leaving the party with them. Brett didn't comment on the parking.

They got out of the car and headed for the house. On the road, broken glass crunched underfoot and Brett had to step around a steaming puddle of vomit on the sidewalk. Standing at the bottom of the driveway, they surveyed the street. Cans and bottles, mostly beer but the odd wine bottle, littered the snow-covered front yards of several houses on both sides of the party house. Next door a youth was staggering barefoot in the snow, a beer can clutched in one hand and a queasy look on his face. *If he's old enough to drive, I'll volunteer to clean up the street; two guesses whose puke Brett stepped around.*

"I'd say we have enough grounds to shut down this party right now even if the complainant doesn't want to." Brett didn't sound impressed with what he was seeing.

"Absolutely." Neither did Jack.

There was another scout car parked in a neighbour's driveway, but there were no cops in sight. Jack and Brett headed up the driveway. The front walk looked like it hadn't been shovelled at all during the winter. They made their way down the side of the house, following a path of packed snow, to where a wood fence separated the driveway from the backyard. Three teens stood by a gate, beers in hand and none too steady.

And, of course, one decided to be an idiot.

"Sorry, officers, but this is a private party." He was smiling the type of shit-eating grin only a head full of booze can produce. "No pigs — I mean cops — allowed."

He was a big kid, but Brett was bigger. Standing six foot six and weighing a solid three hundred, Brett was bigger than most people. Only idiots or drunks would try to stop him from going where he wanted to.

Brett shoved the kid aside without stopping. The kid landed in a pile of slushy snow — warm weather and salt, just his luck — and struggled to get up, a look of indignant anger on his face.

Jack stopped in front of him. Jack was eight inches shorter and a hundred pounds or so lighter than Brett, but his words, delivered in an emotionless voice, didn't need size to back them up. "Is it worth spending the night in the hospital?"

The kid stayed in the snow. He wasn't as drunk as he looked.

Jack gave him and his buddies some advice. "I'd find someplace else to be. This party's about to be shut down."

He joined Brett by the gate. The big cop had a scowl on his face and his words matched. "I hate it when these little shits think they can do whatever they want 'cause Mommy and Daddy have money."

"Yeah, but it gives you a reason to introduce them to the 14 side of you."

The gate opened onto a large backyard, not so uncommon in a neighbourhood as established as this, and they found the party. Or at least the outside portion of it. The house had two floors; a single-storey sunroom jutted out at the back. The roof of this sunroom was a walk-out patio; Jack thought it would be a pleasant place to laze away the afternoons. That evening it was packed railing to railing with happy revellers. Jack had a fleeting concern the patio would end up in the sunroom. Not that it would have slowed anyone down, judging from the amount of alcohol in hand up there.

Brett must have come to the same conclusion. "Man, I'm getting buzzed just looking at all that booze."

Jack nodded and pointed to the back door. The two missing coppers from the other cruiser were knocking ineffectively on the door. They were a pair of older guys from the evening shift. If 53 had a quarter-century club like 51 had, for officers who had lasted twenty-five straight years in the division, these two would be founding members.

Only after it was obvious — painfully obvious in Jack's opinion — that no one was going to answer the door, or could even hear the knocking over the music blaring inside, one of the cops backed up a few steps to holler up at the patio. "Who's Eric? He called the police. We need to speak with him."

The officer's request was met with a chorus of abuse. A number of voices, most sounding drunk and all very loud, told the officers where they could go and what they could do with Eric when they got there.

The officers stepped back from the house as if they were being pelted with more than just words. They shared a look, shrugging in a unison that spoke of a long partnership, and gave their backs to the house. Jeers and more abuse rained down on them as they walked away. They passed Jack and Brett without making eye contact or saying a word.

It was the younger cops' turn to share a look.

"Oh, I don't think so," Jack said.

Brett was in full agreement. "No fucking way."

They approached the sunroom and Jack called out for Eric, the poor underage son of a bitch who was going to have a shit-load of explaining to do when his parents got home.

Bolstered by their successful repulsion of the first attack on their party, the crowd atop the sunroom — a goodly mix of high schoolers and university types, Jack thought — grew bolder still. Jack and Brett were assailed by shouts of "Fuck you!" "Fuck off!" and the catchy "Fuck you, you fucking pig fucks!" A few brave souls from deep within the mob and well out of sight tossed empty and not so empty plastic cups at them. The cups clacked jauntily against the paving stones.

Jack looked at Brett and saw his rising anger mirrored in the big man's eyes.

The verbal assault was growing louder but not much more imaginative until a beer bottle shattered on the ground next to Jack. A shocked silence dropped on the crowd after the sudden, shrill explosion. The partiers waited anxiously to see what the reaction would be. Playtime was very definitely over.

In the quivering silence, Brett asked Jack, "Do you want to kick in the door, or shall I?"

Jack extended his hand. *Be my guest.*

From what Jack could see through a window, the back door led to a kitchen. Brett yanked open the screen door, then found that the inner one was locked. Word from the patio — the cops are going to kick down the door! — must have sped to the kitchen; as Brett raised a fist to pound on the wood, locks clacked and the door snapped open.

But, not surprisingly, the police were not greeted with

heartfelt hospitality. The doorway was blocked by a university-aged kid dressed in boxer shorts, T-shirt and socks. He had a mean scowl on his face, but Jack thought, *It's hard to be intimidating when you're wearing just your undies.*

"You Eric?" Brett growled.

The scowl became a sneer. "No."

"Then get him."

Brett's growl was better than the kid's sneer, but Jack gave the kid marks for balls; he didn't back down.

"He's busy. He says you can go away."

It wasn't often Brett had to look up when talking to someone. That must have been why the kid had been appointed door guardian. Again, Jack gave the kid points for balls. *But balls without brains will only get you hurt. Ask the beer-drinking moron in the driveway.* Door Guardian might have been taller than Brett, but Jack doubted he was half Brett's weight.

"Move," Brett said, stepping forward.

That's when Door Guardian went from ballsy and stupid to just plain stupid. "You can't come in here," he declared and straight-armed Brett in the chest. He might as well have punched an oak tree. A moving oak tree.

Brett kept going forward and when he shoved, the kid flew a good three feet. The only reason he didn't go farther was that he hit a wall. He hit hard enough to rattle the shelves above him, then slid to his butt, a dazed, what-the-hell-just-happened expression on his face.

Brett stepped into the kitchen and Jack was right behind him, giving Door Guardian a cautionary "Stay down" as he walked past.

The kitchen was a crowded mess. Pizza boxes and empty bottles littered every available surface: table, countertops, island. Someone had put a lot of money into upgrading the kitchen and was going to be royally pissed when he or she saw it. One cupboard door had a fist-sized hole in it and another two were hanging from broken hinges. The stainless-steel fridge sported several dents in its door and the pot rack that should have been hanging above the island was a metallic garbage pile on the floor.

Brett stopped in the middle of the room, commanding the attention of the dozen or so teens present. Most of them looked nervous and darted glances at Door Guardian, who had yet to regain his feet. Brett didn't raise his voice; he didn't need to. The party was still in full stride outside the kitchen, but in here it was dead and everyone knew it.

"I want Eric in front of me in the next ten seconds. I won't ask twice."

Two kids bolted from the room and another took a more direct approach. He leaned into the next room and yelled, "Eric! Someone get Eric in here, right fucking now!"

Moments later — it might have been more than ten seconds but not by much — a very frightened yet relieved-looking Eric scampered into the kitchen. His sock feet slid in a puddle of something and he would have ended up planting his ass in the puddle had Brett not grabbed him by the arm. Brett hauled him upright, none too gently and planted him on his feet.

Eric was the type of person who had "Kick Me" permanently taped to his back. Small, scrawny and pimpled, wearing glasses, he was natural bully fodder.

Could this kid be any more of a stereotypical geek? Jack felt pity, remembering his pudgy high school years.

"Are you Eric?" Brett asked, fixing the trembling teen with a steeled stare.

The kid gulped audibly. "Yes, sir."

The music cut off in mid-blare and its sudden absence left a hollow feeling in the air. It was as if the party was sitting on the electric chair, waiting to see if the last-minute reprieve would come through.

"Did you call the police, Eric?"

"Yes, sir." Strike one.

"Did you invite all these people into your house?"

"No, sir." Strike two.

Brett lifted his gaze to take in everyone in the kitchen or peering in from the living room. "And do you want us to remove all these people?"

Eric hesitated, no doubt weighing the wrath of his parents against the ostracism he would face at school. He glanced at the group behind him, then at Brett. He licked dry lips. "Yes, sir." Strike three. Throw the switch, boys.

"Good call."

Brett and Jack waded into the living room, the crowd parting before them almost magically. The living room had fared better than the kitchen, but the carpet was shot to hell. No amount of steam cleaning would remove the spilled drinks, mashed food and mud from what Jack was willing to bet had previously been a pristine white carpet.

"Listen up!" Brett announced. "This party is over. Put your drinks down and leave by the front door. And I mean now."

There were quiet grumbles and protests, but soon a reluctant but steady stream of kids snaked out the front door.

Once the crowd was moving, Jack headed for the stairs to flush out the second floor. He rousted two couples out of bedrooms then made his way to the master bedroom. The parents' — the soon to be very surprised parents' — bedroom was a grand affair dominated by a huge four-poster bed. Sliding glass doors, one of them cracked — Jack was willing to bet the damage was pretty damn recent — led to the rooftop patio. He didn't have to open the doors; one of them was already wide open and letting in one hell of a draft. *Next heating bill's going to be a bitch.* He stepped onto the deck.

"Party's over, everyone. Get out."

"Fuck that, we don't have to leave."

Jack was startled by the voice behind him but tried not to let it show as he looked over his shoulder. A guy definitely too old to be in high school was coming into the bedroom, buttoning his fly.

Didn't check the bathroom, Jack. Getting sloppy.

The newcomer was wearing a University of Toronto leather jacket open over a bare chest. The muscle on display and the perfected swagger screamed jock; the graduation date on the jacket sleeve was from two years earlier and suggested either a grad still hanging out with the university crowd or an idiot who didn't spend enough time studying. Jack was willing to bet on the idiot explanation.

"Sorry, bud, the party's over and everyone has to leave. You first." Jack pointed to the door.

Jockhead screwed his face up and dismissed Jack with a flick of the fingers as he brushed by.

Jack clamped a hand onto his right arm and pulled him back. "I said, you have to —"

Jockhead ripped his arm free and then proved how stupid he really was: he spat in Jack's face. "Fuck you, pig!" He turned to the partygoers while giving Jack the finger.

Jack's anger blazed hot and sudden. Better had the kid just punched Jack: assaulting a cop got you arrested, spitting on one landed you in the hospital. Jack reached for Jockhead, the rest of the party people forgotten.

"All right, fuckhead, you're under —"

The jock spun and Jack saw the fist coming. He jerked his head at the last instant and took a glancing blow to the cheek. Jockhead was cocking his right arm for a haymaker when Jack dug his hands into the jacket collar and pulled the kid forward into a crushing head butt. Jack's forehead smashed squarely into Jockhead's nose. Bone cracked, blood erupted.

The watching crowd *oohed* at the brutal impact and gasped as Jockhead fell limp in Jack's hands. Jack looked into Jockhead's unfocusing eyes. "You're under arrest."

Satisfied he wasn't going to get any immediate resistance from his prisoner, Jack faced the crowd. "Get out. Now."

He stood impassively as the partiers, considerably sobered up after what they had witnessed, scurried past him. Some even mumbled apologies. It wasn't long before the patio belonged to Jack and the still-dazed Jockhead.

Brett came into the bedroom, glancing back as the last of the partiers hurried down the stairs. Then he looked at the bloodied man sagging in Jack's grip. Unfazed, he simply said, "I bet that's going to be a complaint."

"I'll say that's going to be a complaint," Manny laughed, munching on a cookie then washing it down with hot chocolate. "Lawsuit, too, probably."

"Gee, thanks for the support."

"C'mon, dude. This just proves what I've been saying since you started up here: putting a 51 copper in 53 is like putting a shark in the guppy tank."

Jack snickered. "I don't think it's quite that bad."

The scout cars were parked driver's side to driver's side — the universal position for a police coffee meet — in the Loblaws parking lot at the top of the Bayview Avenue hill, just a stone's throw inside 53 Division.

"The man has a point, Jack. You belong in 51." Paul Townsend was one of the biggest and blackest men in 51.

"Ah, the sleeping giant awakes."

"Had court all day, Jack. Have to get my beauty sleep sometime. Might as well get paid for it." Paul stretched massively muscular arms — although wrapped in the bulky uniform parka they simply seemed massive — and cracked his neck from side to side.

"I don't think anyone will blame you for napping all of ten minutes, dude. Did you get any sleep after court?"

Paul shook his head and flashed an amazingly white smile at the same time. "Was gonna, but the old lady wanted to have some fun. If you know what I mean." He playfully nudged Manny and knocked him into the driver's door. Paul was an inch shorter than Brett and had a physique most professional bodybuilders would kill for. He was also stupidly strong, as Manny could attest to.

Manny slowly straightened up, rubbing his left shoulder. "Easy, dude, I need that arm to shoot."

"Baby," Paul scoffed.

Jack grinned at the banter. God, how he missed working with these guys. Paul was one of the nicest people to ever wear the uniform and could quiet a room just by walking into it. If he and Brett paired up, they'd be their own two-man riot squad.

At six feet, Manny carried his own share of muscle but disguised it beneath good eating. As he explained it, he had washboard abs like Paul but had a load of towels in the wash. His shaved head disguised a retreating hairline; his non-regulation goatee was made legal by a thin strip of hair along his jaw. Manny was not your average-looking cop. But then, he was a unique individual.

Manny — William Armsman to most supervisors — was an excitable puppy on a leash. He and Jack had shared a strong partnership until Jack ended up in snoozeville, a.k.a. 53 Division. They hadn't worked together long but had gone through some definite shit and Jack knew he could always trust Manny to have his back. Manny had a huge heart and a huge mouth — the mouth seemed to get him in the sergeants' sights too often when it worked without consulting his brain — and threw himself into the job with a childlike enthusiasm.

"You okay, Brett? Did I get your coffee wrong?" Manny asked Jack's passenger.

Brett started as if Manny had roused him from a deep sleep. "Um, no. Sorry. Coffee's fine."

"Cool. Just checking."

"Is there a SOCO on the air in 51?"

The call came over the radio and Manny promptly snatched up the mike. "5105, talk to me," he said, using his best film noir voice.

"I need you at a B and E for prints and photos."

"10-4, on the way. Dispatch, could you put us on that call?" Manny revved the engine then dropped the car into drive. "Sorry, dudes. Duty calls. I'm off to solve another crime. Later."

Watching the tail lights disappear down Bayview, Brett asked, "How can a guy that hyper stay still long enough to dust for fingerprints?"

"I've often wondered that myself." Jack started up the car. "Well, it's four a.m. in 53. Do you want to cruise the quiet neighbourhoods or the quiet commercial areas?"

Once the bars closed for the night, all activity in 53 generally vanished. Jack sighed. This had always been his favourite time in 51: except for the odd one or two, radio calls were pretty much done for the night and it would be time to play. And playtime in 51 meant chasing the drug dealers. In 53, the second half of any night shift was a struggle to stay awake.

"I miss 51," he muttered as he pulled out of the lot.

"How you holding up, hon?" Karen eased in beside Jack and he slipped an arm around her waist.

Smiling for the other guests, he turned to her and whispered in her ear, "I'm freaking dying."

From one house party to another. And this one was nowhere near as fun as the one he and Brett had broken up the night before.

No, this morning. Today, I think. It's still Tuesday, right? Ah, the joys of shift work.

After busting up the party and leaving poor Eric to clean up as best he could while contemplating his future — if it had been a teenaged Jack and his dad, death would have been a definite possibility — they had taken Jockhead, also known as Matthew

Covingston, to the station. After a stopover at Sunnybrook Hospital, that was. Jockhead's nose had indeed been broken and by the time he was released from the station hours later, he had two beautiful shiners bracketing his nose splint.

As he had left the station, Jockhead had sworn revenge, screaming an all too familiar refrain in 53 Division: "I'll sue your ass! My mom's a lawyer!"

Jack rarely slept well on night shift anymore. Seven years ago, as a squeaky-clean rookie, he was able to sleep anywhere, anytime, but not anymore. Now, after a poor day's sleep, he was at his in-laws' house in Stouffville pretending to enjoy himself while all he wanted was to be somewhere else. Anywhere else.

Karen's dad, good old George Hawthorn Sr. — *Oops, forgot the Doctor, sorry, George* — had published yet another book and was throwing a Congratulations to Me party. He and the missus, Evelyn Hawthorn — no pretentious "doctor" or "senior" attached to her name — had invited several dozen of their closest friends to help Hawthorn stroke his ego. At least that's how Jack saw it.

Hawthorn taught political science at the University of Toronto and his most recent book of six was yet another tome on the post-economic, socially destructive mating habits of the rich and egotistical. Or something like that. Jack's eyes glazed over while Hawthorn was regaling his captive audience with his book's incredible insights. Jack had to admit, Hawthorn was intelligent and no doubt his writing would be beyond Jack's comprehension, but why that didn't excuse him from this fabulous shindig, Jack couldn't say.

But that was sheer bullshit, wasn't it? Jack knew perfectly well why he was here.

Hawthorn resented that his only daughter was married to someone as common as Jack, someone who had not even finished university and was a public servant and, yes, stress the *servant* part. There was an older son, George Jr., and he was off somewhere adding letters after his name and no doubt Hawthorn had expected his daughter to marry someone of equal education. All through their dating, engagement and marriage, Jack's in-laws slapped him down at every chance. And not just good old Dad but both of them, for Evelyn could be just as condescending toward Jack as her husband, although she disguised it as a mother's natural belief that no man was good enough for her daughter. His upbringing, his education, his job, his salary — none of it was good enough for their daughter.

At first, Jack had hoped they would grow to accept him as they realized his presence in Karen's life was more than just temporary. But that had been foolish thinking. If anything, their dislike of the future son-in-law had grown in direct proportion to the relationship. In time, it had become a mutual dislike and distrust, especially with Hawthorn. By the time Jack and Karen were married — on Hawthorn's bill, of course. Can't let the useless son-in-law forget that, can we? — Evelyn had become a side player in the game and the game was simple: every chance he got, Hawthorn reminded Jack that he was unworthy of his daughter and Jack would grin and take it, refusing to respond to the demeaning questions, comments and oh so subtle displays of wealth and breeding.

And why did Jack take it? Why did he tolerate being Hawthorn's punching bag? Because he loved Karen, who idolized her father. She was aware of the tension between the two men in her life and did her best to soothe both of them. For her father, she continued her education despite working full time as a public-school teacher and attended his social functions, smiling and chatting politely with the eligible suitors he paraded before her. Soothing Jack was much easier and considerably more fun. He often wondered what Hawthorn would say if he found out just how uninhibited his special little girl could be.

Jack smiled and sipped his cider. He had developed a liking for it after Manny introduced him to it at a beach party the previous year and now he always brought his own supply to any function of Hawthorn's. Savouring the tart taste, he let his free hand slide down from Karen's waist. He knew she was wearing stockings and a garter belt under her little black dress; she had shown him outside their SUV before the long trek up the driveway. A down payment on the reward he would receive later for enduring the party and he liked to remind himself by feel every so often.

For the moment, Jack was chatting with a couple closer to his age — twenty-nine in a few months, closing in on the big three-oh — than most of the other guests. Whether it was the age or that Scott was the only other guy Jack had seen not wearing a tie didn't matter. Age and an aversion to ties were about the only things they had in common, but they tried.

"Play any tennis, Jack?" Scott asked.

"No. Played some rugby in university. You?"

"Sorry. Do you sail?"

"Some canoeing in the summer."

The small talk fell into a lull and both men filled the gap by taking a drink, Jack his bottled cider and Scott something straight over ice. They were standing by the fireplace, enjoying the warmth and sound as the flames licked the real logs. No gas fireplace for Hawthorn. Jack found it slightly annoying that he agreed with his father-in-law on this one thing. But then again, Hawthorn had had the brick painted and Jack thought anyone who covered up brick or stone with paint was an idiot.

"Your parents have a beautiful home, Karen." Scott resorted to gesturing with his drink hand.

"It is, isn't it?" Karen gave Scott a stunning smile and Jack noticed Scott's wife's eyes narrowing almost imperceptibly. "Mom and Dad just moved in, although they bought it some time ago. It took a while for the contractors to get everything done."

Trust Hawthorn to buy a fixer-upper, a freaking huge fixer-upper, then hire someone else to do all the work. His idea of do-it-yourself was writing the cheques. The house was a turn-of-the-century estate and Jack had to admit Hawthorn's money had been well spent; the old home was magnificent. Jack's only problem with the place, other than the painted fireplace, was its location. Stouffville was a beautiful historic town just north of Toronto and far too close for his liking. Jack would have preferred it if Karen's parents had moved somewhere a touch farther away. Alaska, for instance.

Scott was a likable enough fellow, but, like the rest of the high-end guest list, he was unwilling to ask about Jack's work. No doubt they all knew the story, Hawthorn's version at least, of how Jack had witnessed his partner's murder then shot the killer to death inside Jack's home after his wife, Hawthorn's only precious daughter, had been taken hostage. Jack wasn't quite sure what spin his father-in-law put on the story when he told it but was sure it was not favourable to him. It was as if they all saw Jack as some savage animal or barbarian, only marginally tamed and totally unpredictable.

Don't ask him about work, my dear, you may provoke him and there's no telling what he'll do. Did you know he killed a man? And right in front of George's poor daughter. Poor George, having such a brute for a son-in-law.

Lillian, Scott's wife, was a very beautiful Asian woman with a slinky red dress that seemed a touch too risqué for a cocktail party, but then maybe she was enjoying the slightly annoyed and peeved looks the other wives were shooting her way. Jack wondered if she had shown her husband what underwear she was, or wasn't, wearing before coming to the party. She stepped in to save the two floundering men.

"Do the two of you have children?" she asked, her voice no more than a breathy whisper.

Jack let Karen field that question; it was one of her favourites. She shook her head, tumbling her long blonde hair about her shoulders. Jack cast a quick look between the women, eyebrow raised curiously. He couldn't detect any hostility, but if that little hair manoeuvre wasn't some kind of challenge he'd sit down and gladly read Hawthorn's book cover to cover.

"We don't have any children yet," Karen replied, her voice soft and not dangerous at all. "We hope to start a family soon, though. And you?"

Lillian smiled, a mere baring of teeth. "We haven't decided yet, but that doesn't stop us from practising." She curled herself seductively around Scott's arm.

Jack had seen guys get in territorial pissing contests and out-right fights, but this was the first time he'd been ringside to an alpha-female scrap.

Scott must have figured something was up as well, for he was quick to add, "Any dogs, Jack? We have two French bulldogs."

"I'd love to have a dog," Jack said as he felt the tension ease in Karen. Ease, but not disappear. "But Karen wants to wait until after we have kids."

Scott wanted to know why. Lillian was content to remain quiet, smiling sweetly at Karen every now and then.

"I think it's best to wait until the children are older," Karen explained. "It's safer that way."

"Nonsense," Scott scoffed. "Dogs and babies get along just fine."

"That's what I keep telling her," Jack said. "I grew up with black Labs. Hell, my dad's dog was considered the firstborn son."

"Oh, no," Karen disagreed, shaking her head, and this time there was nothing flirtatious or subtle about it. "My parents had a dog when they were first married and they had to get rid of it when my brother was born. Isn't that right, Dad?"

Hawthorn had obviously decided to see what the barbarian was up to and had casually sidled over to the small group. Jack saw with petty satisfaction that, as he approached, Hawthorn noticed Jack's hand resting on the curve of Karen's buttock. He tried to keep his face pleasant, but a tightening around the good doctor's eyes gave him away. Jack hugged his wife a touch closer.

"Is what right, sweetheart?" Hawthorn had a deep, rolling voice that must have sounded impressive in lecture halls. Jack bet he practised it before going to bed at night.

"You had to get rid of your dog when George was born."

Hawthorn nodded solemnly. Jack groaned inwardly. All Hawthorn needed was a tweed jacket and pipe to complete his Serious Professor look. But Jack had to admit his father-in-law was a good-looking man. A full head of hair, black but greying — distinguishingly, mind you — and a clean-shaven, strong jaw gave him an enviable look. Despite being an avid runner, like his daughter, he was starting to develop a bit of a paunch, Jack noted. Again, with petty satisfaction.

"Dogs and babies just don't socialize that well," Hawthorn explicated for those less knowledgeable and experienced than he. "Canines will commonly grow jealous of the newborn, seeing the baby as an intrusion into the family pack. Unfortunately, this jealousy can at times result in attacks on the infant."

A few other guests had joined the group with Hawthorn. To Jack they were nothing more than parasites, weak social feeders trailing in Hawthorn's wake hoping to improve their status by sheer proximity to the professor. They were nodding wisely in agreement. Normally, Jack wouldn't have bothered to contradict his father-in-law in public; Hawthorn was a natural debater adept at twisting an argument to his advantage, not caring if his opinion was correct, but this was something too close to Jack's heart to ignore.

"Or," Jack offered, "if the parents are responsible enough, they don't ignore the dog. They make him part of the baby's world. My parents said Shamrock slept under my crib and was very protective of me."

"I'm surprised your parents valued . . . Shamrock, was it? . . . so much that they would be willing to risk their son for the sake of a dog." Hawthorn smiled to take the sting out of his words. Not that he was criticizing Jack's upbringing . . . again. "Evelyn and I weren't prepared to needlessly endanger George Jr. or Karen. Anyone who truly loved Karen would never even entertain the notion." Hawthorn smiled slyly as he rammed the barb home.

Karen slipped a calming hand over Jack's and Jack drew a calming breath, his angry words held in check. Typical of Hawthorn to turn every topic into an attack on Jack. As if it was his fault that Anthony Charles had invaded their home and threatened to kill Karen and Jack. And no need to mention that it was because of Jack that Karen was alive today.

A stillness befell the little group, as though they sensed the abrupt and sinister change in the conversation. The bottom feeders were watching their idol closely, adoring faces canted so as not to miss Hawthorn's obliteration of his clearly inferior son-in-law. Jack was aware of the attentive silence, Karen's hand holding, almost clutching, his against her hip, a soundless plea for civility, the fire popping at his back as a knot exploded. Lillian's eyes were fixed on him, watching hungrily, wetting her lips in anticipation of a fight. All this Jack saw and felt in the space of two heartbeats. His thoughts were clear, much as they were whenever he got into a fight on the streets. And what had Hawthorn's snipe been other than an opening jab?

"A parent's first concern should be his child, don't you think so, Jack?" Hawthorn smiled pleasantly, but his stare was challenging. He sipped his drink, the ice clinking loudly in the silence.

"Of course," Jack agreed, hoping to turn this reasoning against Hawthorn. "And any loving pet owner would extend the same consideration to the animal or, at the very least, ensure the pet went to a good home."

"Who did you give the dog to, Dad? I can't remember," Karen said innocently.

Hawthorn favoured his daughter with what Jack thought was a very indulgent smile, as if she had made a poor assumption. "We didn't, dear. He wasn't a pup any longer and a change of ownership would have been just too traumatic on the poor fellow. We had him put down. It was the humane thing to do."

"You what?" Jack hissed. "How old was he?" He already knew in his heart what Hawthorn would say but prayed even he couldn't be that uncaring.

"I can't exactly recall, Jack," Hawthorn said with a hint of hesitation in his voice. If no one else in the group had heard the tightness in Jack's words, Hawthorn certainly had.

And Jack wasn't about to let this go. "How old? Five, ten, twelve?"

"Evelyn and I had had him only a short while," Hawthorn mused, eyeing Jack warily. "No more than four, I'd say."

Jack was speechless but not for long. He pulled his hand free of Karen's — desperate, Karen tried to keep hold of his, but he would not be restrained — and turned to face Hawthorn. "Four years old and you put him down?"

"Of — of course," Hawthorn stammered, obviously wondering what he had said to upset his barbaric son-in-law.

"You lazy, uncaring asshole."

"Jack!" Karen reproached, shocked by her husband's sudden anger.

But Jack didn't hear her or didn't care. He was too enraged to see or hear anyone in the room other than Hawthorn. "You could have found him a home," he snarled. "Or a rescue society or the pound. Anywhere he could have been adopted. But that would have been too much effort for you, wouldn't it? And it was just a dog after all. You lazy, selfish . . ." Jack's words trailed off, consumed by his hate.

"Now, listen to me —"

"How typical of you, Hawthorn." Jack's voice was almost a whisper, but it quivered with anger. "To kill an innocent animal — a pet, no less! — out of ignorance. No, it wasn't ignorance, was it, Hawthorn? That would suggest you'd not known any better and we both know the truth, don't we? The dog was nothing but a possession, right? Bought to project that wholesome family image until you and the missus could upgrade to a child. And when an object's usefulness has come to an end? Why, simply dispose of it. You make me sick, Hawthorn."

Jack's hands were curled into fists, the knuckles of the hand still clasping the bottle of cider white with strain. God, how he wanted to smash Hawthorn. To drive his fists into that self-righteous, snobbish face and feel bones break beneath his knuckles.

Slowly, the red haze receded. Jack became aware of the shocked silence in the room. The silence had weight, an anticipatory feel, as if those watching were waiting breathlessly for Jack to act on his unspoken threat of violence. Hawthorn had taken a step back, his drink clutched to his chest, his free hand raised somewhat defensively. His followers had moved back as well, eyeing Jack cautiously.

Then Karen was there, whispering his name, concern and fear in her voice. Jack forced himself to relax, to back away from that mindless rage. He eased open his fists, felt the joints creak with the release. The tension that had gripped him dissipated, vanished as quickly as it had seized him.

Had he almost hit Hawthorn? Jack knew he had wanted to, but how close had he come to an actual assault? Judging from the shocked faces turned toward him, it had been too close.

Muttering a quick "Excuse me," Jack strode from the room, too proud and embarrassed to hurry in front of Hawthorn and his peers.

"Jack." Karen reached for him as he pulled away, then started to follow him.

Her father laid a restraining hand, gentle but firm, on her shoulder. "Don't, honey. It's not safe. Can't you see what he is?"

"Not now, Dad." Red eyed, she pulled free of his hand much as Jack had pulled away from hers.

Hawthorn watched her go, at a rare loss for words. How do you tell your only daughter that the man she married is dangerously unstable? He had always suspected Jack was capable of violence, long before Jack had transferred downtown. Karen believed the atmosphere of the division, the daily exposure to the dregs of humanity, had darkened her husband's soul, his mind. But Hawthorn knew better. The division hadn't changed Jack, it had freed what had already been inside him and what was now loose, could never be caged again, regardless of where he worked.

Jack's true nature had shown itself the previous fall when Hawthorn and Evelyn had agreed to help Karen confront Jack about his descent into barbarism. When faced with rational, logical arguments, Jack had responded with anger — rage, even — and threats of violence. Hawthorn was man enough to admit his son-in-law had frightened him that evening, standing over him, fists clenched, his eyes devoid of any sane, lucid reasoning.

From the first time Karen had brought him home, Hawthorn had recognized Jack for what he was. A savage, pure and simple.

"That was rather unsettling," Scott commented from beside Hawthorn. "Jack seems . . . unhinged, I'd say. I can now completely understand your concern for your daughter."

Hawthorn glanced at Scott, a junior professor at the university who was rumoured to "grade" female students behind closed doors. Perhaps that was why his wife — Lillian, was it? — was staring after Jack in such a predatory way.

Savages, the lot of them. Hawthorn only hoped he had time to save Karen before she became one of them or fell victim to his son-in-law's brutality.

Karen caught up to Jack on the circular driveway, the crushed gravel grinding loudly under her steps in the cold air. He was standing in front of the fountain — lifeless and sad as it waited, frozen, for spring — with his back to the house. He hadn't bothered with his coat; he had his hands jammed in the pockets of his sports jacket. As Karen neared him, she couldn't help but notice, with his shoulders hunched against the cold and his hands pulling down on the jacket, the rust-coloured material was strained across his back, emphasizing its width.

Karen had always admired his dedication to a fit lifestyle and had spent many pleasurable hours exploring his hard body, muscular yet not freakishly huge like that Schwarzenegger whose movies Jack enjoyed. When he had paired up with Simon, he had spent more time lifting weights than running and had started to grow before her eyes. She thought it would be a temporary indulgence, a way of integrating himself into the new division's social culture. But it wasn't temporary. One kitchen cabinet was devoted to protein powders, amino acids and an array of vitamin and mineral supplements. Bodybuilding magazines appeared in the house. Karen had flipped through one, repulsed yet oddly enthralled by the grotesque physiques. She asked Jack if that was his goal: to be so muscular that he resembled a cartoon superhero. He laughed and assured her, no, he only wanted to get a bit larger and besides, he didn't have the genetic makeup to get that big. To get to superhero size, he'd have to go the steroid route and she didn't have to worry about that.

Now as Karen approached, wrapped tight in her fur coat — a present from her parents the previous Christmas — with his trench coat in her arms, she wondered again about steroids. As soon as Jack had recovered from his gunshot wound — God, how she hated thinking about that — he had been back in the gym, more obsessed than ever. He had been off work until the end of the year and had spent six days a week at the gym, sometimes close to their home, sometimes driving into the city to work out with Manny.

It was as if Jack was physically punishing himself for Sy's death, or the attack on her, or both. Perhaps he was running away from a guilty conscience or hoping to hide in dreamless sleep after exhausting himself physically. His nightmares had become less frequent in the past few weeks. Immediately following the incident — a word Karen preferred over "attack" or "home invasion" — Jack had been plagued with horrific dreams and had repeatedly screamed himself awake. He refused to talk about the nightmares, saying only that they were almost gone now, so infrequent to be of no consequence.

Then he had gone back to work. Although Karen hated the thought of him wearing that uniform, she was at least comforted by knowing he was out of 51 and stationed in a much safer part of the city. She hoped he would come to realize policing was not the career path for him. He was so intelligent and dedicated, he could work just about anywhere, in any field that interested him. And if he wanted to go back to school to get his degree, something that would please her — she never told him, but the fact that he had never finished university still bothered her — she was more than willing to handle the additional financial burden. And they could always borrow money from her parents.

As she slipped the coat over his shoulders, his ever-widening shoulders, she wondered if Jack would ever give up being a cop. And she worried about steroids. The new muscle, the shorter temper, unexplained and inappropriate outbursts . . .

He turned his face to her and smiled. A sad, weary smile. "Sorry, hon. I don't know what came over me."

She laid her chin on his shoulder. With her in heels and him hunched over, it was easy for her to do. "That's all right. Why don't we just go home?"

The wipers beat a slow rhythm on the windshield, intermittently swiping away snowflakes. Spring was close, close enough to feel in the afternoon sunshine, but with the sun banished winter still held sway. It wasn't late, not yet ten o'clock, but the sky, heavy with swollen, pregnant clouds, was as dark as the deepest of night. The Honda's headlights cut a hazy path on the road. Jack could have taken the highway, the faster route home, but chose the less travelled rural roads. Open farmland, still blanketed in snow, alternated with swaths of evergreen forest and suited his current frame of mind. He grinned to himself, the grin sardonic in its bitterness. He was definitely in no mood to deal with speeding, aggressive drivers.

"That's a sad smile, hon," Karen observed from the passenger seat.

"Yeah," he muttered, then more openly, "sorry again for ruining the evening, Kare. I don't know what happened. One minute I was enjoying the party and the next . . ." He shook his head. "I don't know. I guess I just lost it."

It was Karen's turn to smile. "Come on, Jack. You *never* enjoy yourself at my parents' parties."

"Okay, you got me there," he laughed.

"That's better. I don't like seeing you all tense and . . ."

"Ugly?" Jack suggested.

"No," she rebuked gently. "I was going to say troubled." She placed a comforting hand on the back of his neck. "Do you want to talk about it?"

He shrugged. "Not much to say, really. When your dad said he put the dog down . . . I guess it just hit a nerve, that's all." He gave her a sheepish smile; he knew how weak it sounded.

"You really have a soft spot for dogs, don't you? Maybe you should get one."

Jack glanced quickly at Karen to see if she was joking. "I thought you wanted to wait until we had kids."

It was her turn to shrug. "Maybe we should think about it. Just so long as it isn't too big."

He grinned again, happily this time. "No more than a hundred pounds, I swear."

"I said a dog, not a horse." She tweaked his ear playfully, then went back to stroking his neck. "How are you feeling, Jack? Really? The nightmares haven't come back, have they?"

He looked at her, puzzled. "No. Why do you ask?"

"You're restless at night sometimes. Not like you used to be." She shuddered, remembering the nights Jack screamed himself awake. He never described the dreams in detail, but he said enough for her to know the nightmares involved someone dying. Sy, her or himself. "Do you think you should see Dr. David again?"

"Don't think so," he said, casually dismissing the idea. Dr. Michael David was the psychiatrist Jack had seen following the home invasion and shooting. The weekly sessions had been suggested, very strongly suggested, by the service's medical bureau. Jack had gone to them but without much conviction. Dr. David — call me Mikey — was a decent guy who had understood Jack wasn't there by choice and he had dealt with enough reluctant coppers to know not to push. Their sessions had usually followed the same script each week.

How was Jack sleeping?

Better all the time. Getting close to eight hours each night.

Were the nightmares still bad?

Nightmares are always bad, that's why they're called nightmares. But getting less and less frequent.

How was Jack's energy? Concentration? Mood?

And so on and so on.

All that Jack had taken away from his time in Dr. David's comfortable — and damned expensive, Jack was willing to bet — office was that nightmares and bad dreams were to be expected; a sense of guilt, as long as it wasn't overwhelming and persistent, was also to be expected. By mid-December, the good doctor had declared that Jack would be fit to return to work in the new year. No sense going back until after the Christmas party season, he had explained with a wink.

So what if Jack had not been completely honest with the shrink? Especially a shrink who insisted on being called Mikey? Who the fuck wanted to be called Mikey? Jack didn't want Mikey to think he was some kind of nut just because he was afraid to go to sleep some nights, afraid of what he would see in his dreams.

And sure, he felt guilty. He hadn't been able to save his partner. What cop wouldn't feel guilty about that? What he didn't feel guilty about was putting another two rounds into Charles after the murdering fuck had surrendered. As far as Jack saw it, all he had done was hand out the justice deserved. In his nightmares, Charles kept advancing no matter how many times Jack shot him. Those were the worst dreams, for Karen always died in them.

Jack hadn't discussed his dreams or his feelings of guilt with anyone. Not Karen, no one. He figured they would fade in time and they were fading. Although recently, the dreams had picked up again. Jack figured going back to work had dredged up some old memories and feelings. As Mikey had repeatedly said, "These, too, shall pass."

"I guess I'm just having a bit of trouble getting used to the shift work again," Jack said. "I got spoiled sleeping like a regular person all those months."

"It was good having you beside me every night. I miss that." She was quiet for a moment. "Were you really having a good time at the party?"

"Well . . . Scott and Lillian seemed nice."

"I saw the way you were looking at her in her flimsy dress. I never knew you had a thing for Asian women," Karen joked.

"She is good looking, that's for sure. Exotic," he said, a little grin teasing his mouth.

"Oh? And what does she have that I don't?"

Had Karen's words carried any frost, Jack would have been in trouble, but her voice was that low, sultry tone he loved. "I'm not sure," he replied. "Maybe I need a reminder."

"A reminder?" Her hand left his neck, trailed across the shoulder of his jacket. "Aren't you cold without your trench coat?"

He shook his head. "Nah. I know you like it warm in the car.

I'd be baking if I had the coat on. Actually, I'm a little too warm as it is."

"Really?" She leaned forward, changing the radio station from classic rock to something more mellow. "Maybe I can give you that reminder and heat you up at the same time."

At first, Karen was a touch annoyed when Jack decided to take the slower back roads home, but she understood he needed time to cool down after blowing up at her father. Rather needlessly, she thought. It was just a dog, for heaven's sake, and it happened long before she was even born. But she would never say that to Jack. He had a soft spot for animals, dogs especially, and Karen supposed it was from growing up an only child. The closest he'd had to a sibling was the family dog.

Yet his fondness for animals didn't explain or justify his outburst. She'd been having such a good time at the party. She knew Jack and her father didn't get along. But the two men had kept their distance from each other after the initial greeting. Then Jack had gone and ruined a wonderful evening by snapping at her father. Perhaps her dad had been needling Jack some, but still it didn't warrant his reaction.

If only the two men in her life could get along. Karen was tired of being the peacekeeper. She knew her dad didn't approve of Jack, never had, and he couldn't, or more likely wouldn't, see the wonderful qualities that had made her fall in love with him. And Jack couldn't understand that all her father wanted was for her to be secure in life; unfortunately, that wasn't possible on a police salary. At least not in George Hawthorn's eyes.

So Karen was trapped between them, always trying to bridge the chasm separating husband and father, doing her best to please them both. For her father, she was continually furthering her education, building her credentials. She knew he still dreamed of her teaching at a university, preferably following and then succeeding him at the University of Toronto.

Keeping Jack happy was so much easier and more pleasurable. He was an amazing lover and she never grew tired of his touch. There had been that time, for almost two months, when he had lost his sex drive. That had been a dark time, shortly after the incident in their home. Nightmares had plagued him every time he slept and the pitiful sleep he had managed to get did little to ease his stress. His mood at the time grew bleak and his temper unpredictably short. She feared he was suffering from depression. But he assured her, often with a strained smile, that the psychiatrist told him what he was experiencing was to be expected, typical even, and would pass in time.

And it had. Christmas had been a magical time. Even the ever-present tension between her two men had been buried beneath good friends, parties and presents. And after the holidays, Jack had gone back to work but not to that horrible 51 area. Karen had wanted him to quit altogether, use this time as a spring board to a new career, but he had insisted, rather stubbornly, that he was a cop and that it was all he knew how to do. They had finally compromised on 53 Division, which Jack guaranteed was the quietest in the city. Her friend Barb, an officer from Jack's original division and the one who had introduced them, had confirmed 53's status for her.

Everything had been great. Jack, though still a cop, was working someplace safe, his nightmares had faded and with more restful sleep his mood and temper had improved. Until tonight. His overreaction scared her, churning up old memories of the night he had not come home. He said he had spent the night at a beach party with his shift and she believed him; Jack was not the type to cheat. But he mentioned a female officer — PWS they were called — he occasionally chatted with. Barb had done some checking for Karen. What she had learned — all too quickly and easily — did not sit well with Karen. The PW, Jenny, had quite the reputation as a party girl and had, by the sound of it, slept with most of the married officers in the station.

Karen trusted Jack completely, but there was no harm in him staying away from such a woman.

She wasn't looking forward to tomorrow. No doubt Dad would call, wanting to have the conversation she had rudely escaped by going after Jack. But she could worry about her father's lecture later. Right now she had to take care of her husband, thank him — the term "reward" never crossed her mind — for going to the party. She wanted to make sure he didn't dwell on the spat with Dad. Jack had a tendency to keep things inside, letting them fester and bloat until they erupted at inappropriate times and places.

And if, in thanking Jack, she had another chance at fulfilling her own dream — *Don't you mean agenda?* a little voice asked from deep in her conscience, but she brushed it aside — then what was the harm?

While Jack was looking at her with a mischievous grin, Karen unclipped her seat belt and reclined the seat slightly. Not so far that her man would have to turn his head too much to see her but enough to give her some room to play.

"And what kind of reminder would that be?" he asked, sharing his attention between her and the road.

Again, she was happy they weren't on the highway. Playing in the car on the highway was a risky game. Not that she was worried about being seen by other drivers, far from it, but high speeds and foreplay just weren't a safe mixture.

"I could tell you, but I'd rather show you." She let the fur coat fall open, exposing the little black dress Jack loved so much. Slowly, she inched the dress up her thighs to reveal the tops of her stockings. "Did you like it when I showed you my stockings before we went in to the party?"

"Oh, yeah. Did you like showing me?"

"I did," she whispered and she had. Jack loved to be teased and she loved to tease him, so after he had parked the suv at her dad's house she had hiked up her dress, displaying the stockings and garter belt. If she hadn't been wearing the coat, she would have turned slowly to let him see the matching thong. The brief exhibition had him touching her constantly throughout the party, building the sexual tension between them. And now it was time to let it loose.

Karen had intended to give Jack a bit of a show until he could find a secluded place to stop, but now she wanted more. She ran her hands up the insides of her thighs and pulled her thong aside. Stroking herself, she breathed, "Stop somewhere, Jack. Hurry."

"I'm looking, hon, I'm looking."

Her fingers played and the pleasure built. "Do you know what I want to do in this coat?" she whispered and Jack grunted a quick no. "I want to go downtown one evening wearing only the coat and high heels. Nothing on under it. Would you like that?"

"Oh, God, yes." He spared her a tortured look then resumed searching for a side street. Frantically.

Soon she was lost in the fantasy and was only dimly aware of the car bumping over rough ground. Then Jack was kissing her, whispering in her ear as his hand teased her nipple through the thin fabric of her dress. "Don't stop, Kare, don't stop."

And she couldn't. The pleasure, the intensity, was building too quickly, too powerfully, to be stopped or even delayed. The orgasm seized her and thundered through her body, arching her back in ecstasy. Her hips thrust convulsively against her fingers as she consumed Jack's mouth with hers.

In time — a shivering forever gone too soon — her body quieted, quivering as the last few ripples of pleasure ran through her, miniature aftershocks following a massive quake. "Sorry, Jack. I couldn't wait."

He kissed her, tenderly, passionately. "Don't apologize. I love watching you come."

She smiled up at him. A wicked grin her father would never

have thought possible from her. "Your turn."

His hand ran down her body to the sensitive area her fingers had just left. She gasped as his fingers slid into her wetness.

"If it wasn't so cold, I'd take you outside and bend you over the hood," he told her as his fingers began a new rhythm.

"I think we can manage something." She stilled his hand. "Come around to my side."

Leaving the suv running and the heater on high, he climbed carefully out of the driver's seat while Karen freed herself from her coat. Jack had found them an empty field with mounds of dirt. The Honda's tracks — Jack had backed in between piles — came in along a rough road, no more than a wide path, really. There were no street lights in sight, but she was able to see more earthen knolls stretching across the field. Farmland designated for housing? Whatever they were, the hillocks made the perfect spot for a secluded interlude.

Jack opened the passenger door and she met him with a kiss. Her hands dropped to his pants and within seconds she had them around his knees. She twisted in the seat, lowered her booted right foot to the ground, propped her left foot on the suv's frame and leaned across the seat, thrusting her buttocks into the cold. She wanted Jack to fuck her. And quickly, but not because of the temperature.

Jack pushed her dress up to her waist while she pulled her thong aside. She felt him position himself, then push forward, filling her in one wonderful motion. He withdrew almost completely, then eased forward. Back and forward, building slowly, but she would have none of that.

"Fuck me, Jack. Fuck me now."

And he did. She laughed joyfully as he rode her, thrusting into her with ever-increasing speed and power. She could feel the tension gripping him, feel the urgency needing release.

"That's it, baby. Give it to me. Give it to me!"

Jack cried out as he came in her.

Spent and utterly happy, Jack pulled out of Karen. "Sorry, hon, no time for being polite; my ass is freezing." He yanked up his pants as she pulled her leg into the car and rearranged her dress. Belted up, he closed her door and stepped carefully around the truck.

The snow wasn't deep but the footing was treacherous. The evening had turned ugly thanks to Karen's dad and Jack had scared himself with the sudden rage he had felt, but Karen had known just what he needed to feel better. The last thing he wanted to do was slip and fall or twist an ankle. His anger was lessened for now. Not gone — he could feel it coiled inside him, waiting — but banished from his thoughts by Karen's love.

"Breaking an ankle would be a shitty way to end the night," he muttered as he gained the driver's side. He reached for the door and his feet went out from under him. He landed on his ass with a cracking splat.

Karen opened the driver's door. "Jack! Are you okay?" She was leaning across from the passenger side, her arms braced on the driver's seat.

"Yeah, I'm okay," he told her. "I slipped on some ice beneath the snow and —" He stopped, not wanting to believe what his nose was telling him.

"And what? What's wrong?"

He took another whiff and confirmed what he already knew, laughing at the absurdity. "I broke through the ice and now my ass is sitting in semi-frozen cow shit."

Karen was trying to look mortified but her giggles betrayed her look. "Are you sure?"

"As sure as cow shit stinks," he said and threw back his head and laughed.

"All right, maybe you can answer this," Jack's escort surmised over coffee. "No one I've asked knows. Why are the portable radios called mitres? I thought a mitre is the hat the Pope wore."

"As far as I know, it's an old type of radio or something. I don't —"

"Stand by for the hotshot," the dispatcher announced, cutting Jack off.

Jack grimaced. *Like it's coming our way.*

Hotshots — radio calls that needed immediate attention — were more of a rarity in 53 than downtown. He just hadn't realized how infrequent they were in midtown until he was sitting in a scout car wishing something exciting would happen. He could listen to all the fun calls going to the 51 cars. Oh, sure, 53 got its share of hotshots: medical calls, domestics, the odd bank robbery and more medical calls, but nothing like the seemingly endless and sometimes overwhelming deluge of priority calls down in the city's toilet.

Jack sighed. He missed working in the toilet.

"43 Eglinton Avenue East, apartment 1802. Male threatening suicide. Has a history of depression. No means indicated. Ted McManus, age 27. Time 2349."

"He lives on the eighteenth floor, dispatch," Jack muttered into his tea. "Three guesses on how he'll do it."

"5306, that last hotshot is yours," the dispatcher snapped, sounding vaguely pissed. Had she heard Jack's comment? He quickly checked for an open carrier but the mike was closed. Man, he hated when the mike was stuck open. There was nothing more embarrassing than having what you assumed was a private chat get broadcast over the air for everyone's entertainment. And, of course, no one ever bothers to inform you of the open mike at the start of the conversation.

Jack grinned. Last summer a copper on another platoon had been dating a PW from the same shift, which is generally not a good idea. Cops from the same station dating could be considered an office romance; dating someone on the same shift was like dating the person you shared a cubicle with. And if you wound up in the same car . . . well, you had to hope the relationship was going smoothly. The copper had met the PW for coffee and in stereotypical pig fashion had broken up with her while parked next to her — it had been too hot to get out of the air-conditioned car — in the parking lot next to the Beer Store at Gerrard and Ontario. Very scenic. Very classy. No wonder cops had shitty reputations when it came to dating.

Everybody working that day, in 51 and air band–sharing 53, immediately learned about the rather nasty break-up firsthand since the control button on his mike had been stuck open and every word had been transmitted to all the cars, portable radios, the two stations and the dispatcher. And to his wife, who just happened to be a copper in 53. Rumour had it his keys hadn't worked when he got home that evening.

"What's the smile for, Jacky?" Juliet Larson asked as she tapped the Accept Detail button.

"Just something that happened down in 51." He drained the last of his tea and slipped the paper cup behind his seat. "Remind me to toss that out later."

"We get a call for a guy who might take a swan dive onto the sidewalk and it reminds you of something funny? Jeez, you 51 guys are warped."

Juliet had a couple of years on the job and was a nice enough kid but so inexperienced it was like working with a rookie straight out of the college. Two years in 53 taught new officers next to nothing beyond medical complaints and alarm calls. Brett was right the other week when he said that the service needed to get back to training divisions.

But then again 51 would eat Juliet alive; the assholes down there and in any shithole division could spot rookies as easily as seasoned cops could spot assholes. And to add to the whole Officer Friendly image, she was cute. Her hair was done up tight to her head at least, not hanging down in a ponytail some piece of scum could use as a handhold while he pounded her face to mush. But it was so blonde it gleamed when she was in the sunlight. Not as brightly as her perfectly white teeth, though. Jack figured she should be on a billboard or in a magazine ad for toothpaste or soap or some wholesome, not-cop-related product.

But if he had to be bored in a scout car for ten hours a day, he could ask for a lot worse in company than Juliet. As long as he didn't call her Julie. He had made that mistake once and she had damn near bitten his head off. For a cute little thing, she had one hell of a temper. He admired that.

Whenever she wanted to needle him, out came "Jacky." At least she had used the phrase "Jackeo and Juliet" only once. Over the air. Jack had responded by threatening to leave her in 51, unarmed, the next time he jumped on a call down there.

As Jack was pulling away from the curb, a unit from 51 spoke up. "CIT 01 to radio. We're clear. Do you want us to head up to that threaten suicide in 53?"

"10-4, CIT, I'd appreciate the help. I'll put the call on your screen. 5306, are you aware the CIT unit will be attending your call?"

Juliet snagged the mike. "10-4, dispatch," she quipped rather perkily. "We're just around the corner. We'll be on scene in a minute or so, and we'll advise."

Jack suddenly realized he had parked at Yonge Street and Eglinton Avenue after hitting the Tim Hortons. He hadn't even thought about it. This always amazed him: coppers in 53 regularly sat on busy corners when they were not on calls. In 51, if you got a quiet moment for coffee, the last thing you wanted to do was sit where the public could find you.

So now, not only was he parking like them, he was getting used to being able to grab a tea without having to do a call first. *Crap, I'm turning into a 53 cop.*

Aloud, Jack asked, "What is this CIT I keep hearing on the air?"

"Crisis Intervention Team," Juliet explained as Jack waited to turn left onto Eglinton. The intersection, bordered by towering office and condo buildings, was heavy with traffic. "It started up back in the fall. It's a cop with a psychiatric nurse on board. They handle the EDP calls. It's a 51 Division car but sometimes they come up here to help us out. I'm surprised they're still on the air; they usually head in around eleven."

"Sounds like a good idea, but I doubt we'll need them," Jack declared, making the turn on the red.

"Why not? It's that building on the corner. The entrance is on Holly."

"Thanks. If this guy really wanted to kill himself, he wouldn't have called." Jack pulled the scout car to the curb in front of the apartment building. "I mean, if he was serious, we'd be getting calls from other people after he went splat on the sidewalk."

"Are you cynical or just crabby tonight?" Juliet tapped the At Scene button and they both got out of the car.

"Sorry," he muttered. "My wife and I were at her parents' place for a party this evening and I got into a bit of a fight with her dad. Guess I'm still a bit peeved about it." *That and falling in cow shit. But I'll keep that to myself.*

"In-laws can be a bitch, but no need to take it out on this guy. We haven't even seen him yet and you're already declaring him a loser."

"Come on," Jack defended himself as they stepped into the lobby. "How many times have you gone to a call where someone's *threatening* —" he held up and crooked the first two fingers of each hand "— to kill himself and when you get there he's taken half a dozen Tylenols or he's *slashed* —" again with the quotation marks "— his wrists so lightly the cuts are barely bleeding. They just want attention, that's all."

He lifted a quizzical eyebrow her way as he punched the elevator button.

"Okay, I get your point, but that doesn't mean everyone who calls is looking for attention."

"Tell you what," Jack offered as they stepped into the

elevator, "if this guy turns out to be serious, I'll buy you lunch."

Juliet flashed him her toothpaste ad smile. "You're on."

The elevator doors opened with a cheery *ping!* on the eighteenth floor. Jack glanced in each direction. The hall was empty.

"You choose," he told Juliet. "I always go the wrong way."

"Yeah, me too." She shrugged and picked left. Jack followed, keeping an eye on the hallway ahead of them over his escort's head. Just because he was willing to bet good old Ted McManus was simply another attention seeker didn't mean he was going to rule out the chance — a slim one, he was ready to admit — that Ted did want to die and wanted to take some uniformed company along with him when he went. The last thing Jack wanted to be was an example of the complacency instructors used at police colleges.

He never wanted his name attached to *You see what happens when you approach a call thinking it's bullshit? Sometimes it turns out not to be bullshit and that's how coppers die. Take these two idiots for example. . . .*

No thanks.

They realized they were going the wrong way after a couple of doors and turned around. As they passed the elevator, Jack half expected the doors to ping! again, expelling the fabled crisis team. He wondered what type of nurse would want to ride around in a police car. *Some tree-hugging do-gooder, no doubt. Probably volunteered for the job so she could save the poor nuts — oops, Emotionally Disturbed People, I mean — from us uncaring, ignorant cops.*

With luck, they'd have Ted all bundled up and ready for a quick ride to the hospital before the crisis whatsit arrived and wanted to spend the next couple of hours chatting with Ted about his feelings.

Crap, I am cynical.

The door numbers were still climbing and Jack had just

reckoned it would be the last apartment when Juliet announced, "It's the last apartment."

"Always is."

As they approached the door, both of them automatically turned down the volume on their radios. Jack was pleased to see Juliet slide her finger — both of them had donned their Kevlar-lined leather gloves in the elevator — over the peephole before she quickly slipped past the door. She leaned in, not quite pressing her ear up against the wood. Although the building looked clean enough not to have to worry about something crawling into your ear, why take the chance? She motioned for Jack to wait while she listened. Maybe she wasn't such a rookie after all.

A moment later Juliet shrugged, silently to say, *I didn't hear anything*. Jack nodded and tried the doorknob. It turned easily in his grasp. He looked a question at Juliet and she nodded. He pushed and the door swung gently open. Before Jack could step in, Juliet took the lead, pushing the door flat against the wall, achieving a double goal: giving them the widest view of the apartment as possible and removing any potential threat from behind the door.

Jack was definitely impressed. Juliet had not missed any of the little things that could be the precursor to the shit hitting the fan — or what Jack's training officer in 32 liked to call "the fecal matter encountering the oscillating blades."

The door opened onto a small foyer tiled in white with a closet to their left and a tiny kitchen laid out on the right. While Juliet gave the closet a quick peek, Jack scanned the kitchen. It was clean and tidy except for a stack of unwashed dishes in the sink and a deep gouge in the drywall on the far wall. "Far" being a disputable description as the kitchen couldn't have been more than twelve feet in length. Amid a scattering of drywall chunks and dust, Jack saw a frying pan and what might have been a sandwich — it was too charred to really tell. The familiar, unpleasant smell of burnt toast lingered in the air.

Jack pointed it out to Juliet and they both shrugged.

"Ted? It's the police," Juliet called. Her voice was firm but not aggressive. "You called 911? Ted, you in here?"

They paused, listening. A hushed sobbing was coming from farther in the apartment. The living room stretched out from the foyer and kitchen, the sofa, coffee table and TV offering little in the way of concealment. A bathroom and a smaller room, either a den or a second bedroom, lay to the left. Juliet quickly cleared them both. They crossed the living room, heading to what must have been the master bedroom and Jack felt the temperature drop, a chill carried on a breeze from the bedroom.

Open balcony door. Fuck, maybe this guy is serious after all.

The balcony door was indeed wide open, but Ted had not taken that fatal, final step. A man was huddled on the queen-sized bed that all but filled the room. Jack hoped it was Ted and not a grieving roommate.

"Ted? It's the police." Juliet attempted to engage the sobbing man while Jack inched around the foot of the bed to the balcony door. The wind at street level had barely been noticeable, but up this high it sliced into the bedroom, as solid as an icicle. One freaking huge icicle.

Giving Ted a final glance, hoping he wasn't conning them, Jack stepped out onto the balcony. His stomach lurched disagreeably as he peered over the railing at the sidewalk below. Far, far below. Jack wasn't a fan of heights and wasted no time checking the ground for splattered bodies. The sidewalk was clear of people — dead ones at least — and he gratefully retreated to the safe side of the railing.

No way. No fucking way would I ever jump. I'd eat my gun first, if things got that bad. He stepped inside, locking the door behind him. *But then can life ever be bad enough that offing yourself is the answer? Well, let's see what's up with Ted, shall we?*

Juliet was sitting on the end of the bed. A nice, non-threatening position but still well out of reach. Jack passed behind her and leaned in the doorway, crossing his arms casually over his chest. He frowned when he felt his jacket pull tight across his back. *Damn, I have to get a new jacket some day.* He dropped his arms and folded his hands over the front of his gun belt.

Ted's bedroom was in about the same state as the kitchen minus the frying pan redecoration. The walls were painted a nice off-white shade, and the furniture was that rare cross of functional and stylish; the bed had drawers in the frame. *I guess in a small place like this you have to make use of all available space.* The bedsheets were rumpled and had that long-lived-in look. Jack wondered when Ted had last changed the linen.

Speaking of washing, Ted himself had the same kind of ridden hard, put away wet look to him. He was slight in build and, judging from the way his blue golf shirt — also in need of a wash — hung on him this might have been a new body weight for him. He was sitting at the head of the bed, in the middle, with his back up against the wall and his arms wrapped protectively around his knees. His head was tilted back, eyes staring listlessly at the ceiling. His hair was in serious need of trimming and his face hadn't felt the touch of a razor in some time.

Even with his head canted back, Jack could see that Ted's eyes were so heavily rimmed in red they appeared to be bleeding. Tears streamed down his cheeks unchecked to drip heedlessly from his jaw. His mouth was a grimaced slash, his frown lines etched so deeply they appeared carved into his skin. It was as if sorrow was the sole expression he knew.

What the hell could have happened to this guy?

Juliet echoed Jack's thoughts. "Ted, what's wrong? What happened today?"

Ted drew in a ragged, hitching breath. "I . . . I . . . oh, God!" His eyes slammed shut, squeezing out fresh rivers of tears.

Jack felt a shiver chase up his spine. Those stammered words carried such pain, such sheer insufferable agony, it was no wonder the man had thought of killing himself. Compassion, unexpected and sudden, brushed aside Jack's indifference.

Someone's died. Or maybe it's cancer. Or . . . Something. Jack didn't want to imagine what horror could strike someone so deeply.

"Ted, we can't help unless you tell us what's wrong." Juliet was speaking softly, coaxing Ted into trusting them.

Ted lowered his head, rubbed furiously at his eyes. "It doesn't matter," he said, his voice harsh, strained. "It's stupid."

"It can't be stupid if it's hurting you that much," Jack insisted, unable to remain silent.

"Please, Ted, tell us," Juliet urged.

Ted's head whipped to face her, his features a mask of rage. "I burned my lunch! I fucking burned my lunch," he snarled, his voice filled with such hate and anger Jack twitched in anticipation of an attack. But Ted's anger was not directed at them. "I'm useless, so fucking useless." His head dropped to his arms, the fury gone as quickly as it had flared.

Juliet looked over her shoulder at Jack, her eyes wide in disbelief. Jack was sure his own expression mirrored hers. *His lunch? He burned his sandwich and that's why he wants to kill himself?*

"Give me a fucking break." This Jack uttered aloud, once again unable to remain silent. "You burned your lunch?" he asked, not really believing. *"You burned your lunch?"* Louder this time and not without his own touch of anger.

Ted nodded, his face buried in his arms. He was sobbing yet again and Jack had had enough.

"Oh, for fuck's sake, knock it off!" he snapped.

Ted flinched, as if expecting to be hit and Jack was more than mad enough to lay a beating on the wimp.

"Jack —" Juliet began, but he cut her off.

"No. This is bullshit. Bullshit!" he repeated, flinging the word at Ted, feeling a vicious pang of delight when the huddled form flinched again. "He calls 911, says he's going to jump, wastes our time and for what? What? Because he burned his fucking lunch? No, this isn't right, not by a long fucking shot."

"What's all the shouting about?"

Jack turned away from Ted and found a fire hydrant of a cop standing in the bedroom doorway. It wasn't that he was overly short, because he was only a few inches shy of Jack's height. His stocky width created an illusion of shortness. And he was wearing the weirdest uniform Jack had ever seen. He had on a blue nylon raid jacket, the kind plainclothes officers usually threw on during search warrants when they wanted to be easily identified as police, his gun belt and blue jeans. His black hair bristled in a crewcut and he definitely didn't look happy.

"I take it you're the crisis team?"

"Yeah, we are," the half-plainclothes, half-uniformed cop said, not sounding overly impressed.

Jack didn't blame him; he sure as shit didn't want to deal with loser Ted anymore. "He's all yours." Jack stepped aside, waving the crisis cop in.

The cop moved into Ted's bedroom and was followed by his escort, the psychiatric nurse, Jack assumed. At first glance, Jack thought Manny had changed jobs. *Do all guys who shave their heads grow goatees?* But the nurse was too short to be Jack's former partner. About the same height as the cop — book ends, Jack thought sarcastically — the nurse gave Jack a dismissive look as he stepped past.

What's your problem?

Nurse Little Manny tapped Juliet on the shoulder. "Excuse me, officer." He took her spot on the bed when she got up. The cop stood to the side, forming the third point of the triangle between cop, nurse and loser.

"Ted, is it?" the nurse began, speaking slowly and calmly. Jack figured the calm wouldn't last long once the nurse learned Ted had been willing, or at least said he had been willing, to take a swan dive because of a burnt sandwich. "I'm Aaron. I'm a nurse from St. Michael's Hospital."

The cop turned to Jack and Juliet, but his words were for Jack. "You can wait in the other room."

Jack's back went up. First Ted wastes their time and now this jerk thought he could order them around as if being on some stupid team made him special. Jack had been about to step into the living room; he'd had enough of Ted's blubbering. But he decided to stay put. *Fuck this cop and his crisis team.*

Juliet must have sensed the tension growing in the room. It wasn't hard to miss, with two cops glaring at each other. "C'mon, Jack. Let's give them some room." She had to tug on his arm to get him moving.

Once away from Ted and his two holier-than-thou babysitters, Jack relaxed. He blew out a deep breath and some pent-up frustration in the process. "Those guys are supposed to help us out?"

Juliet shrugged, heading to the kitchen. "Seems like everyone's in a foul mood," she declared, looking pointedly at Jack.

"What's that supposed to mean?" First the cop with the fire-hydrant head, then the chubby nurse, now Juliet? As he'd told Ted, this wasn't right, not by a long shot.

"Nothing much," Juliet explained, crouching to pick up the frying pan and sandwich. "I guess Ted likes grilled cheese." She tossed the pan into the sink, adding to the unwashed stack. She found the garbage under the sink and dropped the charred bread in. She went to wipe her gloves on the dish towel, thought better of it and used her pants.

"Well?" Jack asked, impatient.

Juliet joined Jack by the couch, where they could keep an eye on the bedroom door. Officer Hydrant Head had deliberately shut the door. Closing it had not been the wisest of tactics but Jack grudgingly admitted to himself that he might have done the same had the roles been reversed.

"You tore quite the strip off Ted and it seemed a little excessive. Harsh."

"He pissed me off," Jack defended.

"Obviously." When Jack didn't answer, she blunted the edge of her words with an open smile. "You could have toned it down some, that's all."

Jack wasn't so annoyed that he was invulnerable to her smile. "Okay, I guess I was a bit offside, but come on! He was going to kill himself over bad cooking?"

Juliet grinned in agreement. "Some people are just perfectionists, I guess."

Jack snorted and they settled in to wait for Hydrant Head and his nurse to deem the lowly uniforms worthy of notice. It didn't take long. A few minutes later the bedroom door opened and Ted came out, bracketed by Nurse Little Manny and Officer Hydrant Head.

"Ted's agreed to go to the hospital with us, so we won't need you for transport," Hydrant Head announced.

All five of them left the apartment. The ride down in the elevator was quiet. Even Ted was silent, his sobbing all dried up for the moment. With nothing to say, Jack studied Nurse Little Manny and decided that, other than the shaved head and goatee, the man looked nothing like Manny. When Juliet had explained the CIT to him, Jack had just assumed the nurse would be some soft-hearted tree-hugger, but this guy — Aaron, was it? — didn't come across like that at all. Jack noticed that Aaron kept a wary eye on Ted and the slight downturn to the corners of his mouth suggested he wasn't the biggest smiler. Not at work at least.

Aaron was also wearing a jumbled uniform. Unlike his escort's royal blue jacket, the nurse's was a dark blue, almost black, emblazoned with CRISIS TEAM across the back. He wore a ballistic vest over his T-shirt and there was a radio on his hip. Jeans and running shoes completed the outfit.

Semi-casual and pretty comfortable looking.

They left the building and Hydrant Head placed Ted in the rear of the CIT car, an unmarked Crown Vic, plain white but with a caged back seat. Then the cop headed for the driver's side before Jack could say anything, so he spoke to the nurse. Aaron stood in the V of the open door with one foot already in the car. He did not look impressed.

"Listen, I just wanted to . . . apologize for overreacting up there. I guess I've been a little stressed out and Ted looked like a good target to blow up at."

Aaron looked at Jack for a moment, not speaking, then nodded. "Yeah, well, you definitely could have handled the situation better."

"So I've been told," Jack agreed, gesturing to Juliet. "But, honestly, I don't understand it. I mean, I know he's depressed, but he burned a sandwich. I could understand it if he was getting evicted or something, but it was so . . ." Jack groped for a word.

"Inconsequential?" Aaron suggested.

"Exactly."

"That's what made it so bad," Aaron said, shaking his head at Jack's ignorance.

"You've lost me," Jack admitted, truly bewildered.

The Crown Vic roared to life, telling Aaron it was time to go. He ducked his head into the car. "Hang on a sec."

Straightening up, he said, "I've got to make this quick." He ran a hand over his scalp, looking at Jack as if he was searching for the easiest explanation. "Depression is often described as hatred turned inward. A depressed person will think things like 'I'm no good' or 'My family would be better off without me.' They feel loathsome or useless."

"That's what he said," Jack remembered, pointing at the rear seat.

"I don't doubt it. If you or I had burned our lunch, we would've said, 'Shit, I'll have to make another one.' Ted thought, 'I'm so useless, I can't even make a sandwich.' Get the idea?"

Jack nodded slowly as understanding dawned. "I think so."

"Don't they teach you about mental illness at the college?

Depression, schizophrenia, borderline personality disorder?"

Jack laughed, embarrassed. "I've never heard of that last one. They teach us our grounds for arresting under the Mental Health Act, that's about it."

"Unbelievable," Aaron said and in that one word Jack heard a depth of frustration. The car jumped as the engine revved. "That's my cue to go."

"Hey, thanks for the help and the quick lesson. I'm Jack Warren." Jack held out his hand and Aaron gave it a quick, firm shake before climbing into the passenger seat.

"Aaron Wallace. No problem, guy. See you around." Aaron slammed the door but not before Jack heard him say to Officer Hydrant Head, "Jeez, guy. You're one impatient bitch, aren't you?"

Jack's impression of Nurse Little Manny jumped a few notches.

Wednesday, 14 March
1437 hours

Jesse Polan was horny.

If there was one thing worse than needing some crack and not being able to find a dealer, which rarely happened in Jesse's neighbourhood, it was being horny with no one to fuck. Jesse wasn't just a bit horny, he was that blue balls, gonna explode kind of horny. The kind of horny he only experienced when indulging in some particularly fine rock. And he had scored some exceptionally fine crack yesterday, not as good as that Black stuff on the streets last summer, but pretty damn good. He'd also been able to afford half an eight-ball thanks to a couple of easy house breaks. He had spent all of last night high with enough rock at hand so that every time he felt himself coming down all he had to do was light up and he was back to feeling fine.

But he had woken up this morning — or was it afternoon? — with a fucking giant case of blue balls. After a quick hit to get him started, he headed out, looking to get fucked. He hoped to run into what's-her-name with the green hair. She was skinny as shit with a couple of lumps she called tits but could she ever suck a dick. Fuck! He was getting hard just thinking about her. When he found her, he'd offer to share what was left of the half eight-ball if she came back to his room. That would be fucking fine. Nothing like fucking on crack. He was so hard it felt like he had a steel pipe shoved down his jeans.

Jesse stepped out onto the rickety front porch and paused to pull at his dick, trying to find a comfortable position. On the sidewalk, a woman pushing a baby stroller saw him and frowned.

"What the fuck you looking at, bitch? You wanna suck it?" Jesse unzipped and the woman hurried off. He laughed at her fleeing back. "Bitch prob'ly never saw one as big as mine." Fuck, yeah, he was feeling fine!

He zipped up, careful not to snag the equipment and pulled his jacket tight. Still fucking chilly. "Thought it was s'posed to be spring. Fuck." But not even the brisk air could dampen his mood. He had a good coat, army surplus, with lots of pockets to hide things. It was fucking warm and kick-ass black. Jesse liked black. It was tough, cool. Fucking kick-ass fine.

That green-haired chick — what was her name? Linda? Leslie? Fuck her name — usually hung out around Queen and Sherbourne, so Jesse headed south on Sherbourne, following in the steps of the cocksucking bitch with the stroller, though he had already forgotten her. As he was about to cross Shuter Street, who did he spot but the green-haired whore. She was working the corner over on Seaton. One glimpse of her lime spikes and he was steel-hard again. He crossed Sherbourne, his dick leading him like a blood-pumped divining rod.

She was watching the cars cruising by and didn't see Jesse until he was beside her.

"Hey, Greeny." Jesse grinned, proud of the nickname he made up. What the fuck was her name?

She jumped when he spoke, but by the time she turned to look at him she had a twenty-dollar version of a come-hither smile on her face. "Hey, baby, you looking to party?"

"Fucking A, I am." Fuck, but she was skinny. Even skinnier than the last time he'd fucked her and that couldn't have been more than two weeks ago. She must be seriously hooked on rock and that was just fine with Jesse. Fucking kick-ass fine. Any whore who needed crack that much would be more than will-ing to spend the night fucking and sucking. And for a lot less rock than he had originally thought about sharing.

"Twenty for a blow, forty if you wanna fuck too." She opened her ratty old raincoat to show him her stuff. She had on a grungy T-shirt cut off just below her itty titties and Jesse could see her hip bones jutting out above the sagging waist of her jeans. Fuck, she was skanky. Smelled skanky, too. But Jesse's dick had only one thought in its head and it was saying that Greeny, small tits, skanky smell and all, was just what he needed.

Jesse stepped close, digging into his pocket. Shielded by their bodies, he opened his hand to show her six pieces of rock, each pea-sized piece individually wrapped in tiny twists of plastic wrap. Her eyes flared and her ashen tongue darted out, licking her cracked, pale lips. Jesse smiled. He was going to have fun tonight.

"What say we go back to my place and party there?"

"You'll share?" Her voice was no more than a shocked whis-per. She sounded like a devotee enthralled in a vision.

"Three for me, three for you, baby." Which would leave him with plenty more for himself after he kicked her out on her skinny ass. "Let's go." Jesse grabbed her by the arm, but she dragged her feet to a stop after only a few steps.

"I can't," she whined.

"What the fuck you mean you can't?"

"I . . . I'm not supposed to go anywhere."

"What . . . oh." Jesse snickered. "Been caught keeping a bit more than what's yours, eh?" Fuck. If her pimp had her under orders to stay in one place, which he would do so he could keep an eye on her and collect after every trick, then her coming back to his place wasn't going to happen. But Jesse's balls were about to blow out the front of his pants. "All right. Twenty for a blow. But you ain't gettin' any of my rock."

Greeny whined again, a feeble mewling sound back in her throat. "Please, I'll fuck you for free."

"Tell you what. If you blow me real fuckin' good, maybe I'll give you a piece. Maybe. Where to, bitch?"

Seaton Street was a nice little residential road lined with old houses. She led him up to a laneway that ran from Seaton and behind the apartment buildings on Sherbourne Street. She pulled him into a tight gap between two dumpsters and dropped to her knees. Jesse tilted his head back as she fumbled at his pants. Finally! But after a few seconds, he realized she was tugging at his pocket, not his zipper. The bitch was after his rock!

"You fuckin' whore —" The words died in his throat as he felt something cold and sharp press into the soft flesh beneath his ear.

"Move and I'll cut you, motherfucker." An arm wrapped around Jesse's throat.

Jesse froze. "Chill out, man. I ain't doin' nothin'."

The bitch had set him up. Fucking crack whore! Next time he saw her he was going to slice her open from snatch to throat. But for now all he could do was play statue while the green-haired bitch dug the rock out of his pocket.

"Get his money, bitch. Hurry!" The guy behind Jesse smelled almost as bad as the whore and when he spoke warm spittle sprayed Jesse's ear.

The whore was whimpering in excitement as she turned his pocket inside out, dumping the rock onto the ground. She cried out in dismay and began frantically snatching up the precious rock. Jesse felt like stomping on it, crushing and grinding each fucking piece into the asphalt. And maybe her fucking fingers as well. But he stood still, the knife at his neck a strong reminder of what would happen if he moved.

"What the fuck are you doing, bitch? I said get his fucking money!"

"He's got rock, Leo!" She was sobbing hysterically, searching through the garbage at her knees, her fingers splayed like those of a blind man hunting for his dropped cane. Each gem she found disappeared into her pocket.

"What else you got, fucker? Huh?"

The knife jabbed into his neck and Jesse knew he was going to die. Fuck! All he'd wanted was a blow job. It wasn't fair. It just wasn't fucking fair. He'd never done anything to this guy or his whore. Fuck, he couldn't even remember her name.

"Don't kill me, man. Please don't fuckin' kill me." His voice cracked. Hot tears spilled from his eyes. Jesse didn't feel so fucking fine anymore and the woman with the stroller would have laughed if she saw the snivelling boy the tough guy with the dick had turned out to be.

"You make it worth my while," the man, Leo, breathed, almost caressing Jesse's ear, "and maybe I won't cut you. Much."

"You always talk tough when you're sticking a guy, faggot?"

The arm holding Jesse flinched and the knife jabbed him, sharp, hot pain, as his captor spun, trying to see who the uninvited guest was. Jesse whimpered, still in Leo's embrace. Leo stepped back from the shelter of the dumpsters. The whore ignored everything except the precious pieces of crack.

"Who you calling a faggot, asshole?" Leo demanded, digging the knife in as if Jesse had spoken.

"You're the guy with his fucking dick shoved up another guy's ass. Looks kinda homo to me, faggot." The new player in this little game was standing not ten feet away, smoking a cigarette like he had nothing better to do. Despite the cool air, he was wearing only a dark blue sweatshirt and jeans. The sweatshirt's hood was up, draping the upper half of his face in shadow, but the sleeves were gone, no doubt ripped off to expose arms knotted with muscle. Studded leather wrapped each wrist.

"Fuck off, motherfucker. This bitch's money belongs to me." Leo jerked Jesse closer.

"I fucking hate cowards." The man's voice was low, gravelly, his words unhurried. Jesse flashed on an image of Clint Eastwood draped in a poncho, a hat pulled low over his eyes. This guy was talking like Eastwood did in those westerns. Just before people started dying. Jesse was not an educated man; he'd left school halfway through grade seven. But he realized his situation had just gotten a lot fucking worse. As a robbery victim, he would have lost his crack and what little money he had left. But caught between Leo, who kept squeezing him tighter and sticking him with that fucking knife and the new guy, Jesse knew he had gone from robbery victim to shield.

"Hey, man. Leo? C'mon, Leo, just take my money and go. Please?" Jesse liked to think of himself as a tough guy and he'd prove it, too, every time a safe opportunity presented itself, but his real talent was begging. He wasn't a big guy and begging was how he had survived all this time. He'd learned that a lot of predators lost the heart to seriously injure their victim when that victim was wailing and blubbering on his knees. Jesse would rather be spat on in disgust than take a beating like a man.

"C'mon, Leo, please, I don't wanna die." His tears were flowing in earnest. His chest hitched as he sobbed. "I don't know this guy, man. Just let me go."

"A man shouldn't cry." The stranger flicked his cigarette butt away, then reached up to slowly push back the hood of his sweatshirt. A strip of black hair, cut short and about three fingers wide, crested the stranger's head. His face was lean, angular, and the goatee did nothing to soften it. His was not a friendly face but one more prone to cruelty. If the man laughed, Jesse thought, it would be at the expense of others. He radiated violence and in its heat Jesse's tears ran dry.

Something about the stranger tweaked a memory in Jesse's crack-shrouded mind. Something he'd been told? Some rumour on the street?

"Leo?" Green Hair was checking in.

"Stay where you are, bitch. You run on me and I'll kill you too."

The whore had stopped searching for the dropped crack long enough to clue in that something wasn't going according to plan. She scuttled deeper into the dumpster nook.

Leo, his whore and loot secured for the moment, turned his attention back to the man in the hoodie. "Fuck off, mother-fucker, or I'll slice you too."

The stranger shook his head; his eyes never left his prey. "Can't." He stepped toward Jesse and Leo.

"This little bitch belong to you? You can have the mother-fucking loser, but I'm keeping what's fucking mine."

Leo shifted, ensuring his human shield was between him and the approaching stranger.

Jesse might have stopped crying, but his face was sweat soaked, his greasy hair matted to his forehead. He searched frantically for an escape route, knowing he'd have only a brief chance to save himself when the violence started. And he never doubted it was going to get violent; the stranger had blood in his eyes. It was a hunter's look. A killer's.

To the right was the whore, hiding between the dumpsters and a wood fence. Leo was behind Jesse, backed up against an unyielding dumpster. The stranger was in front of Jesse, almost close enough to touch. All Jesse could hope for was a chance to dive to his left. If he could get free, he would run as fast as he fucking could. To hell with the crack and his money.

"Back the fuck off, man!" Leo thrust his knife threateningly at the stranger, slicing the skin on Jesse's neck as he did.

Jesse wailed.

The stranger attacked.

His hands flashed out, ensnaring Leo's wrist and hand. With a pleased grin stretching his tight lips, the stranger began to apply pressure, forcing Leo's trapped hand against his forearm. Leo's knife clattered to the ground and Jesse wriggled free. He was halfway down the alley when a sudden, sharp scream stopped him.

Jesse turned. Leo was on his knees, cradling his right arm to his chest, the hand hanging at an impossibly wrong angle. Now it was Leo's turn to cry. Tears coursed down his black skin.

"A nigger?" Jesse was stunned. "A nigger tried to rob me? A nigger?" Jesse found courage in his outrage and Leo's defenceless circumstance.

"Thought you might come back," the stranger said when Jesse stood beside him. Suddenly, viciously, the stranger smashed his knee into Leo's face, driving his head into the dumpster with a dull, meaty *clang!* The sheer brutality of the strike shocked Jesse, but only for a moment.

When the stranger didn't follow up on the attack, Jesse pounced, laying into Leo with his motorcycle boots. His nigger-stomping, ass-kicking boots. Again and again Jesse slammed the heavy boots into Leo's ribs. A maniacal grin contorted his features. He thought he might be drooling.

In time — seconds only, really; his drug-wasted body was incapable of sustaining such intense effort — Jesse fell back, his cadaverous chest heaving spasmodically as he fought to breathe. Through watering eyes, he watched as the stranger hauled Leo to a sitting position, propping him against the dumpster. The stranger pulled something from a pocket and held it so Leo could see it. Jesse shuffled closer. It was a flat, jagged triangle of black stone, no bigger than his palm. He squatted down to observe, intrigued.

Leo didn't look so good. Blood was flowing thickly from a nose no longer exactly centred on his face. Jesse could appreciate how much it must hurt, touching his own poorly healed nose. *Fucking cop. Shoved my face in my breakfast and for what?*

The stranger tapped Leo on the forehead with the stone. "This is so everyone will know who did this to you." He gripped Leo's neck and pressed the stone — slate, Jesse thought it was called — to the pimp's forehead. When Leo began to struggle, the stranger planted a knee in his chest, pinning him to the dumpster. The stranger drew the tip of his stone knife down Leo's forehead unhurriedly, ripping open the flesh with the stone's cruel edge.

Leo screamed. The stranger ignored him, ignored the blood gushing freely from the jagged tear in Leo's flesh. Jesse knelt on Leo's legs to keep them from bucking. Jesse was enjoying this immensely.

The stranger finished the first cut, a vertical gash not quite down the centre of Leo's forehead. He bore down twice more with the stone as Leo screamed and writhed beneath Jesse's knees. Jesse smiled, elated. He imagined he could hear the stone grinding on Leo's fucking skull as he was carved up.

After the third cut, the stranger stepped back, admiring his work. At first, Jesse couldn't make out the mark torn into Leo's flesh; there was too much blood. He snagged a crumpled ball of newspaper from the ground, wiping cruelly. Leo groaned hoarsely, swatting ineffectively at Jesse with his good hand. Satisfied, Jesse tossed the bloodied wad of newsprint aside. Now he could see what the stranger had written with his stone: the letter K.

Jesse looked questioningly at the stranger.

The man, a stranger no more, smiled grimly. "It's my mark. My name is Kayne."

"Enforcement 51 in foot pursuit! Northbound Bleecker from Wellesley!"

Jack stepped on the gas as Brett flicked on the lights. A heartbeat later the siren started ripping through the quiet residential streets. The scout car skidded around a corner, the four lanes of Mount Pleasant Avenue ahead of them. Jack let the car fly.

A good start to the night. Jack and Brett had just climbed into the car and cleared, then headed for the first coffee of the night.

Foot pursuits and serious medical emergencies involving a child were the two calls any decent officer would bust his or her ass to get to. Not that the lights and siren didn't start blaring for other calls, but kids and foot pursuits always upped the urgency. The only call higher in importance was an Assist PC. A copper calling for help trumped all else.

The radio was alive with 51 units responding to the foot pursuit. Brett waited for a break, then quickly added them to the list. "5302 heading down."

"Units responding, stay off the air," the dispatcher ordered, her words a calm contradiction to the pumped-up officers racing to help one of their own. *"Enforcement 51, keep up your location."*

"Northbound . . . Bleecker, passing . . . 325." The words spurted out between ragged breaths and Jack could hear the pounding of boots, a rhythmic thumping. "Male white . . . black hoodie . . . possession cocaine."

"10-4 on that. Northbound from 325 Bleecker. Male white wearing a black hoody wanted for possession of cocaine. First unit on scene advise."

"Fuck, that sounds like Manny," Jack hissed as he swung into the oncoming lanes to dart around a slow-moving Toyota, the driver too deaf or stupid to get out of the way of the police car with flashing lights and siren. Jack deked into his lane and blasted under the railway tracks that marked the northern boundary of 51. Trees flashed by them as Mount Pleasant dipped into a shallow valley, forested parkland on both sides.

"That the guy we met for coffee the other night?"

"Yeah, Manny's a good guy."

"If he's an enforcement car, then what the hell is he doing

getting into a foot pursuit by himself?" Brett was reclining as best he could in the passenger seat, but Crown Victorias were not designed for those in the six-and-a-half-foot range. He was sipping at a coffee, letting the hand and arm holding the cup sway with the motion of the car between sips. Brett didn't get excited over much and after his time in 14 Division, foot pursuits were old news.

Jack laughed. "Manny could get into a foot pursuit sitting behind a desk."

"Ah, one of those."

The scout car caught a moment of air coming out of the valley and Brett would have lost his coffee had the lid not been on.

"What's your location, Enforcement 51?" the dispatcher prompted when there was no update from Manny. *"Enforcement 51, what's your location?"* A hint of concern rippled her detached calmness.

"5101, we're on Bleecker. What was his last location?"

"Northbound from 325 Bleecker."

"We don't see him out front of 325," the 51 unit advised. "We'll head up to Howard."

Other cars were arriving, fanning out to search.

"Fuck, Manny, where are you?" Jack muttered.

"Where is this Bleecker?" Brett crumpled his empty cup and let it drop. A foot pursuit was one thing; an officer not answering his radio was a whole lot different.

"St. Jamestown," Jack explained. "Like Regent Park but with taller buildings."

Brett nodded. Even though he had never worked in 51, he knew of the park and its reputation. A sprawling government housing project, it was an infamous cesspool of drugs and violence. Brett knew that if St. Jamestown was anything like Regent Park, it was not a good place for a lone officer to disappear from the airwaves.

The road was dipping again, to slide under Bloor Street. If Jack drove under Bloor, he would have to go south, then north again. If they went under Bloor.

"Hang on." Jack hammered the brakes, dumping speed before cutting across the northbound lanes of Mount Pleasant. There was no off ramp *to* Bloor from Mount Pleasant, but there was an on ramp coming down *from* Bloor. Do Not Enter signs really didn't mean much compared to an Assist PC and the moment Manny failed to answer, the foot pursuit jumped to an assist.

Jack flew up the ramp and, if it had been a movie, would have screamed onto Bloor, the scout car dramatically skidding sideways before tearing off to the rescue. But this wasn't a movie and throwing the car blindly into traffic, especially when coming the wrong way out of a one-way, was a damn good way to get into an accident. And once you were in an accident, you were shit useless to the officer who needed your help.

Jack reluctantly came to a stop at Bloor, a main four-lane artery running east-west through the heart of Toronto. Even at night, the traffic was heavy and drivers didn't seem inclined to make way for the police.

"Move, you fuckheads!" Jack yelled, adding his anger to the siren's wail. He pushed the scout car forward. Fuck it. If people weren't going to stop for him on their own, he'd make them stop. Manny's continued silence told Jack he had no more time for politeness. He tromped the gas pedal. If he hit a car, they'd have to wait for him to come back.

"Basketball court! North of 325!" an officer yelled over the radio. The officer didn't say if anything was wrong, but the urgency in his voice said whatever was happening wasn't good.

When Jack hit the intersection of Bloor and Sherbourne, luck was with him: the light was green. He hammered the brakes to dump speed, then wheeled into the turn, foot on the gas as the car straightened out. A pedestrian who must have figured he had the right of way over a police car hauling ass jumped out of the way as the cruiser brushed by.

"Idiot," Brett muttered.

Jack threw the car into the turn onto Howard Street, a small one-way leading out of St. Jamestown, then one more turn and Jack and Brett were on Bleecker Street.

St. Jamestown was a gathering of a dozen and a half or so apartment buildings for low-income and government-assisted families. Like Regent Park, its notorious cousin to the south, St. Jamestown kept the 51 Division coppers busy with drugs, weapons and domestic violence. Unlike Regent Park, which boasted only two high-rises, St. Jamestown was all towering thirty-something-floor apartment buildings. Parking lots, play areas and walkways swirled around the tower bases, serving the good residents by day and the assholes by night.

Bleecker Street was the unofficial western border of the complex. There were apartment buildings on the thin stretch of land between Bleecker and Sherbourne Streets, but Jack never considered them part of St. Jamestown. Two high-rises, 325 and 375 Bleecker Street, often received police visits. The street was northbound only, two unmarked lanes wide. Four scout cars, their roof lights slashing the darkness with strobes of red and white, were stopped between the buildings, two on the street, two on the boulevard, their powerful takedown lights targeting the playground.

Skeletal trees waiting for the kiss of spring encircled the playground in concrete bunkers. A weary-looking jungle gym stood forgotten in a sea of sand, its faded plastic and rusted steel casting gigantic twisted shadows in the takedowns' unforgiving glare. Past the sandbox and jungle gym was the basketball court, its concrete surface home to the nocturnal parasites who preyed on innocence and desperation.

As Jack bounced the scout car over the curb and slid to a

stop on the winter-dead grass, an excited but relieved voice announced, "5102, all in order. One in custody. No more units required."

Jack and Brett were climbing out of the car as the dispatcher advised any units not yet on scene to disregard. Jack wouldn't have given the all-clear quite so quickly.

Clustered between the sandbox and the basketball court Jack saw a crowd of maybe two dozen people. He was behind them, but he could feel the hostility. When Jack and Brett were within earshot, Jack heard angry words and outright threats sparking on the cold night air.

It's another fucking house party, Jack thought. Only this one had considerably more deadly possibilities.

He and Brett pushed into the crowd, breaking its unity and disrupting its violent potential, at least momentarily. People moved aside or were moved aside. Jack and Brett broke free of the mass and Jack breathed easier, relaxing the forearm he had clamped against his gun as he and Brett pushed through the crowd of onlookers. With a quick glance at the coppers on the basketball court, Jack knew all was good.

Manny, looking winded but unhurt, was standing over a prone prisoner and Jack turned to the crowd. "All right, everyone! Time to move on," he bellowed, telling them the show was over and letting the coppers, who either had their backs to the crowd or were searching the cracked concrete, looking for dropped drugs and a possible court card, no doubt, know they should fucking turn around.

A harsh, raspy voice began snapping orders and soon four cops joined Brett and Jack. Within moments the crowd was breaking apart and people were drifting away as if they had been part of a fog bank dispelled by a sudden heavy wind. Soon only one lone straggler was left, huddled in an army surplus jacket that looked as worn thin as its owner. He had the gaunt, wasted look of a long-time crack addict and when Jack caught him staring, the straggler quickly dropped his eyes. There was something familiar about the face and the sunken eyes above jutting cheekbones and a nose that had obviously been broken, but Jack couldn't place him.

Someone sure took a dislike to his face and rearranged it.

But a single crackhead posed no threat and Jack wanted to check on Manny.

Manny's prisoner had already been searched and hauled off by other coppers to a scout car: no sense Manny walking the guy all the way back to his car. As Jack walked up, Manny was brushing at the dirt on his pants.

"That's what you get for chasing someone on foot and not in the car."

"Jack!" Manny gave his pants a final, useless swipe and stood up. "I didn't know you came down to help out."

"Someone's got to keep you out of trouble," Jack replied as they shook hands. "What are you doing chasing someone when you're working alone?"

Manny shrugged. "What could I do? He was lighting up his crack pipe right on the street. I just hope I didn't mess up my hair with all that running." He swept a hand along his clean scalp and grinned. "Listen, Jack, I gotta head to the station with the body. Meet up later for coffee?"

"Sure thing, moron. Try not to get into another chase on your way back to your car."

Manny laughed and mimicked running. Jack shook his head. He really wasn't joking about another foot chase.

"Warren, when are you going to stop pretending you like it up there and get your ass back down here where it belongs? God knows, you spend enough time south of the border as it is."

Sergeant Rose — call her Rosy and she'd punch your lights out — was the owner of the raspy voice that had dispersed the crowd. She was a big woman with short, spiky black hair and a temper shorter than her hair. A self-professed bull dyke, she didn't give a shit what anyone thought about her on the job. As she was known to state, she wasn't here to make friends or hold anyone's hand. Jack thought she liked him, although it was hard to tell with her in-your-face attitude.

"Hey, Sarge. What happened to the blonde hair?"

"The new girlfriend didn't like it," she grumbled. "So? When you coming back?"

"Wish I could, Sarge," Jack said wistfully. "But I can't. After all the shit that happened, my wife would kill me or at least divorce me if I transferred back."

"Better make up your mind soon, Warren. That open invitation from the inspector won't last forever."

"Yeah, I know."

Sergeant Rose started toward her car but turned back to offer a final piece of advice. "Time to grow some balls, Warren, and tell your woman how it's gonna be. Now get your ass out of my division."

Jack tossed her a casual salute and joined Brett, who was leaning against one of the basketball posts.

"Friendly lady," Brett commented.

"Ah, she's okay. Just a little rough around the edges. Let's head back. The division may be falling apart as we speak."

"Yeah, right," Brett snorted, reminding Jack of Sy. Do all cynical coppers snort disbelief the same way?

They walked to the car and Jack never gave the crackhead with the broken nose a second thought.

Thursday, 15 March
0430 hours

Brett slowly manoeuvred the scout car through the old, twisting streets of Forest Hill. Officially, he and Jack were patrolling the wealthy community for suspects stealing high-end vehicles. It was amazing how easy it was to steal an eighty-thousand-dollar car using a tow truck. No one thought twice about a towed car, even in the middle of the night. But really, Brett was trying to stay awake. It was that nowhere time between late night and really early morning and the radio was quiet. 51 coughed up the odd blurb, but from 53? Nada.

Jack was semi-conscious in the passenger seat. Staying awake this time of night when you were driving was hard enough; riding shotgun, it was almost impossible. He tried to keep his eyes focused on the shadows around the old stately homes with their old stately trees, but the patches of heavy darkness kept sucking him down. Then he would sputter awake and realize he had missed a whole street.

Jack sat up straighter, rubbing at his face. "Man, this sucks. At least in 51 there were drug dealers to chase this time of night."

"I hear that. But all the good little 53 Division drug dealers go home when the bars close."

Jack checked his watch. "Oh, fuck. If we've got another two hours of this, then I'm going to need some caffeine. How about you?"

Brett hefted his meaty shoulders. "I could go either way, I guess."

"You sure? I thought you said you didn't sleep all that well today."

His shoulders lifted and dropped again. "I can't remember the last time I had a decent sleep, regardless of what shift it was. Guess I'm just used to being tired." Brett flicked a weary smile at Jack and in the unhealthy glow from the car's computer the dark smears under his eyes were deep enough to swallow his cheeks.

"Trouble sleeping?"

Brett nodded. "I'm lucky if I get a couple of hours in a row. Most of the time I doze for a few minutes in between staring at the ceiling."

"That sucks." Jack knew that a lot of coppers had trouble sleeping. He'd had his fair share of sleepless nights last year, but thankfully the guilt-ridden dreams were fading. "Any idea what's causing it? Is it just the shift work?"

Brett didn't answer. Jack was thinking he hadn't heard the question when Brett blew out a long sigh. "It's . . . complicated."

It was Jack's turn to shrug. "Your choice, but it's not like we're doing anything."

"True." Brett pulled out onto Eglinton Avenue West and headed for Yonge Street. There was an all-night Tim Hortons on Yonge just north of Eglinton. "Remember when I said I left 14 because I didn't like the person I was turning into?"

Jack nodded, not wanting to break the big man's flow of words; it sounded like Brett wanted — needed — to talk about this.

"I'm sure you saw it down in 51: the guys who hated anyone not carrying a badge, always seemed pissed off and ready to kill someone. You know, the miserable old fucks." Again that weary smile. Brett eased to a stop at a red light, the scout car alone on the road. In the harsh, electric light Brett's smile looked like the grimace of a skull. "Well, that was me."

Brett didn't speak again until the light changed. Then, as the car moved forward, so did his words. "I hated work. Hated everyone and everything. I started to have trouble sleeping and that just made it worse; I always felt worn out, edgy. It got to the point my kids began to avoid me and my wife said it was because of my temper. Not that I ever hit them, never that," he added quickly, obviously needing Jack to know that. "Never that. I'd kill myself first."

This last was said so softly Jack wasn't sure he had heard it.

"I didn't want to end up like so many coppers you see: divorced, alone, miserable. So I transferred out of 14. Thought if I got away from all the shit and assholes things would get better. But they didn't." Brett laughed, a bitter, painful sound. "I still can't sleep and I still hate everyone. Only now I have more time to dwell on how much I hate people and the job."

"You hate the job?"

"With all my soul."

"Then why stay?"

Again Brett laughed without humour. "Why?" He fixed Jack with an emotionless stare. "Because my wife left me and took the kids. Because I live by myself in a shitty little apartment. Because my kids are afraid of me."

He pulled to the curb in front of the Tim's.

"Because it's the only thing I have left in my life."

Friday, 16 March
0202 hours

"Hey, man. Whatcha doing?"

"Hey, Manny. Hang on a sec." Jack shifted his cell phone to his left hand and turned down the radio, quieting the dispatcher as she gave a 53 car yet another alarm call in a seemingly unending string of alarm calls. "How are things down in 51?"

"Busy as always, dude. How about you?"

Jack groaned theatrically. "It seems everyone up here has a house alarm but none of them know how to use them. We've done about six alarm calls so far and they just keep coming."

"It's the weather, man. Any sudden change messes up the systems."

Jack had to admit the change *had* been sudden. And drastic. After the warm start to the week, winter had come back, intent on punishing the city for daring to think spring was within reach. The temperature had plummeted, but at least there hadn't been any snow.

"How's your head?" Although their partnership had been short — getting shot can mess anything up — it had been long enough for Manny to learn Jack suffered from migraines and he knew sudden changes in the weather could start a painful chain reaction in Jack's skull.

"Not bad. The pain comes and goes. I haven't had to pop any drugs yet." As if to let Jack know it was listening, the headache he'd had since waking up stabbed him through his right eye. Jack flinched at the sudden jolt of pain. *Damn, I might end up downing some Fiorinal tonight.*

"Who are you working with?" Jack asked to change the topic. Maybe if he ignored his headache it would go away. Yeah, right.

Sounding all smug and happy, Manny gloated, "I'm with Jenny."

"Lucky prick."

Jennifer Alton was another of Jack's favourite people from 51. Jack had never had the pleasure of working with Jenny as she had been on the Community Response Unit, or Foot Patrol in old-time jargon, during his stint in 51. Despite not working together, they had gotten to know each other and had fallen into a very close, very comfortable friendship in a brief period of time. Although Jack had shared his marital problems with Manny, it was Jenny he had confided in, revealing his fear that Karen would divorce him if he didn't transfer out of 51.

It had been strange talking to her about his marriage; he was attracted to her and could easily see himself falling for her had he not been married. What had Sy called her? A modern-day siren, unable to help herself when it came to attracting men. For some it was her smile, others her hair, her legs. For Jack, it was the total package. She was a beautiful, intelligent, fun —

Jack smacked himself lightly in the forehead. One mention of Jenny and his thoughts wandered off down this happy little trail. A siren, all right.

"You with Big Brett tonight?"

Jack groaned again. "Don't I wish. No, tonight I'm stuck with the Earl."

"The Earl? That the guy who gives people tickets for having their licence plates obscured in the middle of a snowstorm?"

"The one and only. I'm sitting in the back lot right now while he's inside picking up a new ticket book. Would you believe he gave a guy on a bicycle a ticket for not having a bell?"

"Was the guy at least an asshole?" Manny asked hopefully.

"It was yesterday when it was so warm. The guy had his bike out for the first time this year and the Earl gives him a ticket. Just a regular guy out for a ride."

"Man, that's low. I can see giving that to an asshole but not someone who has a job."

"Is it any wonder the public hates us? And you should have heard him talking about it. You'd think he had just pinched a guy carrying a gun or something. God, I hate it up here."

"Why can't you pair up with Brett? I mean, it would be better if you came back here but. . . ."

"The staff sergeant doesn't allow permanent partners. I think it's because he knows there's about three guys on the platoon who no one would want to work with." Jack grimaced. "And here he comes now. Gotta go."

"Want to hook up for coffee later if it's quiet?"

"Sure, but you just jinxed us by using the Q word."

Manny laughed. "Take it easy, dude. Talk to you later."

Jack hung up just as Richard "the Earl" Chalmers got in the passenger seat. Jack had learned the first time working with Chalmers not to let him drive, or they'd spend the whole shift pulling over cars for some of the dumbest tickets Jack had ever heard of. Chalmers's defence was the chintzier the ticket, the more likely the person was to take it to court and court cards, those scheduled off duty, meant money for the Earl.

"All set," Chalmers declared, patting his fresh ticket book. "Let's go fight some crime."

More like prong the public, Jack thought.

His headache twinged and he jerked at the pain.

"You okay to drive, Jack?" Chalmers looked more than ready to take over the wheel; his numbers were always low when he worked with Jack. Jack knew the Earl saw himself as the number-one producer in the station, with a reputation to uphold.

"Nah, I'm good. Just a bit of a headache. Let's grab some caffeine before we clear." Jack smiled as he dropped the car into drive. He knew the Earl hated not driving, not being able to pull over every car he wanted to. The Earl checked every car he wanted to pull over on CPIC — the Canadian Police Information Centre — first. He didn't want to deal with someone who was on file for violence, would he? Jack had seen the Earl ignore suspended drivers — usually gold mines for tickets — because the driver also had a caution on him for violence against police. The Earl might have been 53 Division's golden boy when it came to tickets and therefore the staff sergeant's favourite officer, because high numbers on the platoon made the staff sergeant look good to the inspector. But the Earl was also a gutless coward. He'd shown his true colours the first night Jack had worked with him, near the end of January.

A woman had phoned 911 saying her husband was off his schizophrenia medication and was becoming aggressive. She said her husband, a loving and gentle man when on his meds, had a tendency for violence when he was off them and the violence was usually directed at people in positions of authority — namely, cops. She asked for at least four officers, if not more. In a perfect world, or a TV show, the police service would have been operating at full strength and would have had ample officers to send. The dispatcher sent Jack and the Earl.

The paramedics were waiting outside the condo building, looking up and down the street, when Jack and the Earl pulled up and joined them.

Jack looked around, puzzled. "I miss something?"

"There another car coming?" one of the medics asked.

"Nope. What you see is what you get."

"But the call said —"

"Don't worry." Jack cut the medic off. "Chalmers here is actually a ninja in disguise."

The medics didn't look reassured.

The four of them took the elevator up, then paused outside the unit door, cops to one side, medics to the other. No sounds from inside, but the wife must have been waiting by the door because she had it open before Jack finished knocking.

She was an attractive blonde and Jack put her in her early forties, although stress and worry had added a few years. She looked questioningly at the four people at her door, then peered up and down the hallway. "Where's the rest of you?" she asked, concern tightening her voice.

Jack hoped being asked that question twice wasn't an omen. He explained that he and the Earl were the only police available for the call and said they would do their best to talk her husband into going to the hospital.

She paled at the thought. "You don't understand," she cringed. "Last time it took four police plus the ambulance people and he wasn't that bad. He's a lot worse this time."

"He's schizophrenic, ma'am?" a medic asked.

"He is," she confirmed, glancing over her shoulder into the condo. "He stops taking his medication when he feels better. He thinks he doesn't need it anymore."

"How's he acting right now?" Jack wanted to know.

"He's very agitated, aggressive."

"Has he hit you?"

"No," she stated with a firm shake of her head. "But he has in the past when he got like this. Today I told him I thought he should go to the hospital and he started swearing at me, saying I was conspiring against him. He said he'd kill me if I didn't leave him alone." She started to cry. "Please help him."

"That's what we're here for," Jack told her. "Where in the apartment is he?"

"But you don't understand!" she protested in a strained whisper. "He doesn't like the police when he's like this and he'll fight you if he thinks he can win. That's why I wanted more of you."

And that's when Richard "the Earl" Chalmers, who had taken the oath to serve and protect the people of Toronto, suggested, "If he doesn't like police, maybe we should send the medics in first."

Needless to say, the medics weren't impressed with the idea of going in to deal with the violent schizophrenic while the armed personnel waited out in the hall. Jack wasn't comfortable with it either. Jack would have pushed the Earl out of the way had he not been edging his way to the back of the group already.

"For fuck's sake," Jack muttered under his breath as he stepped through the doorway. He didn't know who came in next, the medics or the only other armed person at the call and really didn't give a shit.

"My husband's name is Nathaniel," the wife said. "Don't call him Nathan; only his friends can call him that."

Nathaniel was in his office, pacing the floor. He was a good-sized man who obviously worked hard to stay in shape.

Why can't the violent ones be small and weak?

Nathaniel stopped abruptly as soon as he spotted Jack, who stood just outside the office door, his can of pepper spray concealed in his hand. He had little hope the spray would work on Nathaniel as it rarely seemed to have any effect on the mentally ill, but if the situation ended up in a fight — and from the way Nathaniel was flexing his hands and hunching up his shoulders, it was headed that way fast — Jack wanted to limit the possible injuries to everyone involved. Especially himself.

"What do you want?" Nathaniel did not sound pleased to have visitors.

"We heard you weren't feeling up to par." One of the medics, an older guy with a fringe of grey hair, had come up beside Jack where Chalmers should have been. "We just wanted to see if there's anything we can do for you."

Nathaniel eyed the medic suspiciously. "You look old. Are you in charge?"

"Well, I suppose I'm the oldest here, so that kind of puts me in charge."

"All right, I'll talk to you, then."

Nathaniel told the medic that the neighbours were conspiring against him but he didn't know why. Jack watched in amazement as the medic talked Nathaniel into a chair and then into letting them check his vitals. Ten minutes after Jack and the medic had entered the condo, Nathaniel agreed to go to the hospital.

Jack rode in the ambulance with Nathaniel. "They have eyes everywhere," Nathaniel confided to him. "No telling what lengths they'll go to."

That's when Jack learned he was on his own when he worked with the Earl. But hey, the guy wrote a lot of tickets.

The Earl came from an English background, hence the nickname. The Duke would have sounded way too tough for him and his beard just couldn't hide his weak chin and pasty complexion. He was tall, a couple of inches or so over Jack's five-ten, and thin. Not thin like a runner or swimmer but thin like someone who uses a snow blower to clean an inch of fluffy snow off the one-car driveway.

Jack realized not everyone liked to lift weights. He himself had been more of a runner than a weight lifter until he had started working with Sy and really got into the heavy iron. In fact, Jack had gone from a respectable 185 to just shy of 200 pounds since getting out of the hospital last fall. Most of the new weight was muscle, but like Manny he had a load of laundry covering his washboard abs. Unlike Manny's load of towels, Jack liked to think his was a small one of socks.

But in a job where you occasionally had to fight with people to get the cuffs on, wouldn't it make sense to do at least a bit of training? But on the other hand, if you didn't mind sending in the paramedics to do your job. . . .

Jack didn't know how Chalmers had gotten the Earl nickname or whether it was supposed to be derogatory or not. If he had been labelled — and cops loved to slap on nicknames for good or ill — in sarcasm or jest, then it had backfired because Chalmers seemed to like the handle and never reacted negatively when someone called him the Earl.

After a quick stop at the nearest Tim Hortons, Chalmers wanted to sit at Yonge and Eglinton, the unofficial hub of the division and one hell of a busy intersection. For a change, the Earl wasn't pestering Jack for traffic stops. He seemed content to sip his coffee and watch the women go by, although there weren't many people out at this hour and those who were, were bundled up against the cold.

"5302, call for you at 3000 Yonge Street. Male calling 911, says he's hearing voices and wants to kill himself. See attached CPIC. Time, 0215."

Jack was about to pull up the CPIC hit for the male when Chalmers told him not to bother.

"It's just Willy," he explained. "He calls in about once a month saying he's going to kill himself."

"Bit of a frequent flyer, is he?" Jack caught a break with the light south of them and pulled a U-turn to head north up Yonge Street.

Chalmers nodded, then swallowed some coffee. "He's a harmless little guy. I think he gets lonely and says he's going to kill himself just so he can go to the hospital and talk to someone. This won't take us long."

The rest of the trip was spent in silence, Chalmers running licence plates, looking for an expired validation sticker, Jack sipping his tea. It was funny how he had been a major coffee drinker until Sy, who'd had coffee for blood, had been killed. Ever since then it was strictly tea for Jack. It hadn't been a conscious decision, just something that happened. He wondered what a therapist would make of it.

Okay, Jack. That's enough Sy for today.

He had to be careful. If he thought about his murdered friend too often, he started dreaming about that night in the alley. He couldn't afford another stint of nightmares. What was the old saying? Beyond here there be dragons?

Number 3000 Yonge Street was an old apartment building just south of Lawrence Avenue, the division's northern boundary. Beyond here there be 32 Division, the starting point of Jack's career.

Six years up there thinking I was a cop and all it took was one night in 51 to teach me I knew shit about being a cop. And now I'm stuck in a division so fucking dead it makes 32 look like a war zone.

"I don't know how much longer I can take this," he told himself as he got out of the car.

"You're talking to yourself, Jack. Can't take what?" Chalmers joined Jack on the sidewalk, adjusting his uniform hat. That was another thing: a lot of the coppers in 53 wore their hats. The rule for hats in 51 was simple: they stayed in the trunk unless the media or the brass were about.

"Don't you ever get bored working here? Don't you get tired of doing alarm calls and medical complaints?"

"You kidding?" Chalmers asked incredulously. "This is a great division to work in. Nothing too serious, easy tickets and lots of hot women. They don't call it Yonge and Eligible for nothing. You don't like it here?"

As they headed for the building's front door, Jack considered lying. But why bother? He wasn't happy and he sure wasn't obligated to walk around with a fake smile plastered on his face.

"I'm bored out of my fucking mind."

"Then transfer. I'm sure you could get back to 51. You spend enough time down there anyway." The Earl sounded as if he didn't understand why Jack jumped on 51 calls in the first place. Or maybe he didn't want to understand.

"I can't transfer. My wife would kill me, even though I tell her there are days I'm so bored I could just quit altogether."

"Maybe that's what she wants," Chalmers said as he yanked open the lobby door.

Jack stopped in his tracks. That couldn't be what she was doing, could it? Jack knew Karen wasn't comfortable with him being a cop. What wife would be, after a murdered partner, death threats and a home invasion? But he thought she was okay with him working in 53, a division so quiet it was driving him stir crazy, so crazy he told her he would rather quit than work there. Is that what she wanted? For him to quit on his own, so it would be his decision and not something she forced on him? She wouldn't do that to him, would she?

"You coming, Jack?" Chalmers asked from the doorway.

"Yeah, right behind you."

Would she?

"It's at the end," Chalmers said, gesturing down the hall after they exited the elevator on the eleventh floor.

"It's always at the end." Jack fell into step next to Chalmers and was a little surprised when the Earl moved ahead to knock on the door.

I guess when he knows the EDP isn't violent, he's willing to go first.

Chalmers rapped the corner of his memo book on the door. "Willy, it's the police. Open up."

Willy opened the door and Jack immediately saw why he wasn't considered a threat. Standing all of five-two at best, he was a portly fellow with thin hair. Owlish eyes peered out from behind round glasses.

"Hi, Willy. You need a ride to the hospital?" Chalmers asked by way of greeting.

"No, I don't want to go to the hospital. They never help me." Willy held the door open. "Please come in."

The apartment was a small one-bedroom and impeccably clean and neat. Willy ushered them into the living room, then offered them a seat on the couch. The pillows and a knitted throw looked so precisely placed and proper that Jack didn't have the heart to sit down and he was positive Willy sighed in relief when they declined.

"So what's on your mind today, Willy?" Chalmers hooked his thumbs in his gun belt and rocked back on his heels. Maybe this was his Officer Friendly stance.

If the Earl wanted to handle this, Jack was more than willing to let him run with it. He hung back, surveying the apartment. Everything was as orderly as the couch. The magazines on the coffee table were fanned out decoratively, the glass cabinet holding porcelain figurines gleamed, not a trace of dust existed anywhere.

"The voices are back," Willy explained.

His home might have been tight and organized, but Willy was a ball of nerves. His hands couldn't stop moving. If they weren't smoothing the front of his beige sweater vest, they were patting down his already flattened hair. What was left of it. Willy was a definite candidate for a good toupée or a shaved head.

Willy leaned confidentially toward Chalmers, lowering his voice to a whisper, as if hoping the voices wouldn't hear his confession. "They're telling me to . . . to kill myself."

"And how are they telling you to do that?" Chalmers asked good-naturedly, playing the role of an indulgent father to a troubled child.

Willy darted his eyes at Jack, licking his lips nervously. "I don't know him. He looks mean."

"He's new to the division, Willy. He's used to dealing with drug users, not nice people like you. That's why he looks mean. He's really okay."

"Oh." Willy licked his lips again while he adjusted his glasses.

"Doing a bit of drinking tonight, Willy?" Jack asked.

The way Willy jumped it looked like he expected Jack to

hit him from the other side of the room. When he realized Jack wasn't going to, he settled down. Except for his hands, which went back to smoothing his vest.

"Why . . . why do you ask?"

Jack pointed at the round table outside the small kitchen. Four empty beer bottles littered its surface. One of them was broken, lying on its side and missing its long neck. The bottles were the only sign of normalcy in the apartment.

"The . . . the voices told me to drink them. They said it would help."

"Yeah, I hear the same voice sometimes, too." Jack righted the broken bottle.

"It's okay if you had some beers, Willy, it's your house," Chalmers soothed, glaring at Jack over his shoulder.

Jack held up his hands in an excuse-me gesture. *Sorry for butting in on your big investigation.*

"Are you sure you don't want to go to the hospital, Willy?" Chalmers asked, turning back to the little man. "If you're thinking about killing yourself, it might be a good idea."

Willy tucked his head between his shoulders, almost cowering and jammed his hands into his pants pockets.

If he pulls into himself any more, he'll disappear. Jack's grin turned to a grimace as an errant bolt of pain stabbed his eye. *Fuck! Okay, Chalmers, if we're going, let's go. I need my drugs.*

"Did the voices say how to kill yourself?" Chalmers asked. He seemed to be ignoring Jack's scrunched-up face.

Willy nodded, almost reluctantly, but said nothing.

"It's okay, Willy. You can tell me." Chalmers placed a reassuring hand on Willy's shoulder.

Oh, for fuck's sake. It doesn't matter. Let's go.

"The voices told me . . . told me to . . ." Jack was rubbing the heel of his hand against his right eye in a futile effort to squash the pain and almost missed the furtive glance Willy shot his way. "It's not nice. It'll hurt."

"Well, let's get you to the hospital, then. Okay? Do you need a coat? It's pretty chilly out there. No? Okay, let's go." Chalmers started for the door.

Willy meekly followed, head bowed, muttering to himself.

It's about fucking time. Jack was already waiting in the cramped front hall. His migraine was certainly kicking into high gear. He squinted against the suddenly too-bright light.

Then Willy was standing in front of him. "I'm sorry," the meek little man said, freeing his left hand from his pocket.

Jack had time to think *About what?* before Willy swung at his face. Pain, sharp and instant, ripped by his right eye. He screamed and Willy was at him, slashing backhandedly, the jagged neck of the broken beer bottle clenched in his fist.

Jack got his arms up to protect his face and the glass tore through his jacket sleeves. He lunged at Willy, smashing him into the wall, then flinging him to the floor. Willy was screaming, thrashing and twisting beneath Jack. Almost blind — he couldn't see to his right — Jack groped for Willy's hand, desperate to get hold of the broken piece of bottle.

He felt Willy's hand punch into his side, stabbing at him. Would the Kevlar vest stop the glass? Jack clamped his right arm to his side, pinning Willy's hand between his upper arm and the vest.

"I want to die! Kill me! Kill me!" Willy screamed and went for Jack's eyes with his free hand.

Jack was almost completely blind. He hoped it was only from blood in his eyes. He could barely see Willy and the nut's left arm kept slipping away. Little or not, Willy was fighting Jack with a maniacal strength and it was only a matter of seconds before he tugged his left arm and the bottle neck free.

"Chalmers! For fuck's sake, help me!"

Richard "the Earl" Chalmers stood in the hallway, staring into the apartment, his face a perfect sculpted expression of disbelief.

This wasn't supposed to be happening. What went wrong? Willy had been following him out the apartment like he always did, submissive and cooperative.

There had been a scream from behind him and Chalmers had turned in time to see Willy and Warren falling to the floor. What was that asshole Warren doing? This was supposed to be a quick, easy call. A short wait at the hospital — Willy always knew the right things to say to get admitted at least overnight — then back to the station for lunch, go out solo for the second half of the shift, get away from Mr. 51 Division Tough Guy Warren. Maybe take out the radar gun and set up on Mount Pleasant, no, Bayview would be better at that hour. Now Warren was messing it all up just to prove how tough —

Then Chalmers saw the blood pouring — no, gushing! — from Warren's right eye. The blood was raining on Willy, who was twisting and squirming under Warren, flinging blood everywhere, painting the walls inside the apartment door with it. What the hell was going on?

"Chalmers! For fuck's sake, help me!"

Willy might have been small, but the way he was thrashing about it was like trying to hold down a fucking greased pig. Jack's right eye was gone, cut or full of blood, Jack didn't know, but he couldn't see a damn thing out of it. He was losing his left eye, too, as blood coated his face. He shook his head to clear his eyes, but there was just too much blood.

He finally managed to grab Willy's right arm and pin it to the floor. He still had Willy's other arm trapped against his side, but he could feel it slipping free. A couple more tugs and Jack would be in some serious shit.

"Willy! Stop fighting!" Jack could feel blood, his blood, hot and wet, fly from his lips as he yelled. He pictured his face drowned beneath a mask of red and suddenly it was Sy beneath him, Sy's face covered in blood, Sy's blood pumping out from his severed artery, Sy's blood slicking Jack's hands as Jack fought for his partner's life, Sy's life draining away in rivers of red.

No! I'm not going to die. I won't let this little fuck kill me too.

Willy was still jerking his left arm, trying to free the hand holding the knife. Jack readied himself. Next tug, he was going for his gun.

Let's see this little fucker cut my throat with a couple of rounds in his chest.

Willy tugged. Jack went for his gun.

There was an angry hissing noise from beside Jack's left ear and the unmistakable smell — sharp, hot, abrasive — of pepper spray. Willy's angry screams instantly became wails of agony and still Chalmers hosed Willy down.

The spray burned Jack's throat. "Chalmers! Enough! Grab his left hand." How Jack could hear the hiss of spray over Willy's screams he didn't know, but he knew the hiss lasted another brief second, then abruptly cut off.

Jack felt Chalmers fumbling behind him, tripping over their entwined legs.

"I've got it! I've got the bottle!"

Jack pulled away from Willy and stood up. He didn't care if Willy wasn't cuffed, he had to get away from the pepper spray. God, he hated that shit. Maybe it didn't work all the time on the assholes, but it always worked on him. Just a whiff of it could double him up with hacking convulsions. His throat felt as if it was lined with fire. His left eye was burning but not as badly as it should have been. The blood must have somewhat kept the spray out of his right eye. Thank God for small mercies.

Jack fumbled his way into the hall and drew huge, cleansing breaths. His throat was still a column of fire, but at least he wasn't hacking his guts out. He wiped at his eyes, steeling himself for a slash of pain from his right, but there was none. Another mercy. Willy must have missed the eyeball. The instant his eyes cleared, more blood, rushed back into the right, blotting part of his vision, but not before he glimpsed Willy huddled on the floor, pawing at his own eyes.

Serves you right, you little fuckhead.

Jack gingerly explored the area beside his right eye, wincing when his fingers touched raw, torn flesh. He gritted his teeth against the flare of pain as he pressed his hand to the wound.

There was a choked scream from down the hall. A neighbour, curious or concerned, had stuck her head into the hall and, seeing Jack, uttered a short shriek before slamming her door shut.

Jack looked down at himself with his one good eye. Blood drenched his uniform jacket and glistened on the black cloth. He smiled, then spat blood from between his lips, spraying the wall.

I must look like something out of a horror movie, but I'm alive. But Sy. . . .

Jack's free hand went to his throat frantically checking for a cut, but there was none.

"Jack?" Chalmers slipped hesitantly in front of him. "Jack, you okay?"

Jack turned to him and smiled, a full, teeth-baring grin. "I'm alive, if that's what you mean. Did you get the knife?"

"Um," Chalmers held up the neck of the broken beer bottle. "I got the glass. There wasn't a knife."

"That's what I meant, the glass. There was no knife." Of course there was no knife. Willy had used a broken bottle, not a knife. Sy had been killed with a knife. Sy's throat . . . Jack pushed that thought away. What's done is done. The past is dead.

Chalmers was looking around uncertainly, almost nervously, still holding up the piece of bottle.

Yes, Jack could clearly see it was a bottle, thought he could even see a chunk of his skin impaled on one of the jagged stumps. He grinned at the idea.

Chalmers backed up from that grin. "Um, do you want to call for an ambulance, or should I?"

Still grinning but in an utterly calm, I'm-not-standing-here-covered-in-my-own-blood voice, Jack asked, "Have you cuffed Willy yet?" He couldn't see Willy, who was behind Chalmers, but he could still hear him. His cries had deteriorated to pain-filled whimpers.

"Ah . . . no. I wanted to see how you were."

"I'm good." That same pleasant tone. "Why don't you go cuff Willy before he decides to go get another weapon? I'll call for an ambulance."

Chalmers stepped into the apartment, casting uneasy glances back at Warren. That smile, with blood smearing his face and lips, outlining his teeth and gums, was the freakiest thing he had ever seen. And Warren didn't even seem upset. If anything, he seemed happy! Happy that some nut had just carved up his face. Chalmers pulled out his handcuffs, wondering if he was cuffing the real nut.

"Dude, when I said we should meet up later, this isn't what I meant."

Jack smiled. A normal, true-to-its-depths smile. And blood-less, since he'd had the chance to clean up. "Manny, what are you doing here?"

"Here" was Sunnybrook Hospital. The emergency room, to be exact. While Chalmers had struggled to cuff Willy — the pepper spray might have knocked the desire to fight, to provoke an officer into killing him, out of poor Willy, but he hadn't wanted to pull his hands away from his burning eyes — Jack had radioed for an ambulance and extra units. Willy had been hauled away after officers had gladly and none too gently Jack guessed, decontaminated him by shoving his head under the bathtub faucet.

The paramedics had bandaged Jack up and hustled him off to Sunnybrook. The Earl had followed in the scout car. And here

Jack sat, or reclined, in a hospital bed waiting to be stitched up. The pain had subsided to a sharp ache and withdrawn to the area beside and above his right eye. Curiously, his migraine had taken a back seat to the cut, settling down somewhere at the back of his skull. He supposed the migraine didn't want to share the pain spotlight and was willing to wait until it could have the stage to itself again.

Jack was stripped down to his T-shirt and pants. The pants had only a drop or two of blood on them and could be saved, but his jacket and shirt were history. He had been drifting off when Manny had come in.

"I'm here on official business, brother." Manny held up a camera case. "53 doesn't have a SOCO on the road, so I'm here to take some pictures. But we would have come up anyway, man, you know that. We heard you call for the ambulance but didn't know it was for you until they called me for the pics."

"Is Jenny with you?"

"Yup. She had to hit the little girls' room first. Personally," Manny said, fiddling with the camera, "I don't think she can take the sight of blood."

"Yeah, right." Jenny Alton was one of the toughest cops Jack knew. "I see you're still sporting that goatee. I can't believe no one's given you any grief about it."

"It's a beard," Manny said defensively, pointing at the pencil-thin line of hair outlining his jaw. "And there's been a few complaints," he admitted.

"I still think with that cue ball you call a head it makes you look like a professional wrestler."

"Yeah!" Manny whipped off his jacket and hit a Hulk Hogan pose. Thankfully, he still had the rest of his uniform on; Manny was a big guy and paid his dues in the weight room, but he was too much of a junk food addict to be posing.

"Know any good vets?" He pumped his arms in a double-bicep shot. "'Cause these pythons are sick!"

Jack laughed. He could always count on Manny to lighten things up.

"All I need is a good name." Manny swung his arms down, back to the most muscular pose, quivering exaggeratedly. "Like Manny the Magnificent or Manny the Mighty."

"How about Manny the Mental Midget?" Jenny suggested as she slipped into the tiny room.

Whereas Manny could brighten Jack's mood, the mere sight of Jenny upped his pulse. Tall and slim with just enough muscle to give her curves, she was one of the few policewomen who looked good in uniform. Good? Hell, downright sexy. Her raven hair, done up in a tight French braid, offset dazzling crystal-blue eyes.

Manny the wrestler went back to his camera as Jenny leaned in to give Jack a kiss on the cheek. "That's for being hurt," she explained, then punched him, not playfully, in the ribs. "And that's for getting hurt. How could you let someone get that close with a weapon?"

"Your concern is touching." Jack pouted, rubbing his side. "I could have had broken ribs, you know."

"You don't. We got the story from the Ds when they called for pictures. Seriously, Jack, I'm sorry you're hurt and I'm really happy it isn't serious, but how could you let this happen? It doesn't sound like you."

Jack studied his friends. Beneath Manny's joking and Jenny's anger, he saw their concern and understood it. The Jack who had let a kid sneak up on him at a house party and let a nut dripping with warning signs get close to him with a weapon was not the same cop who had worked the streets in 51.

Jack shrugged, feeling a twinge in his right shoulder. Old pains, new pains. "I was careless, I guess. Getting stale, rusty."

"Dude, you need to come back to 51."

Jack nodded. "I know." A sudden grin split his face. "And this," he touched the bandage, "is my ticket out of here."

Jenny crossed her arms, unconvinced. "You really think that will fly with Karen?"

"How can Karen say it's safer for me in 53? She can't. Not with this staring her in the face. So let's get a look at it, shall we?"

Jack reached for the temporary bandage, but Jenny stopped him. "Shouldn't we wait for a nurse or someone?"

"Nah. The doctor's already cleaned me up. I asked them to hold off on stitches until pictures were taken. Come on, unwrap me."

Jenny gently freed the tape holding a gauze wrap in place and began to unwind the material from around Jack's head. As she removed layers, Jack could feel dried blood clinging stubbornly to the gauze. Jenny pulled it free with a wet, crinkling noise.

"Don't take the dressing off yet, Jenny." Manny moved in with the camera. "I'll take some overall shots first, then some without the dressing. More dramatic that way."

Jenny smirked at him. "Guy takes the soco course and suddenly thinks he's an artist."

Manny was unperturbed. "Some artists take pictures of people or landscapes. I photograph scenes of crime. My work — no, my art — allows the inarticulate to speak in eloquent volumes."

Jack and Jenny groaned in unison. "How many others have you used that line on?" Jack asked.

"You're my first," Manny declared proudly. "I'm really looking forward to saying it in court. Now, get naked for me."

Jenny gently pulled the dressing away, trying not to notice Jack wincing whenever the bandage snagged on clotted blood. When the wound was fully exposed, Manny whistled appreciatively. Jenny frowned.

"You better hope the doctor uses small stitches, man. Otherwise, you'll end up with one big-ass scar." Manny snapped a few final shots, then handed the camera to Jack. "Check it out."

Jack studied himself in the digital display. Manny was right; it was going to be one hell of a scar. The jagged end of the bottle neck had made his wound messy. There was one deep gash, too brutal to be called a cut, starting on the outside of his right cheek, just below the eye. It slashed up on an angle through his eyebrow and faded out as it ran onto his forehead. Above this and beside the eye was a mass of smaller, shallower cuts, like veins branching out from a main artery.

An inch to the left and I would have lost the eye. Lucky.

"And you think if you show that to Karen she'll agree to let you go back to 51?" Jenny was still frowning.

"She'll have to admit that it's not as safe up here as she thought."

"So she and her parents, I bet, will use it as an argument to quit the job altogether."

"It's time I took Sergeant Rose's advice and grew some balls." Jack crossed his arms defensively. "I thought you guys would support me on this."

"We do, man. We just don't want to see you get divorced over it."

"When were you thinking of putting in the transfer?"

Jack laughed. "Hell, I'm thinking of seeing the inspector before I go home today."

A few hours later Jack was sitting in the scout car, his face freshly stitched and still numb from the anaesthetic, though he could already feel the freezing ebbing away, revealing the pain beneath it. He pictured a beach growing again as the tide slowly retreated. He touched the bottle of painkillers in his pocket appreciatively. He was going to need them soon.

"Did you want to stop anywhere before we go to the station?" Chalmers asked as he fired up the car. "Grab a coffee or something to eat?"

Chalmers had been hesitant, cautious even, around Jack throughout the time at the hospital. When Manny and Jenny had arrived, the Earl had disappeared entirely, supposedly to get some lunch. Maybe he thought Jack partially blamed him for what had happened. Whatever the reason, Chalmers was eager to please.

Jack checked his watch. "It's almost eight. We're already on the big clock, so why don't we stretch the overtime a bit?" He tapped the thick bandage wrapped around his head. "I don't think anyone will begrudge me another hour."

"Sure, Jack. You want to get breakfast?"

"Nope. I was thinking we could drive down to 51. I need to have a word with the inspector."

Monday, 19 March
1714 hours

Jesse was feeling good. Better than good, actually. Absolutely fucking fine.

Ever since he had hooked up with Kayne, nothing could go wrong for Jesse. He always had money in hand and there was never a shortage of crack or whores; Kayne was very generous with his friends and he had only one friend. Jesse was intent on keeping it that way. He got to help Kayne on his "quest." That's what the fucking guy called it: a quest to be the baddest mother-fucker on the streets. He wanted to be remembered or some shit like that. Jesse didn't care. As long as Kayne kept the money and drugs coming and Jesse got to crack some bones along the way, Kayne could carve as many Ks as he fucking desired.

But right now putting the boots to someone was not high on Jesse's list of priorities. In fact, Jesse was feeling far too fine to do anything other than lie back on the floor of his apartment and . . . just . . . feel . . . good.

They had just left some poor asshole in a laneway some-where. If Jesse tried to remember where, he might be able to come up with the general vicinity, but really he just didn't give a shit. After relieving the asshole of his stash of marijuana, Kayne had cut open his forehead with the piece of slate he called his talisman. Then they went back to the room, feeling fucking fine on the liberated weed.

Jesse's room faced the street and was one of the two largest in the two-storey rooming house. Prior to hooking up with Kayne, Jesse had had limited cash and been relegated to living in one of the back rooms, a tiny cell he could cross in three steps. The place had stunk like shit and another resident had told him that the previous tenant hadn't left the room in years, not even to go to the bathroom. The talk of the building had it that when the police and ambulance had finally hauled the old fuck away, he had fucking cockroaches living in him. Not *on* him but fucking *in* him. And Jesse could believe it, too, for under that new paint smell had been a stench that made dead fish on the beach seem fucking appetizing. As soon as the warm weather arrived, he'd planned on moving his ass out of that shithole.

But then he'd met Kayne and everything had changed.

All it had taken was a wave of cash under the landlord's nose and Jesse was in the ground-floor front room, the previous tenant not knowing what was happening until his ass hit the sidewalk. Now Jesse had room for a bed, a couch, a chair and the room's crowning glory: a TV. True, the furniture was all old and ratty, having belonged to the last occupant and the TV only pulled in three fuzzy stations, but Jesse was living like a king.

With all the cash rolling in, he was contemplating some new tattoos. When his brain was clear enough to think, that is. Both arms were already sleeved in skull tattoos: skulls with snakes, skulls with knives, grinning skulls, skulls of all shapes and sizes. He was mulling over the idea of one huge, kick-ass skull on his back.

But that was for later. Jesse was sprawled on the floor, the cushions from the couch heaped behind him to prop up his head and shoulders. Kayne was in the chair, one leg thrown carelessly over a padded arm, his chin resting on his chest. Jesse thought Kayne might be asleep but couldn't tell in the shadowy haze: milky light wormed through the threadbare shades to tinge the smoke from the train of joints they had smoked a greyish blue. They had sucked back enough of the weed to envelope the whole building in its sickly sweet stench, but none of the residents had complained. They all knew to steer clear of Jesse's new friend and his new friend's temper. Word was circulating that he was the crazy fucker carving people up, writing his name on their faces with a knife or some shit like that. Jesse was sure the residents knew it was best to leave well enough alone.

Jesse studied his . . . friend? No, not friend. Guys like Kayne didn't have friends. They had . . . followers, that was it. Kayne wanted someone to watch as he smashed people, someone to admire him and gush over him as he ripped open face after face with his talisman.

"Talisman, my fucking ass," Jesse muttered, dragging deep on his rolled cigarette. "It's a fucking piece of rock."

"What the fuck you say?" Kayne's eyes had cracked open, but his chin was still propped on his chest and the words had come out slurred: *Whuh thuh fuck you shay?*

Jesse's heart lurched. "Nothing, man. Just wish we had some rock."

"Get some later," Kayne mumbled — *Geh shum la'er* — as he drifted back to sleep.

Lisa, the green-haired whore Kayne had taken into his troop, was passed out on the floor by Kayne's feet. Her mouth twitched at the mention of rock.

Jesse blew out a shaky breath, then soothed his nerves with another drag. A deep one. If Kayne had understood what he had said . . . Jesse wiped his brow, his sedated mind all too able to imagine a bloody K torn into his skin. And he would be lucky if Kayne stopped there. His attacks had escalated in the last few days; they were more vicious each time he pulled out that chunk of stone. Jesse figured it was only a matter of time before Kayne killed "one of the weak ones," as he called them.

Or was killed himself.

How long before he ran into someone with a gun? Or someone who got tired of his antics and simply ordered him gone? Or maybe, most likely, one of these times Kayne wasn't going to be the baddest fucker in the fight. It could happen.

Jesse wriggled his shoulders, walking them up the cushions till he was sitting upright; he could never think well lying down. He looked at Kayne, drooling on his naked chest. Really looked at him. His torso and arms were heavy with sinewy muscle, not the swollen size of some steroid freak — Jesse had seen enough of them during his time inside — but big like pit bull muscle. Size that said the man behind the muscle could seriously fuck you up, as Kayne had done many times over. But could it last?

Kayne might have worked out like a madman in the pen, but now? Now he was on a steady diet of crack and those muscles would not last long. Jesse had seen it before: guys came out of the pen jacked to the shit, but then they get back on the crack and in no time they were fucking toothpicks. Once that happened to Kayne, people would be lining up for a shot at him. Jesse figured it would be best to get as far from this questing freak as possible. Guilt by association and all that.

But for now life was good. No need to bail quite yet.

Jesse leaned over, shoved a dirty finger up his left nostril to plug it and blew out his right one. Or tried to. Ever since that fucking cop had broken his nose by smashing his face into a plate of eggs — completely undeservedly; he hadn't done a damn thing to warrant such abuse — it always clogged up when he smoked. Breathing through it was a pain in the ass and for months he had endured taunts of "egg face" and "egg snot."

Jesse snotted a yellowish lump onto the floor and sniffed back what was dribbling down his lips. Staring at the snot as it soaked into an old cigarette butt, an idea came to him. He turned from the snot to Kayne and the idea took hazy shape in his cloudy mind.

Jesse fingered his crooked nose and smiled.

Wednesday, 21 March
1200 hours

"Do you really think I'm doing the right thing, Mom?"

"Of course you are, dear." Evelyn stroked her daughter's arm comfortingly. "Now, drink your tea before it gets cold."

Evelyn Hawthorn was a great believer in the therapeutic aspects of tea. Earl Grey in particular. No problem was so great that it could not be viewed rationally while drinking a hot cup of tea. The simple act of brewing and then pouring or serving the tea gave one time to organize one's thoughts in a calm, sensible manner. One could not panic when sipping tea. It was simply impossible.

So, when her daughter had called, frantic with worry, Evelyn had known just what was needed: a mother's knowledge and comfort served over a steaming cup of Earl Grey, the civilized world's tea. Served in China, mind you. None of those garishly large mugs men preferred.

Karen dutifully sipped her tea, as did Evelyn, who studied her daughter intently. Karen's eyes were troubled and unfocused. Perhaps Evelyn had allowed her husband too much of a hand in raising their only daughter. George was a wonderful husband and provider — not that she needed a provider, of course, but his financial success had allowed her to devote herself to her social causes and the plight of the less fortunate. But as a father, he was rather limited in his approach. He raised children the same way he lectured: he presented his theory, established the facts, drew his conclusions and expected everyone to agree. George Jr. had grown up that way. His father had told him which schools to attend, which topics to study, which degrees to obtain. George Sr. had also dictated his son's social life, hobbies, sports, friends, associates and romantic interests. And it had succeeded wonderfully. George Jr. had obtained twin PhDs and was gaining notoriety in the academic world. Evelyn had no doubt her son would one day teach at Harvard.

But that approach had completely failed with Karen. Backfired, in fact. Instead of accepting her father's guidance, she had rebelled, although subtly and never in direct defiance of her father. It had been a fencing match between father and daughter. He, always attacking, pressing his demands. She, always parrying, evading his thrusts neatly but never going on the offensive. He wanted her to go to university and she did, but to York, not U of T. He wanted her to teach at the university level; she taught, but in grade school. She dated the boys George selected for her but never seriously and never for long.

George Sr. never learned that he couldn't lead Karen as he had led George Jr. The more he insisted, the more she parried. No, Karen needed to be guided by suggestion and insinuation, "allowed" to come to the decisions that were best for her, seemingly on her own.

Then had come the Day of Open Defiance. Karen had brought home a young and handsome police officer. Evelyn willingly admitted her daughter had a fine eye when it came to men, but George had been devastated. His daughter had finally attacked and her lunge had scored a winning touch. A police officer! A public servant, no less. And not even a detective or an officer of substantial rank but a lowly uniformed patrolman. And uneducated, too. Jack had attended university but never finished his degree and to George that meant he was uneducated. Evelyn viewed Jack's education as incomplete, temporarily on hold.

Evelyn had agreed with her husband and together, he with his blunt attacks, she more subtly, they told Karen why Jack was wrong for her in every possible way. But the more they pressed, the greater she stood firm. No gentle parries this time. Karen had chosen the man she wanted as her husband and no amount of reason would make her see otherwise.

George continued to hammer away at the relationship. He had been gracious enough to pay for the wedding, but Evelyn knew he had done so to prove his point that Jack was not and never would be financially established. Evelyn had altered her tactics. Altered her whole view of Jack, in fact. Whereas George saw the negative, she saw the potential. George thought policing was a stagnant job. She considered it a temporary occupation, a boyhood whimsy to be satisfied and then discarded for more serious pursuits. Jack was not unintelligent or without a certain manly appeal and with their help he could use his policing background — some people actually viewed police officers favourably — to transition to a new career once he decided, with their help, that it was time to put away boyish dreams and take on the mantle and responsibilities of a man.

It was just taking Jack longer, much longer, to come to that obvious conclusion than Evelyn had anticipated. Which brought her to today.

"Of course it's the right thing to do," she repeated, setting down her cup. "Jack, like most men, needs to be . . . guided, shall we say, to the right decisions. More tea?"

Evelyn refreshed both cups, adding honey to hers. Jack had started her on using honey in lieu of sugar. The boy had potential.

Cup on saucer on her lap, Evelyn faced her daughter. George knew of the visit, but he could *not* learn the reason behind it. Nor could Jack, who was occupied at court this morning. Evelyn was at Karen's home; she and her daughter were seated in the wing chairs in the living room. The chairs had been a Christmas present to Karen and Jack one year. That Karen could sit in this room, let alone stay in the house after what had happened in this very room, testified to her strength. Evelyn was pleased that the new-carpet smell was finally gone.

"But now that Jack is going back to 51 he'll never leave the police!" Karen's voice was strained, almost a whine.

Evelyn had an urge to slap the annoying sound from her daughter's mouth. She kept her hands clasped delicately on cup and saucer. "Nonsense," Evelyn scoffed. "Jack, in many ways, is still rather immature." She held up a forestalling hand. "I'm not belittling him by saying that, it's just that this desire, this need of his to work in such a disreputable area, is a childish way of proving himself."

"Proving himself? To whom?"

Evelyn smiled. The whine was gone. "To himself, to you," she suggested. "To anyone whom he feels may be looking down on him for leaving in the first place."

"That's insane. Jack nearly died because he was in that division. Leaving was the responsible action, the adult thing to do. *Staying* would have been childish."

Evelyn leaned forward to lay a comforting hand on Karen's knee. "*We* know that, dear, but *Jack* doesn't. It's a man thing. What do they call it? Machismo?"

Karen laughed without much humour. "That fits. Did I tell you Jack is getting a tattoo?" She nodded to her mother's raised eyebrow. "Tomorrow, before he goes back to work on Friday. He's had someone working on the design for weeks. He says it's a tribute to Simon."

"How utterly . . . manly of him." Evelyn sipped her tea. "And you're quite right. It does fit with the whole masculine psyche that I'm sure is much more prevalent with the downtown police officers. I'm sure Jack believes that other police officers see his leaving the division as a form of cowardice. That's why he used the first excuse he could to say that it's dangerous everywhere. So he could go back."

"That's not exactly what he said."

Evelyn shooed the words away with a flutter of her fingers. "What you have to convince him of — what we both have been trying to get him to see — is that staying down there and, ultimately, remaining a police officer is utterly selfish of him."

"But if he won't leave for me . . ."

Another dismissive flutter. "He believes you'll stand by him no matter what he does, but I'm sure he'll come to the right conclusion when you tell him."

"Does Dad know?" Karen asked hesitantly.

"Heavens, no!" Evelyn laughed. "And he mustn't find out." She lowered her voice conspiratorially. "Since Jack's outburst at the book party, your father is convinced Jack is dangerous and that by staying with him you're endangering your life."

"That's ridiculous! Jack would never hurt me."

"I know, dear, I know. But your father doesn't. To be quite frank, he intends to see the two of you divorced."

"That will never happen." Karen crossed her arms and scowled as if her father were in the room with them.

This was better. Evelyn hated it when Karen whined or acted less than she was. Stubbornness, although trying at times, was preferable to whining or self-pity. Her blonde hair and sensual figure she got from her mother, but Evelyn knew that stubborn set to the blue eyes and jaw were all George Hawthorn.

"I'm sure it never will, dear. But until you're positive you're pregnant, Jack and your father are not to know. I would wait until you're well into the first trimester. And once you are, both of them will come to their senses. Jack will surrender his boyhood daydreams for something more suitable for an expectant father and your father will be so enraptured with the notion of being a grandfather he'll forget all about a divorce."

"But will he and Jack ever get along?"

Evelyn sipped her tea, then smiled craftily. "Would you like to know a secret about your father, dear?"

"A secret?"

"Jack and your father aren't all that different." Evelyn set her cup down. "Your father will never admit this, not even to himself, but he was once very much like Jack."

"Like Jack?" Karen asked in disbelief. "How?"

"When we met, all those years ago," Evelyn reminisced wistfully, "your father wanted to save the world. He was so handsome back then, so full of life and determination. He even considered joining the police force," she admitted with a devilish smile.

"No!" Karen was shocked. Her father, a cop?

"He did," her mother confirmed. "He often talked about 'working in the trenches' and 'making a difference one life at a time.' I think all men, at one point in life, yearn for excitement and action. I seriously believe that's why sports are so popular."

"But what happened to Daddy?" Karen was still trying to picture her father with a gun and a badge.

Evelyn sighed. "I suppose you could say he grew up," she said, a touch of regret tingeing her words. "He realized you could never save people unless they wanted to be saved, could never achieve any lasting results down in the trenches."

"So he decided to teach?"

Evelyn nodded, then sipped her tea. "What better way to change the world than by educating those going out into it?"

"Daddy a policeman," Karen whispered. She looked amazed and thoughtful. "Is Daddy jealous of Jack?"

Evelyn shrugged delicately. "Perhaps, but he'd never admit it or even entertain the possibility. Like I said, he grew up and one day so will Jack."

"I hope so." Karen sighed. "I just feel a little guilty going behind his back like this. We'd decided to wait to have children until we at least paid off the Honda and were able to put some money away."

"But Jack wants children, right? And who's to say he ever

has to learn the pregnancy was anything but a wonderful accident?" Evelyn patted Karen's knee again. "It will all work out for the best, you'll see. More tea?"

Friday, 23 March
0317 hours

Jack bolted upright in bed, gasping for air, his heart hammering in his chest. He thought he had screamed himself awake, but Karen was still asleep beside him, undisturbed. Her blonde hair, tousled on the pillow, glowed softly in the scant illumination coming through the shutters from the street lights. He drew his knees up, resting his forearms on them as he waited for his heart to quiet and the remnants of the nightmare to fade into darkness.

"Fuck me," he whispered, wiping sweat from his face, wincing as his fingers grazed the still tender scar. Maybe having the stitches removed yesterday had triggered the horrible dream. Jack had thought he was finally done with the nightmares, with seeing Sy's blood night after night. Blood he could never stop from running between his fingers, stealing his friend's life away.

"That's enough, for fuck's sake," he quietly scolded himself. "Just fucking knock it off."

3:17. In the waning aftermath of the nightmare, the clock's red numbers looked like blood. Morning and his first day back at 51 were still a couple of hours away.

Knowing sleep was beyond him, Jack slipped quietly from the bed. The sweat on his chest and back cooled as he padded to the bathroom, then shut the door gently before turning on the light. He leaned on the counter, staring into the mirror. A troubled Jack stared back at him. He checked the scar running through his right eyebrow. It tugged down the corner of the eye, giving him a permanent squinty look. Manny had been right; it was one hell of a scar.

Jack was developing quite the collection. On his right shoulder, in the meat of the trapezius muscle, was a tiny puckered scar. He knew if he checked the back of his shoulder in the mirror, he would see the much larger scar left by the bullet's exit.

Lucky. Twice. If the bullet had been lower or more to the left, it could have killed him. And he knew he was damned lucky not to have lost his eye.

"Yeah, lucky me."

Jack turned on the tap, then leaned down to rinse his face. The cold water felt good on his skin. Refreshing. He straightened up without towelling off, head back, eyes shut. Just enjoying the feel of the water as it dribbled onto his chest. When the drops reached the top of his pyjama bottoms, he reached blindly for a towel. He dried his stomach and chest, then patted his face.

Better. Much better.

Jack opened his eyes and Sy was staring at him from the mirror, blood spurting from his opened throat, splashing against the glass surface. Jack screamed. Or tried to. The scream that wanted to rip from his lips drowned in his throat, in the blood spewing from *his* slashed throat, splattering the mirror in perfect harmony with Sy's blood.

Jack staggered back, slamming into the bathroom door and clutching at his throat, but the blood wouldn't stop. He was going to bleed to death forever.

"No," he gurgled. "No, no —"

Jack bolted upright in bed. Again. Again he gasped for air as his heart hammered.

"Jack?" Karen reached for him and at her touch he screamed once more. "Jack! Jack, it's okay. It was just a dream. Just a dream."

Slowly, gently, Karen laid her fingers on his arm, the muscles trembling beneath her fingertips. When he didn't pull away, she folded him into her arms and rocked him as she would a child. She smoothed his hair, her fingers tracing the fresh scar.

"It's okay, Jack. It's okay. Everything's going to be okay."

In the darkness, she rocked him. In the darkness, they held each other.

"I told you you'd have a kick-ass scar."

"Nice to see you, too, Manny."

"Dude, it's good to have you back." Manny pumped Jack's hand, then pulled Jack in tight, pinning their clasped hands between their chests as he thumped Jack one-handed on the back. "Damn good to have you back. This is where you belong, man."

"It feels like coming home." Jack freed himself from Manny's enthusiastic embrace and headed to his locker. The change room in 51's basement was, like every other room and office in the old building, too small for its purpose. A long but not long enough rectangle, its walls and centre were lined with ancient lockers, the metal doors proudly bearing dents, gouges and, in the odd spot, bullet holes.

Heavy-metal music, cranked to a distorted volume, pounded from the attached weight room. The night shift coppers, getting dressed to go home, bragged and boasted about the night's arrests and shit storms. The day shift coppers, donning the black uniform of Toronto's finest, bitched about the long day ahead of them, the first of seven.

Jack dumped his gym bag onto one of the wood benches that ran the length of the room between the rows of lockers. Some of the benches had been supplied by the station, others had been built in some coppers' garages. All of them were in the same condition as the lockers and splinters were a continual danger.

Jack thought back to the huge change room at 53. The pristine lockers, the ample room, the smooth benches, the peaceful atmosphere. Coppers chatting about family and kids, the tickets they'd given out. So pleasant, so civilized.

God, he was happy to be back.

"This your doing, Manny?" Jack pointed at his locker, only half a dozen down from Manny's.

"We're partners, man. Gotta stay close."

"Next he'll want to shower with you."

"Hey, Paul, good to see you."

Paul standing up was more of a giant than Paul sitting in a scout car. At six-five, he was almost the tallest cop in the station — Marcus Rull topped out at six-eight but was so skinny he looked like a mutant heron when he walked — and easily one of the biggest. His dark skin, midnight black, as he called it, was stretched tight over massive muscles, yet he moved like a man half his size. Paul was known to break up fights simply by getting out of the police car.

"Nice addition, Jack." Paul tapped his right eyebrow. "Gives you a piratey look."

"A souvenir from 53." Jack touched the still tender scar. "And a permanent reminder to keep my eyes open."

Jack hung up his leather jacket and was reaching for a uniform shirt when Manny stepped close and pointed at Jack's left shoulder. "What's that?"

"Had it done yesterday." Jack lifted his T-shirt sleeve to reveal the tattoo.

Paul joined Manny, then whistled appreciatively.

Less than twenty-four hours old, the lines were sharp and somewhat raised, giving the tattoo a three-dimensional look. The ink was a deep, lustrous black. In a week or so, the tattoo would heal and settle into the skin, but until then the harsh rawness gave it that much more life and vitality.

"That is one pissed-off-looking angel."

Jack grinned. Paul had nailed the essence of the tattoo. Capping his left shoulder, the angel glared out from beneath a furrowed brow, powerful wings arced aggressively over his naked and heavily muscled torso. The angel's hands clasped the hilt of a mighty sword held point down and the blade faded into a banner unfurled beneath the heavenly warrior. Writ upon the banner in cursive script was *Simon, Never Forgotten*.

"That's nice, man. Really nice."

"Thanks. Sy said there was a line in the Bible about how, in order to fight evil, sometimes even angels have to do evil."

A respectful hush fell as each man remembered a fallen brother. But time stood still for no one, not even 51 coppers.

"Better hustle, man," Manny warned, "or the new staff'll do you for being late to parade."

"The new staff? What happened to Rourke?"

"Quit, man. Went to work for a bank. Fraud investigations." Manny sighed, sounding utterly disheartened.

Jack was shrugging into his shirt. "C'mon, Manny. Rourke was a good staff, but he wasn't that good."

"It's not how good Rourke was, it's how bad the new one is," Paul informed Jack and there was muttered agreement from the cops within earshot.

"Staff *Sergeant* Greene," Paul said stiffly. "Never just staff."

"Oh, no. Never just staff," Manny grumbled under his breath.

Jack looked questioningly at Paul.

Paul explained. "He's old school, Jack. I mean *old* school."

"He and Moses went to the same kindergarten," another copper declared as he headed for the washroom.

"Hey, Jarjad," Jack said. "How old school?" he asked Paul.

"How about stand-up parades? Old enough for you?"

"You're kidding." Jack was amazed. "I haven't done a stand-up parade since the college."

"Neither had we until a few weeks ago. And not just standing up when he enters the room, oh no." Paul wagged his finger disapprovingly, then gruffed up his voice in imitation. "'The platoon shall be in formation and at attention when I enter the room. Every officer will be thoroughly inspected.'"

"Wonderful." A thought occurred to Jack. "What about permanent partners?"

"As long as both of you maintain your workload. If either of you drops below what he considers acceptable, you're split up." Paul grinned humourlessly. "Can you say 'quota'?"

"Workload also affects time off." Manny slammed his locker closed. "Those with higher numbers get first dibs on T.O. If Greene thinks you don't deserve the T.O., you don't get it."

"Hang on, he can't do that," Jack complained. "If you have the hours in the book and there's enough bodies on the road, then you should get the time off."

Paul pointed a finger at him. "You know that. We know that. Try explaining that to him."

"Wonderful," Jack repeated as he settled his gun belt around his waist. "What else?"

"Hm, let's see." Paul ticked off the points. "Stand-up parades, no T.O., if you call in sick you're weak and should be ashamed of yourself, if you put anything ahead of the job, like family, friends, your health, you aren't a real cop. Anything else, Manny?"

"Don't forget beards."

"Right," Paul said, nodding. "Facial hair, other than moustaches, is severely frowned upon, but since we're allowed to have beards now he can't do much about it. Legally, that is."

"Meaning?"

"Meaning you have a better chance of getting T.O. if you're cleanshaven." Manny looked as unhappy about it as he sounded.

Jack was beginning to understand Manny's impassioned greeting. "He must hate you, then," he said to Manny.

"He does," Manny confirmed, stroking the pencil-thin line of hair along his jaw line that made his goatee a beard. Technically, at least. "He told me to shave it off and I said I wouldn't."

Jack groaned. He could just imagine how unpolitically correct Manny had been as he refused. Manny was a great guy, but he didn't think before he spoke. Even when he was speaking to someone who could royally fuck him over.

"He said the only reason he wasn't documenting me for it is

that he's seen guys on other shifts with similar beards. He's going to bring it up at the next management meeting and push for all the staff sergeants to document anyone who doesn't have a full beard."

Jack was perplexed. "And his reasoning for all this?"

"I told you, man. He's old school." Paul, suited up, closed his locker. "If they did it that way when he was on the road, then that's how we'll do it."

"How long does he have on the job, anyway?"

"Over forty," Manny said. He was leaning against a locker, arms crossed, shoulders slumped. Jack had never seen Manny, the guy he once described as the world's biggest puppy, so apathetic about the job. "He was in headquarters somewhere. We think he was transferred here as a hint to retire."

"What about Johanson and Rose? I can't see this sitting well with them." The platoon's two sergeants came from the same school of policing that many of the division's senior guys belonged to. To them, old school meant you got the job done, didn't take shit from anyone and at the end of the shift everyone went home safe and healthy.

"They don't like it either," Paul confirmed, "but in the end they're the sergeants and Greene's the boss. And Johanson has less than a year till he pulls the plug. Rose is in line for a spot in the CIB. She doesn't want to fuck that up."

"One day when Greene was coming in late —"

"Coming in late?" Jack interrupted Manny. "So he's not perfect?"

"I wish," Manny sighed. "He was coming from a funeral or something. He saw two of our guys checking out some dealers at Oak and River and when he got to the station he had Rose do them up for not wearing their hats."

"Oh, fuck, he's not one of those idiots, is he?"

"He is," Paul confirmed. "The only reason for not wearing your hat is if it got knocked off in a fight. And as soon as the fight's over, you'd better be putting it back on. He even wanted us to wear them in the parking lot to and from the scout cars and while parading prisoners."

"And you didn't think to mention any of this to me when I said I wanted to come back?" Jack accused Manny.

Manny shrugged. "Sorry, dude. We need you."

"What about the senior guys on the shift?" Jack felt as if he was grasping at straws.

It was worse than straws. "There are no senior guys, Jack." Manny looked morose. "Sy's gone and we lost Trozzo, Woolcott and Emberley while you were in 53. Trozzo went upstairs to the Youth Bureau and Woolcott and Emberley both transferred."

"How much time do you have on, Jack?" Paul asked.

"July will be seven years." He had a very sudden, very unpleasant feeling in his gut.

Paul stood up and clapped Jack on the shoulder. "Congratulations, man. You're senior man on the road."

"Welcome fucking home," Jack muttered.

"Officers Warren and Armsman? 5106, 1100 for lunch. Good to have you back on the platoon, Jack." Sergeant Johanson looked up from his parade sheet and gave Jack a brief smile. For the grey-haired, stoic supervisor, it was a gushing display of emotion.

A few other people echoed the sergeant's sentiments but briefly and quietly. The new staff sergeant did not take to unnecessary talking on parade. He glanced from his memo book at the unruly outburst but let it slide.

Too busy with his freaking notes. The man actually took notes about parade. Jack had never seen a supervisor, of any rank, make an entry about parade other than to say when it started and maybe when it ended. And the staff had spent long enough inspecting everyone. Jack hadn't been given such a thorough going-over since his days at the police college down in Aylmer. Greene had done a sock check to make sure everyone was wearing black

socks. A freaking sock check! Several officers, including Jack —
no grace period for the platoon's new addition — had been cautioned about the length of their hair. Jack wouldn't have been
surprised if the old bastard had taken out a ruler to measure the
gap between hairline and collar.

Jack wondered when the basement room at 51 had last seen
a stand-up parade. Its old, tired appearance certainly didn't cor-
respond with such formality. The once-white paint was a faded
and dreary ivory. A feeble light grimed through the dirt-grey
windows set high in one wall. The metal tables, in rows beneath
the windows, were as battle weary and worn out as the assort-
ment of salvaged chairs. No, formality did not belong here.

Jack was surprised when the platoon was allowed to sit as
Johanson read out the day's assignments and alerts. Greene
seemed like the kind of prick who would keep everyone standing. Jack had no doubt Staff Sergeant Greene was indeed a prick
of colossal magnitude.

Astonishingly, Greene was not a big man. Forty years on the
job meant he had been hired in an era when a significant portion of the job interview was whether you had to duck or turn
sideways to get through the door. Greene was neither tall nor
wide. He was unimpressively average. Average in height. Average
in width. His hair, mostly grey, was rigidly cut to regulation
length. The only thing marring his remarkable unremarkable-
ness was his iron-grey handlebar moustache. To Jack, nothing
screamed "prick" louder than a handlebar moustache. Wax the
ends and curl them up and the moustache screamed "colossal
prick." Greene's moustache screamed colossally.

Johanson finished assigning the scout cars. "Anything to add,
Staff Sergeant?"

Jack shook his head at the sad, absurd formality. The parade
room felt empty with only five officers and the supervisors.
Jack, Manny, Paul, Jenny and Boris were the day shift. Morris
and Goldman, both with about four or five years on the job,

were on the early half, having started an hour ago. The platoon's strength wasn't looking too good. Manpower had been a problem last summer but never this bad. Seven on the road plus two on annual training and another two on holidays put the platoon's full strength at eleven and the three senior officers who had left the platoon while Jack was in 53 had created glaring holes in the platoon's seniority. The shift's essence, its strength, was broken. Parade should be the warm-up for the workday. Not quite a pregame pep talk but close enough. This wasn't a pep talk, it was a wake. And the corpse was the platoon's spirit.

What had this prick done?

Jack was about to find out.

"Thank you, Sergeant." Greene stood up as Johanson relinquished the podium, a wood pedestal atop the table just big enough for the sergeant's clipboard. Jack noted Johanson grimace as he stepped aside. The situation must be bad if the sergeant grimaced. Legend had it that years ago Constable Johanson had ended a fight by putting a suspect's face through a car window without so much as twitching an eyebrow.

Greene stood erect and surveyed his officers. Jack figured his gaze was meant to be steely and forceful, but he thought Greene appeared simply . . . well, prickish. At length, he spoke and his voice was as ordinary as the rest of him. Barring the prick screamer beneath his nose, of course.

"I was reviewing the platoon's performance over the past cycle and was appalled to discover that you officers were last in every category." He gripped the podium and leaned over it, as if he wanted to physically force his words onto the officers in front of him. "And not just last but abysmally last. Over the five weeks, your numbers in arrests, POTs and 208s continued to drop until the next platoon was substantially ahead of you. I will not tolerate such a shoddy work ethic!" He pounded the podium, hammering home his decree.

Jack was not surprised to hear workload was down. Why hunt

up arrests outside of radio calls, write tickets or even fill out a 208 after investigating someone? To make this prick look good to his boss? Not bloody likely.

I wonder if he bothered to check what the numbers were like before he got here.

"This platoon is lacking," Greene pronounced. "Lacking in integrity, teamwork and positive attitude."

Can he toss in any more core-value buzzwords?

"Therefore, all time off, including that in relation to annual leave, is cancelled until I deem this platoon worthy of such reward."

A chorus of unbelieving groans churned through the officers. Greene slammed his palm on the podium, silencing the insubordinate din.

"For those of you already planning to use sick time to circumvent my directive, be advised I will be assigning home visits to the road sergeant."

This shocked even Johanson. His face was a dangerous thundercloud.

The beatings will continue until morale improves. That's fucking brilliant.

But Greene wasn't finished. "Constable Warren. I will see you in my office immediately following parade."

The officers of B platoon filed out of the parade room glumly, their heads bowed, their footsteps heavy. Even the world's biggest puppy dog was trudging beneath leaden thoughts.

"The fucking moron doesn't see what he's doing to them."

As Greene had strode from the room, Johanson had signalled for Jack to hang back. Now the room was empty but for the two of them.

"He can't be that blind."

Johanson sighed and, for the first time Jack could recall, the solid sergeant looked his age. "He can and is. The fool actually thinks he was sent here to instill discipline." Johanson nodded when Jack cocked an eyebrow. "He told Rose and me that on his first day here. Unbelievable."

"Why was he sent here?"

Johanson shrugged. "Why does anyone like him ever get sent to 51?"

"He piss someone off?" Jack guessed.

"Either that or they thought he'd retire if he got kicked out of his comfy office at headquarters. Doesn't really matter. We're stuck with him."

"Is there anything we can do?"

"Getting rid of a staff sergeant is a hard thing to do. Technically, he hasn't done anything he's not allowed to." Johanson shook his head. "He's lucky he didn't get sent here even ten years ago. If he'd tried this shit back then, he would've gotten punched out."

"The good old days?"

Johanson snorted. "In some ways."

"Is there something on your mind, Sarge?" Jack wanted to catch Jenny before he headed up to see Greene. They'd managed only a quick hello before parade.

"There is, Jack." Johanson faced him, his eyes steady and, despite what the deep lines around them suggested, still strong. "I suppose you know with the others gone, you're senior man on the road." Jack nodded. "Because of that and what you went through with Sy and afterwards, the young guys on the shift will be looking to you for guidance."

Jack laughed but not with humour. "You suggesting I punch out the staff?"

"No, not yet." Johanson smiled to show he was kidding. Maybe. "A consistently low workload from the platoon will eventually be seen as a symptom of a greater problem, but it has to be across the board. A united front. There can't be any exceptions."

Jack knew what his sergeant was saying. "Borovski?"

"Borovski."

Sean Borovski, known throughout the station as Boris — a nickname he hated — was a slug of a police officer. Lazy, fat and cowardly, he was everything Jack hated to see in a police officer. To Jack, Boris extracted revenge on society for a tormented childhood with his radar gun and ticket book. But if numbers impressed the new boss, then Boris must be burning through the tickets.

Jack thought about it. Boris had looked rather smug on parade, even with his multiple chins spilling over the shirt collar he had undoubtedly just started buttoning up. Appearance had never been his strength. Nor had teamwork.

"I know it's a shitty homecoming." Johanson clapped Jack on the back as he headed to the door. The sergeant was spilling over with emotion today. "But it's good to have you back. Sy would be proud."

The staff sergeant's office was a tiny room crowded by two desks. Although technically it was an office, its chief function, unofficially, was to act as a shortcut from the back hall to the front desk. Except when Staff Sergeant Greene was in residence, that is. During his first day, in his first hour at 51, officers had learned that they were to enter the office only when summoned and were always to leave by way of the same door they had entered. There would be no inadvertent use of the office as a hallway.

Jack stood in the cramped office while Staff Sergeant Greene sat, back stiffly upright, behind his desk. Although, since the desks were butted face to face and Jack was standing to the side, the desk wasn't quite an authoritative barrier. Greene, like everyone else, would have to learn to work with what the station provided.

The office was a squat rectangle with the doors in diagonal corners. Jack had entered from the back hall. Had he stopped when he entered, Greene would have been two desks away. Jack could have taken a casual approach and sat down at the empty desk, but instead he had stepped around it and placed himself beside Greene's desk, forcing the staff to turn in his chair.

It was a petty tactic, but Greene was reminding Jack rather forcefully of his father-in-law: a man used to being obeyed, who had no time for the opinions of others unless those opinions complemented his own. Jack had made a critical error the first time he had allowed Karen's dad to treat him the way he treated everyone else: as an inferior. Jack had assumed his attitude was a facade and would change once he realized his daughter's new suitor was serious. It wasn't a facade and it hadn't changed. Jack had taken a lot of shit from Hawthorn; he wasn't going to make the same mistake with Greene.

Greene was attempting to regain the upper hand by forcing Jack to wait as he took care of important staff sergeant stuff. Too bad all he had in front of him were the day's parade sheets. There was only so much he could do with a list of officer names and their assigned cars, lunch hours and portable radios. Jack wondered when Greene would realize that the longer he looked over the sheet the dumber he appeared.

Pretty dumb, but Jack was tired of waiting.

"You wanted to see me, sir?" No way was Jack going to start by giving this waxed-moustache prick his full title. His training officer had taught him that rank had to be respected but that the person behind the rank had to earn it. And Greene had earned shit so far.

Greene gave the sheets a final check and set them aside before turning to Jack. He surveyed Jack from head to toe and back again, as if he hadn't given him a thorough exam not half an hour ago. Jack was tempted to hoist his pant legs unasked in case Greene wanted another look at his socks.

"I understand you were stationed here once before," he said by way of greeting.

"Yes, sir. Last summer."

Greene's right eye twitched. Jack figured it was because of the "sir." "I also understand you were involved in some questionable activities." His lips tightened as if tasting something unpleasant. "Nevertheless, you are the senior road man and as such I expect you to set an example for the officers beneath you."

Jack held back a retort. If Greene thought length of service was the only factor that made a leader, then in his own mind he would be close to demigod status because of his forty plus years on the job. But if Borovski was one of his favourites, as Johanson had suggested, then Greene had absolutely no insight when it came to judging a copper's worth.

"I will be looking to you to unite this platoon," Greene said, unknowingly echoing Johanson's words. Jack figured he meant unifying them under Greene's control. "Any officer who cannot work toward what is best for this platoon —" *What's best for you, you mean.* "— has no place here." Greene fixed Jack with an authoritative stare. If the quivering tips of his moustache hadn't kept distracting Jack, it would almost have been effective. "I will tolerate no rogue officers."

I think I've just been told no more questionable activities. "All for one and one for all," he said.

Greene appeared not to be a movie buff. "If that's how you wish to view it."

"Is that all, sir? I'd like to get out on the road." Jack had had enough of the prick and his moustache.

"You may go when I'm finished with you," Greene snapped. "I have an assignment for you, Officer Warren. As poor as the officers are on this shift, there is one among them who is rather prominent in his impertinence."

Manny, what have you done?

"I have already formally cautioned Officer Armsman on several occasions about his appearance and disrespectful attitude to those superior to him in rank. If he cannot amend his ways, he will find himself disciplined or transferred. Or both. It is your job, Officer, to influence his behaviour and attitude before my patience runs dry. And I am not a patient man."

Mentally, Jack was rolling his eyes. Manny was a good cop with a huge heart and a resolute, some would say stubborn, view of right and wrong. And there was no doubt that Greene's manhandling of the platoon would fall well within his "wrong" category. His problem was that he vocalized his opinions. He felt everyone should be able to talk "off the record." Sy had once warned Manny there was no such thing as off the record with a supervisor and it seemed Jack was going to have to remind him of that.

"He has one cycle, five weeks, to impress me, or I will rid myself and the platoon of a problem officer. Is that understood, Officer?"

Yeah, nice to meet you, too, prick. "Perfectly, sir. Is there anything else, sir?"

"As it is your first day with us, I realize you are unfamiliar with my supervising techniques."

Oh, no. I'm not unfamiliar. I've run into pricks before.

"Supervisors are to be addressed by their full rank. I expect you to adhere to that rule from here on. Is that understood?"

Jack felt like snapping to attention and giving a sharp *Jawohl!* Instead, he said, "Absolutely, sir," and turned to leave.

"Officer!"

Jack casually turned. "Sir?" There was no rule or regulation, as far as Jack knew, that said supervisors had to be addressed by full rank.

"Don't try and fuck with me, Officer." Greene's face was blooming an angry purple.

"Wouldn't dream of it." Jack smiled. "Sir."

The sky was clear and the sun was shining warmly for a March day. Kayne luxuriated in the feel of the sun's touch soaking into his dark sweatshirt, heating his whole body. He leaned back against a piece of plywood, his legs stretched out comfortably, then dragged deeply on a joint before passing it to Jesse. He felt the heat of the smoke in his throat and sinuses as he let it leak slowly from his nose. Life was good.

They sat on the footbridge spanning the ravine just north of Bloor Street, a link between the wealthy of Rosedale and the less affluent of St. Jamestown. In all his years, Kayne had never been on this bridge, had not known it existed until an unsuspecting weed dealer brought Kayne and Jesse out here to conduct their business.

The ravine was big enough to be called a valley and a street bearing its name, Rosedale Valley Road, snaked along the valley's bottom. Traffic passed in a mechanical hush far beneath them. The trees and brush to either side of the road were bare and lifeless, patches of defiant snow huddling within the ravine's shadows and recesses.

"Bet this looks a shitload better when the trees are all green."

"Huh?" Jesse gazed stupidly at Kayne, his unfocused eyes shifting from his friend to the trees stretching out below them. "What's green?"

"Fuck, you're a dumb shit." Kayne snatched the joint from Jesse's fingers. "You keep smoking this shit and you'll end up as dumb as Lisa. Stupid green-haired bitch." He crushed the last of the joint and tilted his face to the afternoon sun. It felt good to be warm; he'd been cold too often in prison. He knew it was only a matter of time before he went back, he always did, so he intended to enjoy his time outside and that meant sitting on this bridge, comfortably buzzed and soaking up some sun.

There was no need to hurry; they had the bridge to themselves since it was boarded off at either end because it was being repaired. The dealer they had run into in St. Jamestown had led them down to the bridge, squeezing behind loose boards in the wood barrier. A nice, private place for business, he'd said. Kayne couldn't have agreed more.

They had left the dealer, unconscious, bleeding and bereft of his cash and merchandise, by the barrier and sat near the bridge's midpoint, where a section of the chest-high metal railing was being replaced. The long gap in the railing was temporarily filled with plywood and it was against this that they rested. Kayne noted Jesse spent more time hunched over his knees than leaning back against the wood. Kayne knew Jesse was a coward and figured the feel of the wood flexing and bowing behind them had unnerved him.

Coward or not, Jesse was useful. He knew who sold the best rock, knew which dealers were least likely to have a gun or someone watching them. Kayne didn't mind scrapping with a guy armed with a knife, but he hated guns, believed in his heart only cowards carried guns.

Jesse's most useful function was listening to what was being said on the street.

And there was a lot being said. All of it about Kayne.

He thought there must be close to ten people out there — hard-asses, dealers, crackheads — who bore his mark and everywhere those people went, for the rest of their lives, they would spread Kayne's name. Jesse told Kayne the police were looking for him and some of his victims were talking of settling the score themselves.

"Bring them on," he whispered. He'd be ready for them. Next time he'd carve open the rest of their faces.

He reached into his sweatshirt's belly pocket and reverently pulled out his talisman. It felt good to hold it even when he wasn't using it. He loved the way its black surface gleamed in the sunlight, especially the sharp tip that had tasted so much blood since the day he had found it in the prison yard. Kayne had no idea how it had gotten there, but as soon as he had seen it he'd known it was to be his. That fuck Jeremiah had said so many fucking times that if Kayne looked to the Good Book he would find his way, find the talisman that would guide him through life. How right he had been. It was only fitting that Jeremiah had been the first to receive Kayne's mark.

"Why do you do it, man? Cut them, I mean." Jesse was staring at the talisman intently. "Why not just kill the fuckers?"

Kayne looked at Jesse disdainfully. "Because I'm Kayne," he stated absolutely, as if it explained all.

Apparently it didn't, not for Jesse. "I don't get it."

"Use your fucking head, you stupid shit." Kayne smacked Jesse's forehead. Jesse rubbed his brow and continued to smile stupidly at Kayne. Exasperated, Kayne shook his head. "Roll me another one and I'll tell you."

A minute later, fresh cigarette in hand, he began. "Last time I did time, I bunked with this nigger. Big fucking sonuvabitch. Always reading the Bible. Called himself Jeremiah."

"Like the pancakes?" Jesse giggled.

"What? No, you stupid shit. That's Aunt Jeremiah, you fuck."

"Oh."

"Now shut up." Kayne glared at Jesse over the flaring tip of the joint as he sucked in another lungful. "Jeremiah was always reading to me, preaching about my evil ways."

"What was he in for?"

Kayne laughed. "What else? Kiddy diddling, just like all those chest-thumping Christ preachers."

"Fucking faggots," Jesse added.

"Yeah, now shut up and let me talk." Kayne passed the joint to Jesse to keep him quiet. He'd had enough; couldn't get wasted when so many people were gunning for him. "The only part of that book I liked was the story about Cain. You know who Cain was?"

"Sure," Jesse squeaked, fighting to keep the smoke in.

Kayne went on as if Jesse hadn't spoken. "Yeah, well, Cain was the first murderer in history. He killed his brother. Can't remember the fag's name, but that's the fucking point. Everybody remembers Cain. Every-fucking-body. And everybody will fucking remember me."

"But . . . wouldn't it be more . . . bigger if you killed them?" Jesse seemed to be having trouble following his friend's logic.

"You are a stupid shit," Kayne repeated. "If I kill them, they'll just be dead. My way, they'll have my mark on them for the rest of their fucking lives and everywhere they go people will ask, 'Who did that?' And they'll say, 'Kayne did.' I mark them, just like God marked Cain so everyone would know he was a badass motherfucker. And everyone'll know I'm the baddest fucker out here."

Jesse grinned approvingly. "I get it. Fuck, that's smart."

"Fucking right it is. Jeremiah kept telling me to look to the book and when I heard my name I knew what to do. Found this," he held up the talisman, "in the yard one day and carved my mark in Jeremiah's head the day before I got out."

"You found that in the yard? How'd it get there?" Jesse had done enough time to know that finding something that big and potentially dangerous on prison grounds was a fucking one-in-a-million win.

"Fuck if I know." Kayne stroked his talisman lovingly. "Left over from repairs, fell off the roof. Fuck, it could have fallen off a fucking plane for all I care. I found it and that's what fucking matters."

"How'd you get that out, man? Don't they, like, search you?"

Kayne smiled smugly. "They ain't as careful searching you when you go out."

Jesse snorted laughter and it wheezed loudly out of his broken nose.

Kayne tapped Jesse's nose with the talisman. "Who the fuck did that to you?"

"Cops." His euphoric mood dried up as he remembered. "This pig comes into the restaurant where I'm eating and sucker-punches me, man. Busts up my nose."

"Hope you kicked his ass." *Or were you too busy crying?*

"Got a few licks in," Jesse admitted modestly. "But there was another cop there, his partner and they both jumped me. It was the first one, though, that broke my nose."

A foggy silence settled between them for a few minutes. A car horn blared faintly in the valley and then their friendly dealer groaned from his end of the bridge. Kayne glanced his way: the dealer wasn't moving much.

"Too bad that guy's dead."

"What guy?" Kayne asked absently, his thoughts on the beer they had back in the room. Just about time to head home. Maybe see if Lisa was up for a fuck.

"A dealer. Called his crack Black. Can't remember his name." Jesse shrugged.

Kayne nodded. "I heard about him while I was inside. What about him?"

"They say he was the toughest motherfucker ever, killed anybody who fucked with him."

"So?"

Jesse shrugged again. "Dunno. I just hear people say ain't never gonna be anyone tougher than him. Too bad he wasn't still around. If you marked him, then everyone would know who was the baddest."

That caught Kayne's attention. "Yeah, but he ain't here. He's dead. If he was so tough, who did him?"

"Cop," Jesse said simply.

"Figures. Fucking pigs always gang up on you," Kayne declared.

Jesse was shaking his head emphatically. "Wasn't no bunch of cops. Just one." Now it was Jesse's turn to tell a tale. "This guy killed the pig's partner. Slit his throat wide open." Kayne nodded approvingly. "Then when Charles —" Kayne failed to notice that Jesse's memory had suddenly improved "— broke into the cop's house, the cop fucking killed him."

"He broke into the cop's house?" Kayne asked disbelievingly.

"Yup. Was gonna fuck the cop's wife, but the cop killed him." Jesse paused, then added, "Beat him to death with his bare fucking hands."

Kayne was impressed. "No shit?"

"No shit," Jesse agreed. "Hey! If you did the cop who killed Charles, then that'd prove you're the man." He lowered his voice. "Fucking shit, marking a cop."

Kayne nodded slowly, the substance of the idea hot and pleasing to him. "Fucking mark a cop. Yeah. You know which cop it was?"

Jesse smiled, a nasty little grin, and fingered the crooked mess that was his nose. "Yeah, I know which one it was."

"Good." Kayne sprang to his feet. "You find him for me." He gazed lovingly at the talisman, still in his hand. "You find him for me and I'll fucking mark him. I'll cut his whole fucking face."

"I'm an assignment?"

"Yup," Jack replied smugly. "Oh, how the tide has turned, grasshopper."

"How's that?"

They were cruising Allan Gardens, the city-block-square park in the heart of 51. An oasis of normality just up the street from Seaton House, the city's largest men's shelter and a short drive to the constant trouble spots of the division: Regent Park, St. Jamestown and Moss Park. But then everywhere was a short drive in 51, the city's smallest yet busiest division.

Allan Gardens boasted a world-class greenhouse at its centre and paved walkways, all wide enough for a scout car, criss-crossed the grounds in a loose spider's web. The first buds of spring were showing on the trees, giant mature monoliths that would bestow cooling shade come the city's humid summer. Manny kept the scout car on the walkways; the ground, just free of winter's grip, was too soft and muddy to drive on. Once the earth greened and firmed up, the cops would be free to cruise the park as they desired.

The park was relatively empty. Some pedestrian commuters were using its paths to shorten the walk to work, but most visitors were of the four-legged variety. The morning's regular complement of dog owners was out in full force and canines of every size and shape frolicked in the spring mud. Some owners frantically reached for leashes at the sight of the scout car; Jack and Manny waved them off. There were far more serious offences to worry about than a dog running loose. Unless you were a squirrel, of course. Besides, the untethered dogs tended to keep the drunks and crackheads to a minimum.

Allan Gardens had been Sy's special project. According to Sy, in the time before Jack's first interlude in 51, Allan Gardens was a haven for the streets' unsavoury element: drunks, addicts, dealers and prostitutes plied their professions and habits in and around the greenhouse. The public washrooms in the greenhouse had become drug-laden whorehouses. Good people stayed away for fear of being hassled or robbed. Discarded needles, other drug paraphernalia and condoms littered the ground. It had taken a combined and prolonged effort by the community and police to pull the park into the light. Sy's goal had been to keep it that way and Jack had no intention of letting his friend's efforts be undone. Now that he was back in 51, Allan Gardens was his and he intended to keep it that way.

"Remember the first day we worked together?" Jack watched a huge Newfoundland, mud up to his belly, chase an equally muddy tennis ball. The owner, seeing Jack's interest, pointed at the Newfie and held up his leash. Jack smiled and shook his head. The owner smiled in return and gave the coppers a thumbs up. "Staff Rourke told you to keep an eye on me, drive me around, keep me out of trouble."

"Oh, yeah." Manny nodded enthusiastically. "Hey, wasn't

that the day we were in that little restaurant over at Sherbourne and Dundas and you —"

Jack groaned theatrically, knowing what Manny was going to say.

"— smashed that guy's face into his eggs?"

"Admittedly, not one of my prouder moments."

"Dude, that was awesome!"

"Oh, yeah, really awesome. Losing my temper, assaulting someone —"

"Dude, that guy deserved it."

"— in full view of witnesses, I might add," Jack continued. "And I put you in an awkward position. I repeat, not one of my better moments."

"Dude," Manny protested earnestly. "That guy spat on Sy's memory and then he spat on you. I think you showed remarkable restraint."

Jack wouldn't admit it, but driving that asshole's face into his breakfast plate was one of the most satisfying feelings he had ever experienced. At the same time, though, he had a weird feeling, but he couldn't nail it down. Something about the guy, a crackhead judging from his scrawny build. Jack couldn't picture his face, but he remembered arms sleeved in skull tattoos.

He shrugged the weird feeling off. No big deal. "Getting back to my point. Our roles have been reversed. I'm the babysitter and you are the babysat."

"Oh, mannnnn. . . ." Whining did not become Manny. "What did Greene say about me?"

"Surprisingly, it had something to do with your attitude, appearance and behaviour, if I recall correctly. I told you that goatee was going to get you in trouble."

"It's a beard," Manny defended automatically. So automatically Jack wondered how many times and to how many supervisors he'd said it. "I'm not getting rid of it." Manny protectively stroked the emaciated strip of hair running along his jaw line.

"The *beard* aside, what else have you done to piss him off?"

"Nothing! Dude, I swear —"

"Save it for the courtroom," Jack scolded. "Come on, Manny. I know you and there's no way you'd stay quiet about Greene."

Manny stopped at the Gerrard Street edge of the park and avoided answering Jack by easing out into traffic. Pedestrians might have been light in the park, but in the still-wintry weather, rush hour was alive and bloated. Despite the heavy traffic, drivers in both directions were eager to stop to let the police car in. Drive around in a white police car and other drivers would needlessly yield the right of way so often it was almost irritating. But throw on the lights and siren and the police car became invisible. Go figure.

Manny slid into the street's sluggish flow and Jack pounced on him.

"What did Sy tell you about talking with supervisors?"

Manny made a point of not looking at Jack. "Dude, I didn't —"

"What did Sy tell you?"

"Dude, you gotta —"

"What did Sy tell you?"

Manny's bald head drooped between his shoulders. "'There's no such thing as off the record with a supervisor,'" he quoted sheepishly.

"Very good, grasshopper. Now, what did you say *off the record* to our new glorious leader?"

"Not much, really." Manny cast a quick look at Jack. "I just told him things were different now than back when he was on the road."

"Uh-huh," Jack snorted disbelievingly. "And did you happen to use any words like *ancient, prehistoric, antiquated?* Anything along those lines?"

Staring straight ahead, Manny confessed, "I may have said something about him being an outdated relic."

"Fuck, Manny. You're lucky he didn't document you for insubordination. He said something about formally cautioning you?"

Manny nodded.

"More than once?"

Another nod.

"He told me he's looking to document you or transfer you." Jack let that sink in for a second or two. "Or both."

"Dude, he can't make me leave 51!" Manny protested.

"He can and he will. Greene strikes me as the type of guy who knows rules and regs inside out. So far he hasn't done anything wrong, just stupid. He wants me to bring the platoon together as a team while he stomps on our morale."

"You got any ideas, man?" Manny asked, looking hopefully at Jack. "Like what you did with the gloves? Dude, that was beautiful."

"This is a little trickier than just tuning up any asshole you find wearing leather gloves." Jack slumped in the passenger seat, chin propped in hand. It seemed everyone was expecting him to take on the mantle of leadership, whether he wanted to or not.

"All right, Manny, it's four-thirty. Time to get out of the laneways."

"Aw, c'mon, Jack. We've still got time."

Jack levelled a steely glare at Manny, using his new scar to its best advantage. "Listen, you've been crawling around the laneways looking for trouble for the last half hour. Time's up. You find anything and you're doing the overtime on your own."

Manny shuddered comically. "Dude, don't do that. That scar makes you look all evil like."

"Really?" Jack brightened. "What kind of evil? Dracula evil or Terminator unfeeling cyborg type?"

"Definitely Terminator, man. I'm jealous."

Jack laughed. "Well, maybe if you're lucky, you'll screw up one day and get one of your own. Now, out of the alley. Don't make me say it." He gave Manny his best cyborg stare.

Manny giggled. "Do it, man. I gotta hear it."

Doing his best Arnold impersonation, Jack slowly faced Manny and said, "Get. Out."

Laughing, Manny manoeuvred the car through the laneway's tight corner behind the beer store on Gerrard. He'd spent at least the last half hour cruising the division's labyrinthine laneways hoping to stumble over something that would kill the time. The day had turned out to be on the slow side and instead of rushing to get the calls done before the end of shift they had found themselves clear with nothing on the pending screen. A crackhead smoking up, a whore blowing some guy, a hound sucking on a bottle. Anything to pass the time, but the laneways had been as quiet as the radio.

Manny turned north on Seaton Street and eased to a stop at Gerrard.

"Oh, for fuck's sake," Jack grumbled. He nodded toward his window, then leaned back so Manny could see.

"That's rude."

Not ten feet away, on the thin stretch of grass between the sidewalk and the beer store's west brick wall, a man stood, swaying gently, as he urinated in full view of the pedestrians, rush-hour drivers and police car. And it was a hell of a good piss, judging from the blissful expression on his face. Almost too blissful; he was coming awfully close to pissing on the twelve-pack Jack figured the guy had just bought.

"There you go, grasshopper. A quick ticket for pissing in public and then we head in." Jack laughed at himself. *Quoting movies, calling him grasshopper. I'm turning into Sy.*

Jack advised the dispatcher and they got out of the car, Manny armed with his ticket book, as the man shook off the last few drops.

He noticed the cops as he was zipping up. "Thorry, offithers," he slurred around a happy grin. "I hadda go."

"Apparently. You know, you could have gone around the corner into the alley."

The man, unkempt from his ripped runners to the tips of his greasy hair, nodded in solemn agreement with Manny.

Manny, standing in front of the man with his gun side bladed away, gestured to the busy street, its cars and pedestrians. "Do you think all these nice people on the way home from work needed to see you pissing on the sidewalk? Didn't your mother raise you better?" Manny shook his head in disgust. "Let's see some ID, bud."

"I'm thorry," the man repeated as he dug out a battered wallet.

As he dropped his head to dig through the wallet, he teetered forward. Manny reached out a gloved hand to gently set him upright. Jack, positioned on the man's right and slightly behind so as to be out of sight, raised an anticipatory hand, but it wasn't needed. The drunk wobbled but didn't go down. Showing off his remaining teeth with a shit-eating grin, he proudly handed Manny his ID.

"A Seaton House card? This all you got —" Manny consulted the hostel's card "— Eric?"

Eric nodded, big loopy nods, each one threatening to overbalance him.

Manny reached for his mitre, then looked at Jack. "Should I run him?"

"And if he comes back wanted on some chickenshit warrant?" Jack asked around Eric's tilting shoulder.

"Right." Manny tucked the radio in its carrier and flipped open his ticket book.

"You ain't givin me a ticket, is you?" Eric suddenly perked up.

"'Course I am. Can't have you pissing wherever you want, now, can we? What would my mother think if I let you walk away from this without suffering the appropriate consequences?"

"Fuck your mother!" Eric proclaimed defiantly and snatched his ID back.

Or tried to. Manny neatly stepped away and Eric reeled forward, saving himself from an embarrassing face-plant in his own urine by thrusting out an unsteady leg. Bent nearly horizontal with his legs stretched out beneath him, he swung blindly at Manny and once again almost dumped himself.

With an amused grin, Manny placed his hand on Eric's head and pushed ever so gently. Pinwheeling his arms, Eric tottered backward. For the briefest of moments, he paused, his balance within reach, his arms and one leg thrust out like some fucked-up scarecrow. Then gravity, aided by brain cells stewed in cheap alcohol, won the contest and down Eric went. He fell on his ass, avoiding his steaming puddle but still making a decent *splat!* in the soggy ground.

"Sorry, dude." Manny shrugged apologetically and snapped open his handcuff pouch.

Jack shook his head. By the time they got mumble-fuck to the station, searched, lodged and the paperwork done, it would probably be close to an hour of overtime. If they didn't have to wait long to parade him, that was. Overtime on his first day back at 51. Jack, thinking of Karen, could hear the argument already.

They flipped Eric over in the mud to snap the cuffs on and then hauled him upright. At the car, they leaned him over the trunk for the search, more of a thorough patdown; the complete, smelly, disgusting strip search, one of the things they didn't tell you about at the police college, would come later at the station.

"I've got this, Jack." Manny quickly swapped his leather gloves for latex; Eric was muddy and damp and leather tended to absorb fluids.

"I want muh beer! Don't you forget muh beer!" In his indignation, Eric's alcohol-induced speech impediment had cleared up.

"Shut up," Manny advised Eric. Finished with his lower half,

Manny raised him off the trunk to search his threadbare lumber jacket. Jack stood by, his left hand clamped around Eric's right arm.

"I want muh beer." Eric turned to Jack, his face dripping soupy mud. With all the dogs in the neighbourhood, Jack wondered how much of the goop on Eric's nose and chin wasn't mud. "Go get my fuckin' beer," he ordered and jerked his head at Jack to emphasize his earnestness.

Jack turned his head, but mud still splatted onto his cheek and neck. It was cold and he could feel the slime trail as the mud slid to his collar. Jack let go of Eric and wiped his neck and face, flinging globbing muck to the sidewalk.

"I said, get muh fuckin' beer."

"That's it, fuckhead." Jack reached for Eric, murder in his eyes, but Eric was too drunk to notice.

"Jack, people are watching," Manny cautioned fervently, his voice pitched so it wouldn't carry to the small group of curious spectators.

Jack stopped, one hand on Eric, the other twitching at his side, eager to draw back and let fly the punishment. He looked at Manny, who shook his head ever so slightly.

"Witnesses, Jack."

"Yeah, Jack. Wit-sees. Go get muh beer." Eric grinned like the moron he was, too drunk, too stupid to know how close he had come to a trip to the hospital.

"You finished the search?" Jack asked through gritted teeth.

"Yup, all done."

Jack yanked open the car's rear door. "Get this shit out of my sight."

They stuffed Eric into the back seat and Jack slammed the door on his demands for them to "get muh beer." Jack reached into the front seat and grabbed some napkins from under the visor — there were always napkins under police car visors; cops were notoriously sloppy when it came to eating in cars they didn't have to clean — and wiped the mud off his skin. *And it's only mud*, he kept repeating until he was satisfied he was clean.

"Dude, that was close. You looked like you were going to kill him."

Jack drew a deep breath, held it and blew the tension out with it. He balled up the napkins and tossed them onto the passenger floorboard — notoriously sloppy — before trusting himself to speak.

"Tell the truth, I felt like murdering him. I haven't lost my temper like that since ... I can't remember when."

Oh really? How about with Karen's dad? Hm?

"If'n I was you, I'da slugged 'im one."

The tiny crowd of onlookers, hoping for some real-life police brutality, had drifted away disappointed. But standing at the front of the scout car was an ancient black man bundled up in a thick parka despite the flush of spring in the air. At his feet was a small and equally ancient dog.

A grin banished the scowl from Jack's face. "Phil. Good to see you."

"I thought it was you, Officer Jack, but I wasn' sure. Haven' seen you aroun' much these days." A matching smile stretched the already taut skin around Phil's mouth.

"They had me tucked away someplace safe and boring. How are you doing?" Jack took Phil's hand gently, not wanting to cause the elderly gent any pain; his hands were misshapen lumps, the knuckles swollen grotesquely by arthritis. "Manny, this is Phil, we met last year."

"I remember meeting this gentleman." Manny shook Phil's hand. "I came out to take the photos when you were assaulted."

"Whatever happened to that prick?" Last year, while Jack was working with Sy — *Was it the first day we worked together?* — they had responded to an assault call at a rundown rooming house on George Street. Phil, eighty-odd years old, had been punched and knocked to the ground by a much younger and bigger resident for the crime of being black. The asshole had called him a nigger. Jack and Sy had taught the asshole a lesson in respect. Before dragging his ass off to jail.

Manny shrugged. "Pled guilty, far as I know."

"Has he been around, Phil?"

The old man carefully shook his head. "Ain't seen 'im since you and Officer Simon busted down 'is door. That was good t'see!" Phil laughed his way into a coughing fit. Jack and Manny waited patiently for the old guy to get his lungs under control. "Sorry 'bout that," he apologized, wiping away a tear. Whether from laughing or coughing or both, Jack couldn't tell. "Damn cig'rettes gonna kill me yet."

"You kicked down his door?" Manny inquired innocently.

"He didn't want to be arrested. Nothing big." Jack knelt down. "And how is Bear?" Jack held out his hand to the little guy who was trying to hide behind his owner's legs.

"Gettin' old, like me, but he's doin' good. Go on, Bear. Say hello."

Bear, a tiny Heinz 57 of a dog with a bit of a paunch, hesitantly stretched his nose out from between Phil's legs to sniff at Jack's offered hand. After a few investigative sniffs, Bear waddled stiffly out from hiding, his stub of a tail twitching happily. He butted his head into Jack's palm, seeking an ear scratch.

"Damn if he don' like you, Officer Jack. But then, he took to you that day, too."

"Bear and I understand each other. Don't we, Bear? And it's just Jack, Phil. None of that officer crap."

Bear, moving slowly and deliberately, eased down onto his belly, then tried to roll onto his back, but he lacked the flexibility. He settled for lying on his side and lifting his front leg while whining. Jack knew a tummy rub request when he saw it.

"I'll be damned," Phil wheezed as Bear's tail thumped ecstatically on the sidewalk while Jack's fingers scratched his belly. "You certainly got a way with 'im. Maybe I was meant to meet up wit' you t'day."

"Why's that, Phil?" Jack looked up but didn't stop the tummy rub. Bear's back leg had joined his tail in a happy dance.

"Been seein' this guy 'round. Got a pup with 'im. Beautiful shepherd, 'tis. And he beats 'im som'thin' bad."

Jack stood up. Bear lay where he was, his tail and leg slowly winding down, a dopey doggy grin on his face.

"What's this guy look like? White, black, Asian?" Like most cops, Jack could endure violence against adults, at times even partake of it himself — Eric really didn't know how lucky he was — but hurt a child or an animal and it got personal.

Phil nodded, seeing the change in Jack's attitude and approving. "Little white guy. Red hair. Got a nose on 'im looks like it's been busted up a few times."

"Joey Horner," Manny said without hesitation. "He's a little shit. Hangs around the Seaton House. Didn't know he had a dog, though."

"We'll keep an eye out for him, Phil. Thanks."

A muffled cry came from the scout car. It might have been *I want muh beer.*

"Manny, go shut him up."

"No problem."

"Where you headed, Phil? You need a ride home? We can always make that mumblee ride in the trunk."

Phil smiled his thanks but declined. "Jes' 'eading to the beer store. Gonna pick me som'thin' to sip on."

Jack smiled as a very nasty idea came to mind. "Hang on a sec, Phil." Still smiling, Jack stepped over to Eric's twelve-pack, careful not to step in any puddles and scooped the beer up.

"That's right, motherfucker! I better get muh beer back when I get out! Where the fuck you going?"

Jack waved at Eric before handing the beer to Phil. "There you go, Phil. Compliments of the Toronto police."

Phil smiled and it was as evil as Jack's. "Why, thank you, Officer. I really 'preciate that."

"No problem, sir. You have a good night. You, too, Bear."

The little dog had made it back to his feet. Jack stooped to give him a final ear scratch.

"That was nasty, dude. Nasty." Manny beamed approval over the car roof.

"It was, wasn't it?"

Inside the car, Eric's scream was loud and long. Sometimes a trip to the hospital just wasn't necessary.

Saturday, 24 March
0700 hours

"Hey, Jack. Good to see you. I'd heard you were back. Couldn't stay away, could you?"

Jack gripped the offered hand. "Hey, Rick. Yeah, I'm back. This place kind of grows on you, I guess."

"That it does, that it does." Rick Mason was the detective in charge of 51's Major Crime, an old-clothes unit that targeted the drugs, violence and serious property crimes in the division. In other words, most of what happened in 51.

Mason was a big, solid man, with forearms the size of most people's legs. He kept his greying hair cropped short, but his goatee, as grey as his hair, scraped at his chest as he talked. Together, he and Jack had orchestrated the arrest of a vicious drug dealer, Anthony Charles, the man responsible for Sy's murder. If the details of Jack's identification of Charles ever became public, the two of them and members of Mason's inner circle could lose their jobs or end up in jail. But with Charles dead — killed by Jack after he had taken Karen hostage — the secret could rest easy.

"Seems like 53 didn't treat you all that well." Mason touched the fresh scar running through Jack's eyebrow.

"It was my own fault; I got careless."

Mason nodded. "Quiet divisions can make a copper rusty."

"You don't look like you've been suffering." Jack tapped Mason's belly, which was protruding more than it had in the fall.

Mason grinned sheepishly. "Yeah, well, after you took out Charles, the rest of the dealers spent the winter fighting each other for turf and I was able to go home some days."

Jack glanced at his watch. Almost seven. "You got something for us, or did you just come down to say hello?"

They were standing in the hallway outside the parade room. Inside, the platoon was grumbling as officers lined up for inspection. Mason cocked his head at them. "Your staff really does stand-up parades?"

"Just for inspection," Jack told him dryly. "He lets us sit down after that."

Mason whistled softly. He was about to say something when Staff Sergeant Greene, followed by an unhappy-looking Sergeant Johanson, came down the stairs, senior officer's white shirt pressed and starched, handlebar moustache waxed and curled. Greene stopped, almost stepping between Jack and Mason, a small man made smaller by standing next to the burly Major Crime D.

But his attention was on Jack, not Mason. "Constable Warren," he clipped. "It is seven o'clock and by standing here you are late for parade."

"My fault, Staff," Mason jumped in. Did he know Greene hated to be called Staff and not Staff Sergeant? Jack expected so; there was little that happened in the division, let alone the station, that Mason didn't know about. "I was just catching up with Jack, welcoming him back to the division."

Greene turned his intimidating gaze — at least Jack thought it was supposed to be intimidating — on the big detective.

"Constable Warren is on my time now. And he is late." He snapped his head back to Jack. "And you can consider yourself officially cautioned for being late. If this happens again, you will be documented. Is that understood?"

For the second day in a row, Jack wanted to give Greene a hearty *Jawohl*. "Yes, sir. Perfectly." *Prick.*

Jack fell into line and Greene spent extra time going over him and, yes, he did a sock check. As he was bent over examining the colour of Jack's socks, Manny caught Jack's eye and gave an exaggerated eye roll. Jack had the smirk gone from his face by the time Greene straightened up.

Jack could feel Greene's eyes on him, daring him to meet his stare, but he kept his eyes focused on the wall above Greene's head. He was not about to be suckered into anything that could be construed as insubordination.

At last Greene snorted, in disgust or satisfaction Jack couldn't tell and really didn't care. But if he thought he had received a detailed scrutiny, it was nothing compared to the attention given to Manny. Greene checked his socks and asked him to remove his magazines so Greene could count the number of rounds in each one. Greene checked his memo book to see if he had underlined the date.

Jack had to give Manny credit; he kept still and quiet throughout the examination. Jack had no idea what it was costing his friend to remain silent. At least Mason was enjoying the show. He was at the front of the room with Johanson, leaning comfortably against the chalkboard, his meaty arms folded casually across his chest. He gave Jack a wink and a disbelieving head shake.

Again, there were five officers on parade and two on the early half. Seven cops for the division. Manpower was definitely tight. When Greene finished his inspection, he stomped his little feet all the way to the front of the room. Something had their steadfast leader in a snit.

Maybe he curled his moustache too tight.

Johanson stepped up to the podium to read out the assignments, but Greene brushed by him and seized the podium with a white-knuckled grip. He glared silently at the officers while he drew several deep breaths and Jack realized he was trying to calm himself. Something was unquestionably out of kilter in Greene's perfect, orderly world.

"I was going over your memo books this morning before parade," Greene announced at last. He did not sound happy. "What I found was shoddy, unprofessional and unacceptable." He paused, perhaps to let the officers ponder the heinous crime they had committed. "Officers are not filling out the duty stamps in their memo books at the end of shift prior to reporting off duty." Greene's eyes burned with a fevered intensity.

Oh, for fuck's sake. This guy has got to get a life.

Muted murmurs floated up from the officers and Jack had to fight to keep a smirk off his face.

If rolling eyes had a sound . . .

Mason was having a hard time schooling his features. He finally cupped his chin in a thoughtful pose, but the points of a smile kept creeping out from behind his fingers.

Greene wasn't done. "Officers are not breaking down the hours spent at the station, on radio calls or on general patrol. Nor are they indicating the number of tickets issued during the tour of duty. By not providing this information, officers are contravening the service's regulations. I believe this is more than gross negligence and there is an ulterior motive behind this . . . this . . ." Greene's moustache twitched uncontrollably. A vein throbbed in his neck as his face darkened with anger. Finally, Greene found the word he wanted and spat it out like a cobra spitting venom. "Conspiracy!" He raked the parade room with frenzied eyes and clenched hands trembling at his sides. "I know this is a combined and determined effort to prevent me from evaluating this platoon on a daily basis and it . . . will . . . stop . . . now."

There was silence in the squad room. *He's not a prick, he's a fucking loon.*

Jack could hear Greene's ragged breathing. The staff sergeant glared at the officers, daring them to challenge him. When no one stepped forward, he blew out a final, huffing breath, his absolute authority intact. Jack watched as his tension visibly evaporated. The heated crimson drained from his face, the vein that looked ready to rupture with every surge of blood sank back into the side of his neck and his hands eased open.

"Then I shall consider this matter resolved. Sergeant Johanson, you may carry on." Greene strode from the room, his spine ramrod straight.

Jack noticed a hint of unsteadiness in the staff's walk. *That man is seriously off balance.*

"Not a word. Not a fucking word." Johanson held up a forestalling hand as he took the podium. "I'll talk to the superintendent after parade. Now listen up."

It didn't take long to get through the assignments. Coverage was thin; Jack and Manny were the only two-man car in a division where the majority of calls required two officers. Two men in each car would mean fewer cars and the public might clue in to how few officers there were on the streets.

Can't have the public — or the assholes, for that matter — learning how thin the thin blue line really is, can we?

"Rick, you have something for the troops?"

"Yeah." Mason pushed off from the chalkboard and dropped a sheaf of papers in front of Jack. "Pass those along, would you?"

Jack took a sheet, slid the papers to Manny, then looked at what was important enough to get Mason out of his second-floor cave.

Speaking of assholes . . . The face staring up from the officer safety bulletin had asshole written all over it. A hard face with sharp angles, stony eyes, eyes that, even when reproduced in black and white, held a thousand-yard stare.

"Take a look at our latest problem. Randall Kayne. Released last week and residing in our neighbourhood." Mason studied the officers before him. "Most of you probably don't have enough time on to remember Kayne. He's 51 born and bred and has spent his whole waste of a life in and out of prison. He just finished a four-year stint for robbery and I can guarantee you he will reoffend."

Mason paused, levelling his unyielding gaze on the young coppers. His stare carried weight and demanded attention. "Kayne has a history of going to the pen wasted on crack and coming out pumped up and jacked up. He'll get back on the crack and wither away soon enough, but until then do not —" he rapped the podium with solid knuckles for emphasis "— do *not* try to arrest him on your own. I am not fucking around. He's a hard-ass and will hurt you. I wouldn't try him on my own. Neither would Tank."

That caught everyone's attention. If the division's one-man riot squad took this guy seriously, he must be a hard-ass.

"He's already back in business, or so we believe."

Mason passed out more sheets of paper. There were two photos. One showed a black male reclining in a hospital bed with an injury to his forehead; the second was a close-up of the injury. Just as the intensity of Kayne's eyes came across in a stark picture, so did the brutality of the wound. It filled the centre of the man's forehead from hairline to eyebrows. The cuts were deep, jagged and wide and Jack was willing to bet they went down to the skull.

"Is that. . . ?" Manny was holding the photo up, turning it this way and that, trying to make sense of it.

"A letter K, yes," Mason confirmed. "K for Kayne."

"The mark of Kayne? Oh, fuck me." Paul said it for all of them.

"Exactly," Mason agreed. "We believe he's carved his initial into at least three people since getting out, as well as his cellmate before he was released."

"Whoa. He does this while he's inside and still gets out?" Manny was still rotating the picture.

"No one's talking to us. Most of them just clam up when we talk to them." Mason chuckled. "That guy in the picture claimed to have fallen on some broken glass."

Jack spoke. "They don't want to report the guy who's scarred them for life?"

Mason shook his head, his goatee swinging like a tiny, furry pendulum. "They're either scared shitless of him, or they're planning on taking care of it themselves."

"No one's talking to us?" Jack was puzzled. "Is he only targeting other assholes?"

"Yup. Dealers, small-time hoods. Whoever he runs into, by the sound of it." The Major Crime boss rapped the podium again. More emphasis. "There's a rumour going around on the streets that Kayne's out to prove he's the toughest badass on the streets. I imagine it would go a long way in cementing that rep if he managed to carve that K into a copper's face. And I sure as fuck don't want to see that happen."

Sombre nods all around.

"This picture recent, then?" Paul was folding the photo, slimming it down to fit on the car's visor.

"Except for his hair. Fuck, I'm getting old. Starting to forget things. He's sporting a mohawk now. A wide strip down the middle of his head, cut short. That's it."

"Thanks, Rick." Johanson added his two cents' worth. "I've dealt with Kayne before. He's asshole to the core and won't hesitate to kill you. You see him, you get as much backup as you can before you arrest him."

"I thought he wasn't wanted for anything yet," Borovski pointed out.

Johanson stilled his objection with a simple "Find something."

Knife call. An anonymous complainant had called 911 saying there was a male on the second floor of a rooming house threatening people with a knife. Jack and Manny were guarding the bottom of the staircase while Paul and Jenny cleared the first floor.

"Just one resident and he hasn't heard anything," Jenny reported quietly.

Jack nodded, whispered, "Okay, up we go. By height."

They slowly ascended the stairs in order of height so everyone could see ahead, Paul at six-five bringing up the rear behind Manny. Jack and Jenny were about the same height, but Jack could see around her thinner frame, so she went first. Paul had to turn sideways to fit his shoulders in the narrow stairway. Guns out and pointed down in two-handed grips, they crept up the stairs as quietly as they could, but the old wood steps creaked under their feet and groaned in agony when Paul shifted his weight.

The landing was as tiny and cramped as the stairs. A doorway on the left opened onto the second-floor hall. Jenny crouched on the landing and Jack straddled her back; the rude comments and suggestions would come later. The hall dead-ended to the right. To the left, it ran to the front of the house, parallel to the staircase.

Jenny leaned around the door frame and darted head and gun into the hall. After a moment's pause, she muttered, "Oh, fuck me."

Still astride her — after that "fuck me" comment, the crude comments were going to be a lot cruder — Jack leaned past the door frame, taking the hall. It was almost as narrow as the stairs and had three doors, two closed and one open. Unfortunately. The closed doors were on the opposite side and were probably bedroom doors. The open door was at the end of the hall and Jack wished it was closed too. And barred.

"Hey, guys. What's the holdup?" Manny squeezed past them into the hall. And froze. "Oh, crap."

Paul stuck his head past Jack's shoulder. He was silent for a moment, then asked, very quietly, "Should we run?"

"Only if you want it to chase you," Jenny advised in a strained whisper.

In the front room, lying on the bed to catch the cozy morning sunshine coming through the window, was the biggest pit bull Jack had ever seen. It rolled from its side to its belly, its massive head cocked quizzically as it studied the four strangers in front of it. The dog stood up on the bed and stretched slowly, its powerful jaws cracking open in a huge yawn, revealing equally huge teeth.

"It's freaking immense." Paul's voice was hushed. Paul didn't do well with dogs. "I bet it weighs more than you, Jenny."

"No shit," she said, never taking her eyes off the monster.

"Fuck that," Manny breathed. "I think it weighs more than me."

All of them were frozen, fixated on the dog, guns half raised. Jack suddenly imagined what the dog was seeing: four cops — Jack hoped it hadn't been trained by an asshole owner to recognize and attack uniforms — at the end of the hall, three of them stacked neatly from smallest to biggest and leaning out the door, the fourth flattened against the wall. It was something out of a Keystone Kops routine. Jack hoped the pit bull had a sense of humour.

The dog's fur was a dark burnt orange slashed with streaks of black. Jack could see the muscles in its chest and shoulders rippling beneath the fur as it shifted its weight on the mattress.

"Do you think our guns can stop it?" Manny asked, not sounding too confident.

Jack seriously doubted it. "You see the size of that head? It's fucking armour plated."

"Um, guys? It's moving." Jenny shuffled slightly, adjusting her position.

Jack prayed there would be time later for crude comments.

The dog let out a great huff, then hopped off the bed and thumped heavily onto the floor. Four guns came up on target.

The dog huffed again and trotted toward them, its claws clicking in an almost merry way on the floorboards. Its jaws slipped open in what Jack swore was a grin and its tongue lolled out as it panted its way to them.

"Ease up, everyone," Jack cautioned. The dog wasn't charging them. If anything, its gait had a happy bounce to it. Jack lowered his gun and stepped in front of Jenny.

"Jaaack," Manny moaned, but Jack waved him to silence.

The dog stopped when Jack moved but jounced forward when he knelt down. Jack had his Glock by his right side, but he knew he wouldn't need it. The pit bull barrelled into him hard and would have knocked him over if Manny hadn't been there to support him. The great head butted Jack's stomach and the dog simply stood there, head nestled comfortably, whipcord tail wagging in happy anticipation.

Jack holstered up and set both hands to scratching behind tiny, floppy ears. The tail flailed in frenzied ecstasy. Jack grinned at his cohorts. "Why don't you guys clear the rooms while me and my new friend get acquainted?"

Manny and Jenny stepped past — Jenny reached down for a pat as she passed — but Paul inched by, so tight against the wall he was almost a part of it. Bikers, crazed druggies, guns, knives, Paul had faced them all. Usually with a smile on his face. He really didn't do well with dogs.

The dog — Max, according to the bone-shaped tag on his collar — was on his back, one hind leg jerking uncontrollably as Jack rubbed his belly, when Manny declared the rooms clear.

"No victim, no crime."

"That Bob Marley?" Jenny joked.

"Kind of. You about finished, Doctor Doolittle?"

"Yeah, guess so." Jack reluctantly stopped the belly scratch and Max flopped onto to his paws.

After a vigorous shake, he followed the officers down the stairs. Except for Paul. Paul let Max go ahead of him.

They met one of the house's tenants, who looked rather perplexed at the four cops coming down the stairs as he came in the front door with an armload of groceries. "Anything I can do for you, officers?" He was a wisp of a man, older, with rough leathery skin.

Jack briefly explained why they were there. "Any idea who'd call in a bogus knife fight?"

The old guy was quick to respond. "That little fucker," he spat. "There's this guy, a little soft in the head, I think. He keeps coming by. Wants Max to fight his dog. Came by earlier and I told him to go fuck himself." He shook his head in disgust. "He's got himself this beautiful shepherd and it can't be much more'n six months old."

Jack and Manny exchanged a knowing look. Joey Horner. The dog abuser Phil had told them about. Jack's hands unconsciously curled into fists. Jack was going to have to track this fucker down.

"See you met Max, though." The tenant called Max over from where he had been leaning companionably against Jack's legs. He gave Max a quick ear rub, then shooed him upstairs. Max trotted up the stairs, seemingly eager to resume his interrupted nap.

"Max your dog?" Jack listened to the fading clicks of Max's nails on the stairs.

"Nope." The old guy stepped onto the old porch with them. "He just showed up one day. Skinny as a twenty-dollar crack ho." The cops cracked grins at the reference not many would understand. Except for Paul. He was keeping a watch behind them in case Max's friendliness had been a ruse. "We all pitch in for his food and walks. He's kind of the house mascot, I guess you could say." He noticed Paul's wary expression. "Scary looking, though, ain't he?"

Paul gave the man an uneasy grin. "I'm just glad he didn't want dark meat."

"5106, in 5111's area. At St. Lawrence Street and King Street East, behind the Mr. Big and Tall for an industrial accident. Male has fallen behind a truck. Time, 1149 hours."

"Doesn't sound like much, does it?"

Jack shrugged non-committally, his hands never leaving the steering wheel. When they had worked together in the fall, Manny had driven most of the time, but Jack had requested to drive and Manny had reluctantly relinquished his position in the driver's seat. Manny didn't handle being a passenger very well. Jack didn't know if it was because he got bored or needed to be in control. Probably a bit of both.

Greene had paired them up for the second day in a row, no doubt so Jack could fix the problem that was Armsman. They were cruising Allan Gardens and Jack was being careful to keep the car on the paved paths.

He stopped to let a mother with a stroller pass before crossing the sidewalk into traffic. A light drizzle was falling, mixing with the salted road slush thrown up by every passing tire. The car's wipers screeched across the glass, smearing the gunk more than clearing it. The scout cars came with factory-grade wipers and Jack doubted this pair had ever been replaced.

"Miserable weather," Jack commented needlessly as he sprayed the windshield yet again to clear it.

Manny craned a leery eye at the heavy grey clouds. "How's your head?"

Jack snickered. "Fine, but you probably just jinxed me. If I get a migraine, it's your fault."

Manny perked up. "Does that mean I'll get to drive?"

"Your compassion is touching."

"Hey, man, I just have your best interest at heart, that's all."

"Uh-huh." Jack gave his partner a skeptical look.

Manny grinned like a happy puppy. A very large, bald puppy.

The Mr. Big and Tall store sat on the southwest corner of King and St. Lawrence Streets. King was a four-lane road and a key route into and out of downtown for daily commuters, but for a few blocks it was lined with low-rise commercial and residential buildings, most of them with that older, red brick charisma. St. Lawrence was a very short but very wide street that went not much of anywhere. Its west side held an old three-storey factory that had been converted into lofts. Farther down the street was an old car lot, part junkyard and part mechanic shop.

The street's greatest feature was the multi-lane bridge that crossed its lower half, known as the Waterfall among the division's coppers. The bridge's underbelly was a desolate wasteland of hard-packed earth and grim, massive concrete support columns. Toss in a few burnt-out car husks, add some wretched tin and cardboard shacks, populate with filthy people dressed in rags and oozing sores and you had the perfect post-apocalyptic shantytown. It was a favourite movie-shoot location.

It was also the perfect foul weather meeting place for cops because there was a huge expanse of shelter. And it was during the rain that the reason for its nickname became evident. A major waterspout carried runoff from the bridge and in heavy rains could produce a thunderous waterfall. More than one unsuspecting rookie had been driven under the cascade with his passenger window locked open by his coach officer. At least that was the story according to Manny, who denied, rather fervently, that he had ever fallen prey to the cruel initiation. Jack had his doubts.

He pulled up behind an ambulance on King Street, right in front of the big man's clothing store. The drizzle had dwindled to nothing but left a damp chill in its wake and Jack shivered as he zipped up his jacket.

"A coffee would be good after this," Manny suggested, unknowingly echoing Jack's exact thought.

The entrance to Mr. Big and Tall was on a diagonal corner at the intersection of King and St. Lawrence. The paramedics were helping an older male who slumped on the store's steps. There was no truck in sight.

Manny saw Jack looking around and pointed to the building's west end. "There's a cube van parked in the laneway beside the store. That might be the one he got hit by."

"Can't be that bad if they moved him out front." But as they approached the medics, Jack began to change his mind. The man wasn't that old, early fifties tops, but from the limp, boneless way he sat on the steps Jack thought he might have had a stroke. He looked like he might sag to the concrete if the medics weren't propping him up.

Can getting hit by a vehicle cause a stroke?

"Hey, guys. What have we got?"

One of the medics was a pretty blonde with dark smears under her eyes, another victim of shift work, Jack figured. She was kneeling in front of the man but looked over her shoulder at the two coppers. "Your guy is around back."

Jack gestured to her patient. "This isn't the victim?" he asked, puzzled. Looking at the man's empty, slack face, Jack was more certain than ever he was a stroke victim.

She hushed Jack with a quick slash of her hand, then jerked her head in the man's direction, a very dark, unfriendly look on her face.

Jack held his hands in front of him compliantly and he and Manny backed off.

"What was her problem?" Manny asked, his voice hushed as they headed for the laneway.

"Fucked if I know."

They turned down the laneway and saw a balding man huddled in a parka waiting for them by the front bumper of the cube van Manny had spotted. The laneway was short and wide and it T-boned with another laneway behind the building.

"Oh, thank God you're here, officers." The balding man, his chubby face pale and worried, wiped his damp brow.

Sweating in this temperature? What's got everyone so spooked?

"The . . . the . . . the other . . ." He groped for a word. "The other gentleman is over there." He swept his hand behind him, taking in the truck and both laneways. It was clear he didn't want to look.

What the fuck is going on? "And the guy out front is . . . ?"

"That's Jim. He's one of our drivers. He was making a delivery when . . . when . . ."

"When the other guy fell behind the truck?" Jack offered and the man nodded enthusiastically, sweat flicking off his forehead. "Manny, you want to take down this gentleman's info? I'll go check on the other guy."

"Sure thing, man." Manny pulled out his memo book and lifted a quizzical eyebrow Jack's way. Jack pumped his shoulders in a quick shrug and headed for the back of the van.

The east-west laneway behind the store was much narrower than its intersecting neighbour and Jack could see why the driver would have had a hard time navigating the corner, especially if he was backing up. The five-ton cube van, its white paint grey with slush, sat on an angle, the driver's side rear bumper aimed at the lane's southern wall.

Jack realized the other building was the old, converted factory, its red bricks and looming windows darkened by decades of soot and pollution. *Sure hope they cleaned the inside before turning it into condos.*

He squeezed between the van and the corner of the clothing store. He noted some heavy scrapes on the van's body, worn and dirt filled, and figured this wasn't the first time old Jim had had problems turning in the alley.

As Jack neared the rear bumper, he spotted a pair of legs on the ground, blue jeans and winter boots wet from the brief rain. The loose lace of one boot lay in a puddle.

Ambulance just left him here? Is he pinned or something?

"Hey, buddy, you — Jack stepped around the van and the words died in his throat. He could see the rest of the victim: a well-worn brown leather jacket, a jaunty green scarf knotted loosely around the neck. And nothing else.

Man fallen behind truck. Yeah, that's one way of putting it.

Jack could tell it was a man from the stubble on the neck and chin, but he was missing his head from the jaw up. No, not quite missing. It was there. Mostly. Just not the way it should be.

Blood, amazingly red among the grey slush, pooled where the head should have been. A flattened sack of skin and hair that used to belong to a living, breathing person was all that was left after the head was crushed between a brick wall and a steel bumper. Jack looked more closely and saw the bumper's grid-like pattern pressed into the skin of a squashed cheek.

His stomach heaved. He looked up, wanting to see anything except that . . . that thing that used to be a person's head. He fixated on a patch of bright red and green on the grimy bricks. The green was the man's toque, caught between the corner of the bumper and the brick wall. The red was his blood, sprayed when his head was popped like a ripe tomato. It looked as if someone had decorated the crown of a Christmas tree by taking a shotgun to the flesh-and-blood angel perched on top.

Manny came up behind Jack. "Hey, Jack. That guy was saying something about — oh."

Jack nodded, his eyes never leaving the congealing blood as it dripped sluggishly from the cheery green toque.

"Yeah. Oh."

"I heard you guys had a messy one this morning."

Jack pushed away from the keyboard and arched his back, groaning in contentment. "Yeah, you could say that."

The on-scene investigation had taken hours. Sergeant Rose had attended as the road supervisor; then the detectives had come, then the coroner, then finally, body removal. Store staff had been interviewed, statements taken. Jack and Manny finally went back to the station to do the paperwork in the tiny room ridiculously labelled the report room. It had space for three computers along one wall and, on the other walls, ranks of shelving holding outdated paper forms.

"What happened?" Jenny boosted herself onto the countertop next to Jack's computer. She waved her fingers at Manny and he smiled at her around his sandwich. Ever since his girlfriend had become a live-in girlfriend, she'd been making his lunches for him and, apparently, was rather hurt if he came back with any of them uneaten.

"Pretty stupid, actually." Jack rotated his head, feeling the vertebrae in his neck crack pleasurably.

Jenny hopped off the counter to stand behind him. She slapped him lightly on the side of the head to get him to hold still, then began working her fingers into muscle at the base of his neck. Jack had taken off his jacket and vest before settling in at the computer, so she was able to really dig into the muscle. "Keep going."

"As far as we can tell — ah, that feels good — our victim was cutting through the laneway — he lived in the converted lofts there — and stopped to tie his boot and while he was kneeling the truck backed into him."

"He didn't hear it coming? Jeez, Jack, don't you ever stretch after your workouts?"

"No. I mean yes. Yes, I stretch. No, he didn't hear the truck." He tapped his ear. "Had his headphones on and the tunes cranked. Stupid way to die."

"I'll say." Jenny dug her fingers in deeper, eliciting another groan from Jack. "Do you have to notify next of kin?"

Jack grunted no, too involved in the feel of her fingers to talk.

"Sergeant Rose did it for us," Manny explained as he wiped the crumbs from his fingers and reached for a bag of grapes. He popped one into his mouth. "She said she wanted us to get started on the report as soon as possible."

"Well, at least you didn't have to do that. I hate having to notify families about deaths. I'd rather clean up the body than talk to the family. What did it look like?" Nothing seemed to interest coppers like a really gross story. Except maybe for a gun call.

"It looked like. . . ." Jack plucked free one of Manny's grapes and held it up between his thumb and forefinger. "Like this." Its innards spewed over his fingers as he squished it.

Jenny giggled. "That's gross."

Manny had a different reaction. "Oh, dude." He pushed the bag of grapes away, a queasy expression souring his face. "I'm never going to be able to eat another grape ever again."

Jack and Jenny laughed, but their levity was cut short as Sergeant Rose stepped into the report room.

"You okay, Sarge? You look tired."

Rose smiled at Jenny and it eased the hard-ass expression Sergeant Rose normally wore. But Jack agreed with Jenny. Rose did look wiped out. Telling parents their only son had his head popped like a grape between a truck and a wall would probably wear out even the most callous bastard.

"I fucking hate day shift," she grumbled and with that the smile faded and her sergeant's mask slid back into place. "You're on lunch, right, Alton? Use my badge for cancelling your lunch and head out. The calls are starting to back up."

"Sure thing, Sarge. See you guys later." Jenny gave Jack a final pat on the shoulder before leaving.

"How much more do you have to do?"

Jack considered the screen in front of him and shrugged. "Not much. Fifteen, twenty minutes I guess."

Rose nodded. "Good. Get it done as quick as you can. You're the only two-man car on the road today and a domestic just came in with your name on it."

"Oh, joy." Jack snuggled up to the keyboard again.

"What's wrong with Armsman?"

"Hm?" Jack looked at Manny. His partner was still staring

at the bag of grapes like he expected them all to suddenly start exploding. "Nothing major, Sarge. His lunch just isn't agreeing with him."

Jack lay in the dark, staring at the bedroom ceiling. By all accounts, he should be fast asleep; it had been a long and tiring day. An adrenalin rush thanks to Max the pit bull, then the industrial accident — *poor fucking bastard* — and, to finish off, a wonderfully unoriginal domestic in which the husband had beaten the living snot out of the wife. Jack had taken her statement while Manny had snapped photos of her and the trashed apartment. Only three calls, but they had filled the day. And then some.

Jack had called home from the station when overtime looked inevitable to tell Karen not to wait for him. She had dinner plans with her mother but had hoped to see him before heading out. Jack had, of course, been invited to join the ladies for dinner but had declined; day shift and evenings out really didn't mesh. As it turned out, he wouldn't have been able to make it anyway.

Not that missing dinner with his mother-in-law was all that distressing, although he had to admit Evelyn had certainly been treating him nicer this last month. Or was it longer than that? His occupation was her favourite topic of conversation; her husband liked to bash Jack any way he could. Jack tried to remember the last time Evelyn had gotten on his case about the job and couldn't. But it was definitely more than a month.

Wonder if she's up to something?

If a particularly nasty supervisor at work, Staff Greene for example, suddenly changed demeanour the way Evelyn had, Jack would expect a knife in the back. Could Evelyn have finally realized her daughter wasn't going to leave her cop? Had Evelyn decided to make the best of it?

Yeah, right. And Santa Claus is real.

Jack had crawled into bed before eight-thirty. He and Manny had agreed to forgo tomorrow's workout before shift, so he didn't have to get up until half past five. He had hoped to bag a good nine solid hours of sleep. And here it was almost ten and sleep was still as elusive as it had been an hour and a half ago.

The room lit up briefly as headlights swept across the front of the house before blinking out. Karen was home. He heard the engine cut and smiled as he heard her try to quietly push the Honda's door shut. He could picture her swearing under her breath as she shoved against the door; Karen didn't do quiet well. She was a slammer and stomper.

He listened to her moving around in the kitchen, the fridge opening and closing. Leftovers? Or had she brought him home something? Maybe dessert? Sundays were typically his cheat day, after all.

Jack followed her progress up the stairs by the faint creaking; he should tell her to walk on the outside of the steps if she wanted to be quiet. Then she stepped into the room. She must be feeling her way through the dark.

"It's okay, Kare. I'm awake."

"I'm sorry, Jack. I tried to be quiet. Did I wake you?"

"Nope," he said. "I just got to bed a few minutes ago."

She clicked on the bathroom light, silhouetting herself in the doorway. "But you sounded so tired on the phone. I thought you'd be in bed as soon as you got home."

"Got home around eight-thirty, had something to eat and watched some TV. If I'd known you were on your way, I'd've stayed up." No sense letting her know he'd been lying here for more than an hour; she'd worry that he was having trouble sleeping again. She'd blame it on his return to 51 and he didn't need to provide her with any more ammunition for that argument.

"You didn't have to," Karen called from the bathroom. "I'll be out in a minute." The door clicked shut, muting the sound of running water.

A few minutes later she was sliding next to him, a T-shirt with dancing teddy bears on it covering her to mid-thigh. She lifted his left arm and snuggled in against his chest. "Bad day, hon?"

"Nope, just long."

"That was terrible about the young man. Are you okay?"

He shifted his gaze from the ceiling to her. "Yeah, I'm okay. I mean, yeah, it was a pretty horrible sight, but —" He laughed, a brief, harsh exhale of breath that even to his ears sounded forced. "But I've seen worse."

"How do you handle it? Seeing stuff like that all the time."

"Well, I don't exactly see stuff like that every day," he said carefully, weighing her question. Was she concerned? Or was this another assault on 51?

"I know," she said quietly, hugging him tight. "People shouldn't have to see what you see. I don't know how you do it."

"Well," he mused, shrugging beneath her comfortable weight. "You get used to it, after a while."

"But how can you get used to that?" Her breath tickled the hair on his chest.

He sought an answer that would explain it and finally opted for the words cops had been using since there were cops to say them. "You just do. That's all." He stroked her hair, watching it gleam softly in the street light that stole past the curtains. "You have to, otherwise you can't do the job. I mean, after the accident, Manny and I handled a pretty nasty domestic where the husband laid one hell of a beating on his wife. I had to take her statement and if I let the sight of her get to me, then I wouldn't have been much use to her, would I?"

"I guess not." Karen hugged him again and held him tight. "Did you catch the husband?" she whispered into the dark.

He nodded, a grim smile on his lips. "Yeah. We found him hiding in his mom's basement."

"Did he fight with you?" She rose up on her arms as if suddenly afraid she was hurting him by lying against him.

He snorted contemptuously. "Nah. Like most wife beaters,

he's a coward. When faced with someone their own size who'll fight back, they usually give up. Like I said, cowards. That's why they beat their wives. Or girlfriends. Or children."

"You really like it down there, don't you?" Karen asked as she snuggled close.

Jack smiled again. It was still a grim smile but a satisfied smile. "I do. I know shit happens all over the city. But down there. . . ."

"You really feel like you're making a difference?" she suggested.

"Exactly." He hugged her, kissing the top of her head. She shifted in the dark and her lips found his. "You know," he whispered as his hand trailed down her back. "We're in bed together and one of us is already naked."

"Really?" Her hand trailed down his stomach and lower. She stroked him to hardness, then slid a leg across his hips. She straddled him, then pulled off her T-shirt and flung it aside. The teddy bears would have to find somewhere else to sleep.

Sunday, 25 March
0615 hours

"Karen, what's this?"

She heard the words, the sound of them, but didn't understand them. She mumbled something, not really awake, then rolled over and burrowed deeper beneath the covers. She was dimly aware of the bed shifting as Jack sat down; then his hand was on her hip, gently nudging her.

"Kare, I need you to wake up for a minute."

"It's Sunday," she grumbled, still more asleep than awake. "I don't have to work today."

"I know, Kare, but I need to ask you something. Then you can go back to sleep." Her hip was nudged again, not as gently, more persistently.

Grunting with displeasure, she rolled over to check the clock. Not even six-thirty. Her eyes swayed groggily to the windows. It was barely light out. Jack should know better; she never got up on Sunday until it was time for church.

"C'mon, Kare, I have to go to work soon."

Fine. She pushed herself upright and sat up against the pillows. "Jack, you know Sundays are the only time I get to sleep in," she snapped, hoping her irritation came through loud and clear. They'd had such a wonderful time last night. Why did he have to spoil it by waking her up? "What's so impor —"

"What's this?"

An icy fist squeezed her stomach. Jack was sitting on the edge of the bed as he had done so many times when he wanted to say goodbye before heading off to work. He had even sat there — on a different bed in a different bedroom — when he had proposed to her, a beautiful ring held in trembling fingers. His fingers were trembling now, but she knew he wasn't nervous.

"What's this?" he repeated, his voice calm, but she could hear the effort it required.

What could she say? He knew what it was. "A pregnancy test."

His hand dropped to his lap. He fingered the damning piece of blue plastic, turning it slowly in his fingers before wrapping his fist around it. "Are you pregnant?" he asked, sounding tired.

It hurt her heart to hear him sound so tired. "No," she whispered, shaking her head as if that would make this moment go away. *Please, God, let this be a bad dream.* But she knew it wasn't.

"Are you still on the pill?" Still calm, still tired, still not looking at her.

"Jack, let's not talk about this right now. We can discuss it tonight when you get home from work."

He nodded as though he had heard words other than what she had said. He laughed, that short, cynical snort she had come to hate. If that damned division had a noise for her, it was that laugh. Harsh and utterly devoid of the Jack she knew and loved.

He bounced the test in his hand. "Guess you didn't shove it down deep enough into the garbage." It was his turn to shake his head. Finally, he lifted his eyes to look at her. "Are you trying to get pregnant?"

Such a simple question. Asked so softly, so explicitly. She couldn't answer it, but then she really didn't have to answer it.

Again that laugh, that fucking laugh. "Was this your idea or your mother's? I'm betting Evelyn's." His words came through clenched teeth, his voice quivering with effort. "What was the plan? Blackmail me? Give me an ultimatum? The baby or 51? Or am I not thinking grand enough? The baby or policing? That's it, isn't it?"

"Jack." Karen reached for him, her fingers tracing the wound that had come so close to taking his eye. Every time she saw it, it terrified her, screamed at her, reminded her what could happen. If that could happen to him where he said it was safe, what could happen to him down there in that hellhole? How long before it was more than a scar? "Jack, I love you and I want you to be safe."

She cupped his cheek, but the muscles under his skin were tight, unyielding. His eyes brimmed with tears, yet his gaze was cold. Wordlessly, he pulled back from her hand and slowly stood up.

"Jack, please." She threw back the covers, made to get up, but he stopped her with an outstretched hand.

"Don't, Karen. I . . . I have to go to work." He walked to the door, then stopped, his hand on the frame. He looked at her over his shoulder and she could see the tears were free. "I really hate . . . this." And then he was gone.

Karen sagged onto the mattress, feeling empty and scared. Was it just her imagination, or had he paused before that last word? She thought he had and it horrified her to think of what he had meant to say, what he really hated.

She jumped as the car door slammed shut; then his car — that poor old beast Jack kept alive so she could drive the Honda — coughed to life. She waited for him to drive off, but the sounds from the engine remained in the driveway. The engine quit and her heart began to beat again as the car door opened. Now it was her turn to laugh, a huge sobbing gasp of relief.

She was out of the bed and partway down the stairs when the door slammed again and the engine roared to life. This time there was no hesitation, no second thought. The tires screeched over the engine's howls of protest and he was gone.

Jack sat in the car, his hands fisted on the steering wheel, his grip tight and painful. It was either that or hit something.

"I don't believe it. I don't fucking believe it." He choked back sobs, felt them burning in his throat. How could she? How could she betray him like that? "Fuck!" He smashed his fists against the steering wheel. Again. And again. Screaming with each blow. As his hands slammed down the third time, something in his fist screamed back at him.

"Fuck," he swore once more, but softly this time, the anger vanishing in the flare of pain that shot up his forearm. He cradled his right hand against his chest, wondering if he had broken anything. "My luck, I probably fucking have."

The emotional pain, gut wrenching and foul, that gripped him as soon as he had seen the pregnancy test was gone, leaving him wrung out, spent.

Why did I have to look down when I threw out the razor blade? Why?

And the things he had said to Karen and the things he had almost said. Part of him wanted to go back in, apologize, make things right with his wife. He flexed his hand and the painful twinge decided him. He was acting like a prime fool.

He snapped off the ignition and opened the door. *We can talk this out; Karen's not like her mother.* He stopped abruptly, one foot on the asphalt, the thought of Evelyn Hawthorn freezing him half out of the car. Hadn't he wondered just last night why she had been nice to him lately, questioned what she was up to?

So that's it. Well, fuck me.

Karen letting herself get pregnant out of concern for him he could understand and deal with — but not if Evelyn was behind it. Karen would use the baby as a lever, something to strengthen her arguments against policing, against 51. But Evelyn . . . she would use the pregnancy the way a puppeteer used strings to make toys dance.

"I'm no fucking puppet." Anger rose up from his belly, hot and righteous. It burned through his veins, exploded behind his eyes. He cast a final, hateful eye at the house, then dropped back into the driver's seat. Slamming the door felt good. Blasting the engine to life was better. Roaring away from the house as fast as he could felt the best.

The sickly sweet stink of marijuana smoke barely masked the stench of dried urine in the stairwell. Ah, the sights and smells of Regent Park, the unofficial heart of all the crap that was 51. A sprawling housing complex, home to the low-income, welfare and no-income. A breeding ground of violence and despair. Walking its halls and searching its apartments, Jack had met third- and fourth-generation welfare recipients. Why work if the government will pay you not to? And he had met crackheads and crack dealers, people who preyed on the weak and scum, who fed on fear and brutality.

Wonderful place to live, Jack thought, stepping on a "crack can," a pop can turned into a makeshift crack pipe. He had to remind himself there were also good people living within the park's sad buildings, although it was easy to forget the good when all he dealt with was the shit. And as corny as it sounded, the good people of Regent Park were one of the reasons he had come back to 51, but at the moment he had no idea if he and Manny would meet some of the good having a bad day or some of the shit being themselves.

They were trudging up the stairs to the third floor at 259 Sumach Street in answer to a frantic 911 call. It had come over as a domestic hotshot, but details were sketchy. The caller was a hysterical woman, her words incoherent between her sobs and a prominent language barrier. The call taker had heard a male yelling in the background. Coupled with a crying female, it added up to a domestic.

I'm not really in the mood to help other people with their domestic problems right now. But Jack stepped out of the stairwell, then quickly scanned the hall in both directions. There was no need to check apartment numbers; the cinderblock tunnel of a hallway echoed with the sounds of the fight. All they had to do was follow the screeching.

Jenny was already by the door and so was Boris. *Holy shit! Maybe there is a Santa Claus after all!* The dispatcher had detailed an additional unit to attend with Jack and Manny's two-man car and Boris had been clear.

Too bad all the dispatcher sees is a badge number assigned to the car, otherwise she'd know Manny and I are still on our own. Guess Jenny knows that, too.

Sean Borovski — Boris to the shift just because he hated it — was not Jack's favourite person, let alone copper and Jack could have done without seeing his pudgy face today. Boris was grossly incarnate: grossly fat, grossly lazy, grossly embarrassing. His idea of good police work was measured by how many tickets he wrote and how many radio calls he could avoid. Jack had no problem slapping some paper on Mr. Average Joe if he deserved it, but there were enough assholes in the division who warranted special attention that there was no need to beef up your workload at the expense of people who actually paid taxes. Boris took the phrase "pronging the public" to new and nauseating heights.

Boris should head up to 53 and work with the Earl.

Which explained Jenny putting herself on the call. Jack was surprised, astounded really, that Boris was standing there with her. He had a knack of showing up when the cuffs were on or the report already started. Less chance of actually having to do something that way.

"Holy shit, Batman. I think this is the first time I've ever seen Boris not be the last one at a call," Manny declared, echoing Jack's thoughts.

Jack just grunted.

"Hey, guys. I think it's coming from in there," Jenny joked, pointing at the apartment door.

Boris just blinked and nodded.

The steel door, painted a thick, cloying blue, did little to mute the noise coming from the apartment. A woman was screaming in Chinese, raw and ripping. A male bellowed back at her, also in Chinese.

This sounds like it's going to be fucking pleasant. "Just the two inside?"

"That's all I've been able to make out," Jenny said. "Shall we?"

Jack made an *after you* gesture and Jenny unholstered her collapsible baton, then rammed the butt end against the door. Steel clanged on steel, silencing the shouting mid-screech. Locks clacked loudly in the sudden stillness and the door swung open. As soon as the uniforms were visible, the shouting began again, hers at the police and his at her. At least that's the way Jack thought it was going.

The woman had a baby tucked in the crook of one arm; her free hand was busy jabbing angrily at a man who stood across the room. Even the baby's wails couldn't drown out the woman's hellish screeching.

"Shush. Don't yell," Jenny said calmly, stepping into the apartment.

The guys followed, Boris bringing up the rear. *Of course.*

Jack grabbed Boris and they headed down the apartment's short hallway to check the rest of the place while Manny and Jenny corralled the man and woman in the living room. The unit was a small one bedroom and floor space was at a premium. A double bed and a crib fought for dominance in the bedroom and it took only seconds to clear the room and the closet.

"Nothing in the bathroom," Boris advised as Jack joined him in the hall.

"Good." *Would Boris say anything if he found a dead body laid out in the tub? Or would he pretend nothing was there so he could get back to avoiding work? Damn, I'm in a crappy mood.*

He and Boris headed to the living room. The place was clean and tidy, albeit a bit cramped with furniture that seemed too big for the room. Nothing broken and no blood splattered in fancy, decorative patterns across the wallpaper. So far, so good.

The woman had slowed her rapid-fire monologue. Jack thought she was in her early twenties, if that, and other than eyes red and puffy from crying she appeared unharmed. Jenny had her in a corner and was talking to her in hushed tones. Manny had the guy, who easily looked twice the woman's age, in the kitchen. The man had his arms crossed defensively and was emphatically shaking his head to whatever Manny was saying.

"At least they're speaking English."

Jack nodded. Every once in a while, Boris could say something inoffensive. Obvious and unnecessary but inoffensive.

It only took a few minutes for both sides of the story to be heard and assessed. There were always two sides to a story, if not more. That was one of the first lessons a cop learned, no matter where he worked.

Jenny and Manny met by the front door to compare notes. The wife — she was the man's wife, not his daughter, thankfully; the two had been yelling at each other with an intensity only an intimate relationship can create and Jack didn't want to think about that — sat on the couch sniffling into a tissue with the baby in her lap while the husband glared at the kitchen cabinets. Jack stood where he could keep an eye on both of them while Jenny and Manny conferred. It didn't take long.

Jenny gave Jack the heads-up. "The husband's taking off to stay with his mom while he cools down."

"No assault?" From the ferocity of the screaming, Jack would have bet his mortgage someone had been hit.

"Nope, just a loud-ass argument."

"It sounded like they were getting ready to kill each other. What the fuck were they arguing about?"

"Would you believe diapers?" Her mouth crooked in a sardonic grin at his perplexed expression. "Yup, hubby refuses to change the diapers and she called 911."

"You're fucking kidding me." Jack shook his head. "For fuck's sake."

They stuck around while hubby packed a bag — *guess he's staying with mommy for more than the night* — then walked him out of the apartment. The wife slammed the door behind them and Manny had to hop to avoid getting smacked in the ass. They all took the stairs and it was a quiet trip.

Diapers. They were fighting over diapers. Is that what Jack had waiting for him? Not that he thought he and Karen would ever fight over something as stupid as that, let alone call 911 about it, but what if she was pregnant? She said she wasn't, but how accurate was that test? And when had she used it? *Fuck, she could be pregnant from last night.*

His mood, which had been sour all morning thanks to images of him dancing woodenly as his mother-in-law jerked strings attached to his limbs, dropped even further. *God, I want to hit someone.*

When they reached the ground floor, hubby exited through the back door; the cops turned for the door that opened onto the hallway. Jack yanked the door open and almost walked into a crackhead stepping into the stairwell. That he was a crackhead was obvious, considering the crack pipe he had held to his mouth and the way his eyes widened in shock and fear over the flame of the lighter he was touching to the pipe.

"Hi there." Jack snagged the guy by the front of his parka and hauled him into the stairwell. One good thing to say about the buildings in Regent Park: the stairways had enough room for four cops and one shit-out-of-luck crack addict.

Manny pulled on his search gloves and plucked the pipe and lighter from the man's unresisting hands. "Just a twenty piece," he estimated, examining the rock resting on the aluminum foil wrapped over the short end of a copper-piping L joint.

"Keep your hands where I can see them. You got any more on you?" Jack asked as he tugged on his Kevlar-lined gloves.

"N-no," the guy stammered. Old at a young age and burned skinny by the drug, he shivered in his heavy parka. His eyes darted nervously from face to face.

"Of course not."

Jenny came into the stairwell. "No one else." She had checked the hall to make sure buddy had been alone. She took up a position by the stairwell door, keeping an eye on the hall and the stairs. Where there was one crackhead, there could be more. Boris leaned against the railing, a bored look on his face.

Jack unzipped buddy's parka, grimacing at the stagnant body odour. "Fuck, buddy, don't you ever wash?" *Bloody fucking hell. First a couple of morons fighting over a shitty diaper and then some asshole who smells like one.*

"Sorry," the kid muttered.

"I'm sure," Jack growled. He grabbed the crackhead by the jaw, forcing the bloodshot, fearful eyes to meet his. *Calm down, Jack. No need to lose your temper over some crackhead.* "You have anything on you that I'm going to cut myself on? Knives, razor blades, needles? Anything like that? Tell me now, 'cause if I cut myself I'll put you in the fucking hospital."

"No . . . nothing."

"Uh-huh." Jack started with the coat pockets, patting down the outside before reaching in — no sense sticking his hand in blindly, Kevlar or no Kevlar — and when he smoothed the fabric of the second pocket he felt it, grabbed it from the outside as cold dread slid up his spine. "What the fuck is this?" he snarled.

The crackhead panicked, knowing he had fucked up. "Nothing! I'm sorry! I forgot!"

Holding the crackhead's jacket with one hand, Jack pulled the knife free of the pocket. It was a folding buck knife and he flicked it open with his thumb in front of the crackhead's terrified eyes. Against his sickly complexion, the blade's gleam was sinister. "Fuck!" Jack punched the crackhead in the ribs, knocking the wasted body across the landing.

Jenny jumped out of the way and the man crashed into the door. She darted to block Jack as he advanced on the crackhead, murder in his eyes. "Jack, that's enough. Enough!"

He bumped into her outstretched hand without seeing her. "Stop, Jack. Please."

"She's right, man. He's learned his lesson." Manny was at his side, firmly pushing down the hand that clasped the knife. "Right, bud? You won't lie to the police again, will you?"

The crackhead shook his head and clutched his chest. "No, boss."

Jack shook his head to throw off the red haze that had saturated his vision. He looked at the man sprawled on the floor. *Did I do that?* He didn't remember hitting him or pulling out the knife, but he must have, because there it was in his hand. Numbly, he handed the knife to Manny.

"Thanks, man." Manny closed the knife, then studied it. Grinning, he snapped it open with a flick of his wrist. He pointed the blade at the crackhead, still grinning. "Flick knife, bud. That's prohibited and you're going to jail, dude."

"Where to, man? Allan Gardens?"

Jack thought about it for a second. "Nah, too many people. Somewhere a little more secluded."

"You got it, dude." Drinks from the Second Cup at Church and Wellesley on board, hot chocolate for Manny, tea for Jack, Manny headed south on Jarvis Street. Traffic was light for a Sunday afternoon and in minutes they were deep in the division's south end, away from well-travelled roads. There was less chance someone would walk up to them with a problem down here.

Processing the crackhead on the weapon and drug charges had been a cinch with the three of them helping on the paperwork — Jack the arrest, Manny the drugs and Jenny the knife, court cards for all — and they had been back on the road in no time. Boris had declined to join in on the arrest and potential court card, saying it was their pinch and they didn't need to feel obligated to include him. It wasn't like him to turn down a free court card and as he had left the stairwell he had given Jack a peculiar look. If Jack had to label it, he would say the fat copper had looked devious and rather pleased with himself.

Manny turned off Cherry Street into a deserted dirt parking lot just north of the raised CN train tracks. Old wood loading docks, relics from a bygone era, abandoned and choked with weeds and garbage, framed the V-shaped lot. Much of the southeast corner of the division was like that: abandoned and forgotten. Like the Waterfall parking lot, this area was popular for film and TV shoots because of the neglected buildings and vacant lots.

Manny swung the scout car in a hard U-turn, churning up a lethargic dust cloud and then reversed into the lot's far end and tucked the car next to the loading dock, concealing the white car with its distinctive red and blue striping. Out of sight, out of mind.

He killed the engine and they both got out and leaned on the hood. No clouds barred the sun and beneath its mild touch the air smelled of spring. Jack popped the top on his tea and inhaled deeply. Warm sunlight, hot tea and no radio calls. If only it could stay that way for a few minutes. . . .

The work station beeped in the car and Manny went to check on it. A minute or two of tapping on the keyboard and he was back.

"That was Jenny. She's on her way."

Jack nodded and sipped his tea. "Warm weather, hot tea, no calls and a beautiful woman. Things are getting better all the time."

They stood in companionable silence, enjoying the warmth and solitude. Across from them on the west side of Cherry Street stood the old Gooderham and Worts distillery. The aged red brick buildings sat empty and forlorn, waiting to see what the future held. The surroundings weren't cheery, but they fit Jack's mood perfectly.

"You okay, man?"

Manny's question broke Jack's dark thoughts of a wife who betrayed him and a mother-in-law who wanted to control him. "Yeah. Why?"

"I dunno." Manny shrugged beefy shoulders and squinted at Jack. The sunlight gleamed off his shaven scalp. "You seem kind of tense today. Angry, maybe."

Jack shook his head, his lips pursed as if his tea had suddenly turned bitter. "Just a bit of trouble at home. Nothing major, really. No need for me to ruin the fantasy of domestic bliss for you."

A lot of people, supervisors especially, mistook Manny's childlike exuberance and cheerfulness as stupidity and were constantly underestimating Manny. Just like Jack had done, hoping to blow him off with a bullshit, lame answer.

"C'mon, dude. We're partners, right? No offence, but the way you reacted in the stairwell . . . I mean, it was cool when you knocked him like ten feet through the air with one punch and all and I bet he won't lie to the police again, but, dude, we're lucky you didn't stab him when you hit him. And the way you went after him with the knife still in your hand." Manny chuckled. "Dude, it looked like you were getting ready to carve a J into his forehead."

"A J? What are you babbling about?"

"You know, that Kayne guy, carving the letter K into people's heads."

Jack pulled a face at his partner. "I don't think it was that bad."

Manny drained the last of his hot chocolate and set the cup on the car hood. He shielded his eyes from the sun and looked at Jack. "You sure?" he asked simply.

Jack paused with his tea halfway to his mouth. "Put on your sunglasses, moron." He drank his tea.

"Did that thing yesterday bother you?"

Something in Manny's voice, more than the question itself, told Jack his partner wasn't making small talk. "It was messy," he replied cautiously, knowing which thing Manny was referring to. "I don't think I'll be able to look at a Christmas tree the same way ever again. You okay with it?"

"I guess so," he said quietly but didn't meet Jack's eyes.

It was Jack's turn to say, "You sure?"

Manny heaved a deep breath, slowly shaking his head. "The guy's head was gone, man. One minute he was tying his shoe, the next he was dead. It sucks. It really sucks."

Manny had joined the TPS at twenty-one, coming straight to 51 out of the police college. Despite more than three years on the job, he was a young guy, still a kid in many ways. Jack had only five years on Manny, but he felt much older. He had aged a lifetime in the past six months.

"Yeah, it sucks and it's a really fucking stupid way to die. But shit happens and we have a job to do. We all see things that upset us, and it's different for everyone. Some guys can scrape bodies up off the road without a thought, but they may have problems with anything involving animals or kids. I'd be worried about you if yesterday hadn't bothered you."

"Thanks, man." Manny sighed, looking like the weight was suddenly lighter. "You won't tell anyone, will you? I mean, I don't want the guys thinking I'm weak or anything."

"Of course not." Jack grinned. "For a price."

Manny groaned. Then Jenny's scout car rolled into the lot. Jenny pulled up close and got out.

"Hey, beautiful. Glad you could join us."

"But not glad enough to buy me a coffee," she complained, pointing at Jack's cup.

"If I'd known you were . . . available, I would have grabbed you one," Jack said defensively, flashing her a smile.

She smiled back and some of the darkness encasing Jack's heart melted away. "For you, I'm always available."

"Did you guys want to use the back seat of the car?" Manny opened the door for them.

Jenny wrinkled her nose at the suggestion. "The back seat? Yuck. You know the type of people we put in there. No thanks."

Manny shrugged apologetically. To Jack, he said, "Sorry, dude. I tried."

"I just said no to the back seat," Jenny corrected. "We could always use the hood."

"You seem in an awfully good mood," Jack noted, hoping to distract her from the blush he felt creeping up his neck. It was amazing how she could make him feel, even when she was joking. And he was pretty sure she was joking, unfortunately.

That was one of the things he liked and admired about Jenny. She could give as well as, or better than, she got when it came to sexual innuendo and ribbing. Coppers who tried to embarrass her often found themselves the ones being laughed at. But the two-way teasing sometimes backfired on her.

Cops, primarily the dinosaurs but also a good number of impressionable young guys, viewed policewomen as bitches, dykes or party girls. A PW who dated cops was usually known as a party girl who'd fuck anyone in uniform. If she didn't date guys on the job, she was a bitch. Or a dyke. Maybe a bit of both.

Jenny's rep was bitchy party girl. She had dated a couple of cops early in her career. Neither of the relationships had ended well. In general, cop-cop relationships had a tendency to self-destruct. Gossip had it that Jenny had dated several dozen cops. Guys at the station claimed to have dated her, or at least slept with her, but Jack figured those guys had been shot down quickly and decisively. Hence the bitchy part of her reputation.

Cops could be such assholes.

Jack knew Karen had heard of Jenny's supposed exploits through her friend in 32. He was always careful when he mentioned Jenny to his wife. Karen could be jealous, and it didn't help when she pictured Jenny spreading her legs for anything with a badge. If Karen and Jenny met, it could make the divisional Christmas party this year rather interesting.

"Maybe now that you're here, Jack will tell us why he tried to punch a hole through a guy's chest this morning." Manny smiled smugly. "Thought I'd forgotten you didn't answer the question, huh?"

Constantly underestimated. "I didn't. . . ." Jack looked from Manny to Jenny, the two people he trusted the most. If he couldn't be honest with them . . . He drew a deep breath, let it out slowly. "All right. Ever since Sy died, I've had a problem with knives. I dream about them and when I found that one today it shook me. I imagined what would happen if he pulled it out when I was that close."

"He would have died, dude. That's what."

Jack snorted, just shy of laughing. "I know. So that's all it was. That and a bit of stress brought in from home. And no, we don't have to go into that."

Jenny and Manny exchanged a glance then nodded and Jack suddenly felt the little discussion had been far from spontaneous.

"You guys satisfied?" he asked.

"Dude, we're concerned, that's all."

"What type of friends would we be if we weren't?" Jenny hugged him. Jack preferred hugging her when there weren't two Kevlar vests between them. "You've been through a lot, you idiot." She touched his newest scar lightly. "We would've been stupid not to ask how you are."

"Thanks, guys. I appreciate the concern." Time to change the topic. "Now it's your turn to answer a question. How come you're so happy?"

"I," she announced proudly, "have a date tonight."

"This the same guy you mentioned last week?"

Jenny nodded happily and for an instant the cop disappeared and Jack saw her as the beautiful woman she was. *Lucky bastard.*

Manny had to ask. "He's not a cop, is he?"

She grimaced. "Fuck, no." *Yeah, party girl. Riiiight.* "And he's not a fireman or paramedic."

"Well, that eliminates the obvious. What does he do?"

"Computer stuff. He has his own business, but I don't understand it." She waved that away, unimportant. "I'm meeting him after work. He's taking me to this amazing Japanese restaurant."

"Is it just me," Jack asked, turning to Manny, "or is she acting like some giddy little schoolgirl?"

"She is." Manny leaned in conspiratorially but spoke loud enough for Jenny to hear. "I think someone's getting lucky tonight."

She smiled slyly. "Maybe. It is the fifth date and I really like him. If dinner goes well, we may just end up back at my place."

Very lucky bastard. "Well, I hope all goes according to plan."

Jack had gathered that Jenny didn't have the greatest luck when it came to relationships. He figured guys saw just the physical side of her and were shocked when they discovered she was smart as well as attractive. And, being a 51 copper, she probably wasn't used to taking the submissive role in a relationship.

He doubted most guys, cops or not, could handle the woman being the dominant one. He smiled. If he was single, he figured he could take being dominated by Jenny for a bit. Okay, more than a bit.

She caught him daydreaming. "What are you smiling about?"

"Oh, nothing you need to hear about."

The can of Diet Coke hit the dispensing slot with a tinny clunk. Jack gratefully ran the cold can across his brow before popping the tab and downing a huge swallow. Fuck, what a day. Scratch that. What a fucking weekend. First the poor bastard who got his head smooshed, then the fight with Karen, and he capped off the day by almost killing some crackhead with a knife.

Jack summed up the day by ripping loose a satisfying belch.

"My thoughts exactly." Jenny stomped into the lunchroom and angrily dumped her purse and jacket into a chair.

The lunchroom was right above the parade room and its twin in size and shape but with larger windows in the south-facing wall. Despite the extra glass, the room was dim in the late winter/early spring evening light. Jack could clearly see that Jenny looked as pissed as she sounded. Gloomy light or not, foul mood or not, she still managed to flutter Jack's heart by the simple sight of her.

Her jeans were still new enough to have that dark blue colour yet hugged her hips with an enticing familiarity. Her belted blouse was that deep indigo a summer sky could hit just before the setting sun painted it in colours. Her hair tumbled in soft raven waves to her waist; her blue eyes flashed crystal fire.

What did Sy call her? A siren? Jack fully understood what his old partner had meant. She was the type of woman men would gladly sign over their mortgages for.

"Can I have a sip?"

"Huh?" Jack realized he had been staring and shook his head to clear his thoughts. It almost worked. "Sorry?"

Jenny pointed to the Coke. "Can I have a sip?" If she noticed his mental fugue, she didn't mention it.

"Oh. Sure." He passed her the can and watched, mesmerized, as her lips touched the wet metal. *Easy, Jack. You're a married man.* Her tongue slipped out to wipe those amazing lips. *A married man who's pissed at his wife, so shut up.*

"Thanks." She handed him his drink. "Everything okay? Do I have something on my face?" She raised a tentative hand.

"Um, no. I've just never seen you wear lipstick before."

"Big load of good it'll do me." She hopped onto one of the metal tables running the length of the room, kicked her booted feet.

Jack was reminded of the abrupt twitching of an angry cat's tail. "Thought you had a date tonight."

"So did I." More foot twitching. "But Richard had other plans." She might as well have hissed the words.

"What did he do?" Jack felt an unreasonable flair of anger at a man he had never met.

"We had this great night planned and he didn't know the half of it."

Another flair in Jack, this time . . . jealousy? "Yeah." His throat hitched a bit. Just a bit. "It was supposed to be *the* night."

"Well, he can forget that," she snapped.

Jack eased in next to her, resting his butt against the table. "What did he do?" he asked again, handing her the Coke.

Jenny smiled her thanks, then sucked back a healthy gulp. She passed the can back in time to cover her mouth before croaking out her own carbonated belch.

"Sorry. Guess my stomach's a little unsettled."

"Because . . . ?"

"He called me. Not ten minutes ago. I was still getting dressed." She flapped her hands in useless frustration at her clothes. "We were supposed to have this special night and he cancels on me. And do you know why?" She caught his eyes with hers and Jack thought he had never seen anything so beautiful. He managed to shake his head. "A buddy of his called him up with hockey tickets. He cancelled on me for the fucking Leafs." It was her turn to shake her head. "I mean, I could understand it if they were in the run for the playoffs, but they're done for the season. I doubt any of the top players will even dress for the game."

"That sucks." As soon as the words were out, he cringed. *Way to go, Jack. That sounded really intelligent.*

But apparently Jenny thought it was appropriate. "Yeah, it does suck." She hung her head and her face slid behind a curtain of glossy hair. Her feet stopped twitching. Her anger was spent. "What are you still doing here?" she asked after a moment.

"I'm not exactly in a hurry to get home, so Manny and I are heading out for wings and some cider." He dropped his voice conspiratorially. "Don't tell him I told you, but that industrial accident yesterday really got to him. I think he just needs to talk for a while."

Jenny patted his thigh and a thrill flashed through him. "You're a good friend, Jack."

"Why don't you come with us?" he suggested with a hopeful smile. "We can take turns crying on each other's shoulder."

She swept her hair back with a smile. "You wouldn't mind?"

"Hell, no. Misery loves company." *Another good one, Jack.*

She gave his thigh a quick squeeze. "You are one of the good ones. I hope Karen knows that."

Before Jack could answer, Manny bounced into the room. "Not interrupting anything, am I?"

Jenny slid her hand seductively up Jack's thigh. "I was just telling Jack why he should dump you and work with me."

Manny glanced at her hand caressing Jack's leg, then smiled at her. "Well, you do have some assets I don't," he conceded, "but Jack loves me and would never leave me. But you can have him tonight if you want."

"I thought we were grabbing some drinks?"

"Sorry, dude, but my girlfriend called. I told her about yesterday and she's waiting for me wearing nothing but chocolate sauce."

Jack laughed. "I hope she waits until you get there to pour it on, otherwise she'll be a bit of a mess by the time you arrive."

"No worries, dude. She knows how long it takes me to get home, so she'll put it on her —"

Jenny shot up a hand. "Whoa, I don't need to know."

Manny smiled. "Like you've never used chocolate."

She held up both hands suppliantly. "I didn't say that," she admitted with a grin. "I just don't need to picture you covered in chocolate sauce. I might not be able to ever look at another sundae again."

Manny grinned, a grin that wiped away the day's trauma, at least temporarily. "You don't mind if I bail, do you, Jack?"

And the amazing thing about Manny was that Jack knew if he said he really needed to talk, to shake off the memories from this shitty day, Manny would call his girlfriend and postpone without a second thought. Not that he didn't want to indulge in some chocolate fun — from the way he was bouncing on his toes, chocolate fun was the only thing occupying his thoughts — but if Jack needed a friend he'd be there. No questions asked.

How anyone can not like this guy is beyond me.

Jack waved Manny on his way. "Go, man. You don't want the chocolate to get all runny."

"Thanks, dude. I owe you. See you guys tomorrow." With that, he was gone, nothing but a slap of shoes running down the half flight of stairs to the back door.

"They grow up so fast," Jack said wistfully. "So, what do you say, my dear? You still up for some wings even if it's with just me?"

Jenny smiled at him and his heart melted. "You want to take one car or two?"

The bar was in the division's south end and a favourite watering hole for end-of-shift parties. This being Sunday, Jack and Jenny were the only cops in the place. They were in a corner booth, well away from the crowd and their noise at the bar. Jenny was sipping a beer, and Jack held a cold bottle of cider lovingly between his hands.

"Manny really got you hooked on those, didn't he?"

Jack took a swig, then nodded. "Yup. I don't think I've had a beer since that beach party last year."

"That was the one where Sergeant Pembleton had you burn those gloves, right?"

"It was," he said simply, then thought about that night. The night the division's coppers had said goodbye to a brother and friend. The night war had been declared on anyone daring to wear black leather gloves in honour of a cop killer. A killer who died at Jack's hands. God, he missed Sy.

As if reading his thoughts, Jenny raised her glass. "To Sy."

Jack smiled, a little sadly, and tapped the neck of his bottle to her glass. "To Sy."

They drank in companionable silence until the basket of wings arrived, half honey garlic for him, half suicide for her. Over the food, they did what coppers always did: they talked about the job.

"That was a pretty gruesome scene at the industrial accident," Jenny commented, then nibbled at a wing.

Jack devoured his wings; Jenny took them apart with small, meticulous bites. It let her thoroughly enjoy the hot sauce, she said.

Jack nodded in agreement. "Poor bastard. I've never seen anything like it. Funny, though. The call came over for a man fallen behind a truck and Manny and I both think, 'Okay, guy got hit by a truck. No big deal.' When we get there, everyone's running around in a panic, but I'm still thinking it's just a guy who needs to go to the hospital or something. Then I walk around to the back of the truck and he's lying there without a head."

"That's one of those 'I see' moments."

"That's for sure." Jack hooked another wing and tore off a strip of meat.

"What are you grinning at?"

"Was I?" Jack sucked the last of the meat from the bones and tossed them aside. "Just thinking how Sergeant Johanson says you know you aren't a rookie anymore when you can have lunch with a corpse."

"We're not exactly eating with the corpse right now," she pointed out.

Jack shrugged. "Close enough."

"Was Manny really upset by it?" The concern in her voice was genuine and it touched Jack. A lot of cops would have seen Manny's reaction as weakness.

"I think he was. And it wasn't the sight of it. We've all seen our share of gross things. I think it was the whole situation, you know? Suicides and homicides are one thing, but this . . . it was just sad, really. A sad, stupid way to die."

"How about you? You okay?"

He shrugged again. "I've seen worse."

"No, you idiot," she derided with a smile. "How are things with Karen? Have you talked to her today?"

"Nope." Jack wiped his fingers with a napkin, then wadded up the paper and tossed it in among the chicken bones.

"What are you going to say when you get home?" Jack had given Jenny and Manny a brief recounting of the discovery he had made that morning.

His face twisted and he shrugged again. It was his day for shrugging. "To tell you the truth, Jenny, I really don't feel like going home. I'm just way too pissed off."

Jenny smiled sympathetically. "You have to go home sometime."

"Yeah, I know, and I will, but . . ." He didn't have the words to express what he was feeling.

Jenny reached across the table to take his clenched hands in hers. "Tell me how you feel."

He was silent, sorting through the thoughts and emotions running rampant in his head. Finally, "Hurt. Betrayed." He laughed, a short, rough bark. "And really, really pissed."

Jack drained his cider, using the opportunity to free his hands from hers; it was too distracting having her touching him. He knew she did it in friendship, but she had that effect on him, got him thinking what it would be like to be single and free to ask her out. Definitely something he should not be thinking about.

"I thought you wanted kids." She eased back in her seat, giving him some room.

"I do." He signalled to the waitress for another round. "But we agreed to wait, pay off some bills, build up a reserve. You know, build a good financial base. It's not like she's too old and we have to hurry. If she had gotten pregnant by accident . . . that would have been one thing, but now . . . I don't know. And to be *plotting*" — the word came out between clenched teeth — "with her mother, to use a baby to control me, to get me to quit. . . ." He shook his head, at a loss.

The waitress came with refills and Jack chugged half the bottle.

"Easy there, Jack. Getting drunk won't help."

He wiped his mouth with the back of his hand and nodded. "I know. It's just that if it wasn't for her parents . . . Her mom wants me — fuck that, *expects* me — to be some puppet for her and Karen. Mostly her. And Karen's dad . . . Hell, at least he's straightforward. He just wants Karen to divorce me." He frowned in frustration and took another drink. A sip this time.

Jenny paused, then asked the question that had to be asked. "Do you still want to be married to Karen?"

It was a question Jack had asked himself repeatedly since the morning. "Yeah, I do. I mean, I think I do. Fuck!" He scrubbed his face with both hands before letting them drop limply into his lap. "I don't know what to think, Jenny. I'm too fucked up right now." He gave her a weak smile, then reached across the table for her hands. She gave them to him willingly. "All I know right now is that I'm very thankful to have friends like you and Manny. I appreciate you letting me vent to you."

She slid her hands over his and squeezed. "Any time, you big idiot."

He smiled, a real smile this time. They sat quietly, holding hands. Jack was content to let the silence grow. It wasn't uncomfortable and the feel of her hands in his was doing weird and wonderful things to his spine. A minute later, he thought he had to let go before things got awkward.

"What about you?" His hands were around the cider bottle. It was a poor substitute.

"I'm not having problems with my wife," Jenny joked.

"Haw haw. Very funny. I vented, now it's your turn. C'mon, give."

The smile faded from her lips and the room became a touch less bright. "I know how you feel. I'm pissed too but for different reasons. Things were going so well. I thought I'd finally found a decent guy." She stopped, embarrassment showing on her face. "Actually, he reminded me a lot of you. Oh, relax, I'm not hitting on you. I told you before, I'm not a home wrecker. It's just that ever since I got to know you at that beach party —"

"The one where you slept with me?" It was either make a joke or have his insides rupture from twisting up at her words.

She rolled her eyes. "Yes, the night I fell asleep with my head on your lap. If that's what you mean by sleeping with you."

"Hey, just pointing out the facts, that's all." *Way to go, Jack. Now open wide and see if you can cram the other foot in.*

But Jenny smiled as if she appreciated the levity. "It's just that you're one of the good guys, Jack, and I hope Karen realizes that."

"Thank you," he said honestly. "I hope you make this Richard guy realize how much he messed up tonight, because he obviously doesn't know. I mean, if I had a woman like you, there's no way I'd be passing up on a night with you. Not for a hockey game. Not for anything."

She rewarded him with another smile and he decided he liked it when she smiled. Especially when the smiles were for him.

"You're an amazing woman, Jenny." He wanted to banish her sadness. "You're smart, confident, caring and you have a killer body."

Her blush deepened. "Now you're just trying to make me feel better."

"Just repeating what I hear in the change room. I mean, if I had naked pictures of you to sell, I could have retired last year."

She laughed. "That has to be the most backhanded compliment I've ever been given."

He laughed with her. "All I'm saying is that you're a great woman and one day you'll find a guy who realizes that. And if Richard doesn't, it's his loss, not yours."

"Thank you, Jack. I'm glad we're friends."

It was his turn to smile. "Me, too." But if they were just friends, why did he have an urge to punch out some guy he'd never met?

Monday, 26 March
0010 hours

Lisa was working her corner at Shuter and Seaton, but she didn't mind much now that Kayne was looking after her. In fact, life had been sweet since she had hooked up with the Man. He took real good care of her. She had a place to sleep, food if she was hungry and all the rock she could smoke. The Man was real generous when it came to sharing his rock. Not like that fucking asshole Leo. He had used her to set up the johns and had only tossed her a few bucks. And he had beaten her when he thought she wasn't working hard enough. But a girl had to have protection out here on the streets.

Now Lisa had the best protection in the world. No one messed with Kayne, so no one messed with her. Why he kept that little shit Jesse around she'd never know. All he did was kiss the Man's ass and smoke rock that could have been hers. True, she'd grudgingly admit, they were staying at Jesse's place, but Jesse wouldn't have that bigger room if it wasn't for the money Kayne brought in. Jesse was a little punk-ass bitch and if Kayne hadn't saved his ass Leo would have cut him up. She always smiled when she thought of how Jesse had cried like a punk when Leo had him. What a bitch.

Guess guys just like to have other guys around.

Not that Kayne was a fag, that was for fucking sure and when he wanted to fuck she was there for him. Whatever way he wanted it, she'd do it for him. She even let Jesse have a ride if her Man told her to, but she liked it better when Jesse watched, waiting for his turn and then Kayne would want to sleep, his strong arms wrapped around her. Those were the best, knowing Jesse had a major case of blue balls and couldn't do anything about it. What a bitch.

But now she was back working, helping her Man. She loved watching him beat the fucking shit out of guys, then slice them up with his . . . watchamacallit . . . his talisman. All that fucking blood. She got horny just watching.

Kayne had taken up Leo's old scam, using her to bring the johns to him. They didn't do it much, just enough to make some quick cash and they never rolled a regular john, someone who might go to the cops. Not that her Man was afraid of the fucking cops. Fuck no. But if the cops started looking for them, then the party was over, so why fuck up a good thing?

And Lisa was good at spotting the vics — she'd learned that word from watching that TV show, whatchama call it, *Lawyer's Order* — the ones who wouldn't go crying to the pigs. Crackheads, wannabe tough guys, little bitches like Jesse.

And here was one right now.

"Hey, honey, you looking to party?" Lisa had on her best come-fuck-me smile for the vic when he turned around. He'd walked past her, pretending not to check her out, but she'd seen the look in his eyes. He wanted to fuck.

She stuck a leg out, planting her hand on the other hip — she'd seen the pros stand like that on TV — and let the vic check out the goods. And she was looking fucking good. Kayne had said her old clothes stunk like rat shit and sent her to the Goodwill store to buy some new ones. That was the only time he had hit her and she knew she deserved it; she had used the money to buy some rock. The next time he had told her to buy clothes, she did as she was told.

She had on a blue jean skirt and a black tank top, but what she was most proud of was the leather jacket. She'd never owned a leather jacket before. Jesse said it wasn't real, but what the fuck did he know? He also said the skirt made her legs look like skinny crack whore legs, so he didn't know shit.

She waited, smiling her come-fuck-me smile, for the man to make up his mind. He was eyeing her up and down, so she opened the jacket to show him what could be his. The night air was cold, but she kept the jacket open. It had been a slow night and Kayne would not be happy if she let this one get away.

The vic was a young guy with a hard face. Not much skin on it and a mean set to his jaw. A tough guy for sure. Lisa smiled. Kayne would show him what tough was. Nice leather jacket, though.

"So, honey, like what you see?"

The vic stepped closer, reached out to feel up her left tit. His eyes were fixed on her chest like he'd never seen a pair of tits before and Lisa let him fondle her for a few seconds before pushing his hand away.

"Any more and it's gonna cost you, honey. We can go back in there and party." She tilted her head up Seaton Street, in the general vicinity of the laneway Leo used to use.

The vic looked at the laneway, then back at her. He nodded. Lisa took his hand and led him up the sidewalk, shivering at the thought of him behind her. There was something wrong about this vic, something that spooked her and if Kayne hadn't been around there was no fucking way she'd be going anywhere with this guy. He fucking creeped her out.

But Kayne was there, waiting in the shadows across the street from the laneway. He'd give her enough time to get the vic all happy and horny; then the real fun would begin. Maybe Kayne would let her have his jacket. It sure as fuck didn't look fake.

The laneway was heavy with shadows and the narrow space between the two dumpsters was darker yet. Smiling, Lisa walked backward into the gap, tugging the vic in after her. "C'mon, honey. Ain't no one gonna bother us here."

But the vic didn't want to be dragged into the confining shadows. Was he just changing his mind or had he caught on? Fuck, she'd been so eager to get him in between the dumpsters she hadn't even talked about price or what he wanted. Of course he'd figured something was wrong.

He grabbed Lisa by the throat. "You fucking whore." His voice was raspy and it perfectly mimicked the hate that blossomed in his eyes.

Lisa knew she was in deep shit. But that was all right.

Kayne appeared behind the vic and Lisa's fear vanished as her Man grabbed the vic by the shoulders and rammed his head into the dumpster. The vic dropped to one knee but didn't go down. Maybe he was a tough guy after all. No matter. Kayne dug his fingers into the vic's spiky black hair and smashed a knee into his face.

"Do him, baby!" Lisa hissed. "Who's the fucking whore now, bitch?"

The vic was on both knees, his mouth and chin drenched in blood. Lisa hoped Kayne had knocked the fucker's teeth out. But fucker or not, he was tough. He clutched at Kayne's sweatshirt, tried to pull himself to his feet. Kayne smiled and let the vic get back to his feet before kicking him in the stomach. Kayne's heavy boot blasted the air out of the vic and this time when he went down he stayed down.

"I want his jacket." Lisa began tugging at the leather. "Can I have it, lover? Can I?"

Kayne laughed. "Sure, baby. Let's see what else this fuck has on him."

He hauled the vic up into a sitting position, ripped the jacket free and tossed it to Lisa. She clutched it to her chest, laughing happily.

"Got your jacket, bitch," she crowed. "Who's the whore now, bitch?"

Kayne went through the vic's pockets. No wallet but a bit of cash. Kayne stuffed it in his pants.

"You gonna cut him now, baby?" Lisa's eyes were wide with excitement and Kayne saw her hand sneak under her skirt.

"Horny little bitch, ain't you?" Kayne laughed. "Yeah, I'm gonna cut him. Give me a fucking min — what the fuck?"

"What is it, baby?" Her Man had been checking the vic's shirt pockets and now a slow smile was spreading across his face. "He got some more money?"

"You ain't gonna believe this." Kayne grabbed the front of the vic's denim shirt and ripped it open.

"Holy shit!" Lisa couldn't believe her eyes. No fucking wonder she'd gotten a weird feeling from him: the vic was a woman.

"Her titties are smaller than yours," Kayne declared as he dragged the vic to her feet.

"Whatcha gonna do, baby? Ain't you gonna cut her?" Lisa wailed quietly from where she squatted between the dumpsters. She was all set to frig herself off watching Kayne do his thing.

"I don't cut women," he stated as he flung the vic across the hood of a nearby car. "But I've got something else for her."

The vic was moaning and trying to push up from the car so Kayne slammed her face into the metal. The laneway rang with the impact. The vic slumped but was still conscious and that made Lisa happy. She knew what Kayne was going to do and she wanted this bitch to be awake for it.

"Fuck her, baby, fuck her," she chanted, prancing around the front of the car.

Kayne fought the vic's jeans to her knees before unbuckling his own. Lisa laughed delightedly. Her Man was hard and ready. He slammed himself inside her and the vic screamed.

"Who's the fucking whore now, bitch?" Lisa spat into her face. "Who's the fucking whore now?"

She was sitting on the edge of the bed, looking incredibly sexy in a tight black dress. She smiled at Jack as he stepped toward her and he knew she was his for the taking. He didn't know who she was, had never seen her before, but she was beautiful and she wanted him.

What am I doing? I don't know her.

Jack ignored his doubts and reached for her, sliding first one then the second thin strap off her shoulders. He knelt before her and still didn't recognize her but didn't stop. Slowly, tenderly, he tugged her dress down, freeing her small, lovely breasts, the nipples already stiffening to excited points.

What am I doing? I'm married!

He paid no heed to his honourable thoughts. He cupped her breasts, his thumbs flicking gently across the nipples. She sighed and arched her back, pushing her flesh firmly into his hands.

I can't do this. I'm married.

She was lying on the bed, naked, smiling over her shoulder at him as she raised her buttocks enticingly, urging him on. And he needed no further invitation. He was hard and ready. He crawled onto the bed, positioned himself above her. As he thrust into her, he screamed in his mind.

I can't do this! I'm married! I can't cheat on Jenny!

Jack snapped awake, the quiet darkness of the bedroom greeting him. He lay still, listening, but Karen slept on beside him. They had barely spoken when he got home from work and had gone to bed with a cold chasm between them.

What the fuck was that about?

To cheat on your wife in a dream was one thing. Dreaming your wife was someone else and still be cheating?

I have no idea what that's supposed to mean. This was one nocturnal fling he could do without remembering.

Karen rolled over to face him. "Everything okay?" she mumbled, her face nestled comfortably in her pillow. She must have become attuned to his restlessness and nightmares; she awoke easily if he was having a bad night.

"I'm fine. Go back to sleep, hon," he whispered, caressing her cheek with a tender finger.

She murmured something as she kissed his finger, then snuggled deeper into the covers. Seconds later her breathing was deep and regular again.

But sleep did not come quickly or easily for Jack. He lay awake for a long time, wondering what his dreaming mind had been trying to tell him.

53's lobby was everything 51's wasn't: big, airy, bright. It even had plants. Except for the cops behind the front desk, it could have been the foyer of any commercial building. When Jack had left 53 Division to return to the place where he really belonged, he had hoped never to set foot again in the station at the corner of Eglinton Avenue West and Duplex Avenue. But here he was, less than a week in 51 and dragged back for some bullshit he'd forgotten about.

Well, the kid warned you, said his mommy was a lawyer.

"Hey, Jack. Thought you'd left us."

"So did I, Kimmy. Buzz me in, please? I need to see the boss."

The station operator, a buxom blonde with a heart of gold and no patience for cops who talked to her bust and not her face, hit the button at her desk to let him in. Every platoon had a civilian operator — the real boss of any shift, most staff sergeants were willing to admit — and Kimmy was one of the best. She logged the work hours, knew who was on holidays, did the thousand and one little tasks needed to keep the platoon running smoothly and acted as the staff's first line of defence. Anyone coming into the station to talk to an officer or a supervisor had to get past her and only people with real problems got past her. She would have made an awesome cop.

Jack had asked her one day why she hadn't gone that route and she had laughed. "Me with a gun? Are you serious? It's all I can do some days not to reach over the front counter and slap some of these idiots."

As he walked in, she said, "Good luck, hon," and gave him a thumbs-up. He thumbed her back and headed to the second floor.

Seems like my summons isn't much of a secret.

Staff Greene had advised him on parade that he was due at the superintendent's office at 53 at nine o'clock sharp. Greene had told Jack to be early because, as Greene understood it, Jack was "in serious enough trouble without adding tardiness to the list."

Tardiness? Who used words like tardiness nowadays? Jack glanced at his watch. Oops, seven minutes late. He knocked on the super's open door and stepped in.

"Come on in, Jack. Glad you could make it."

Superintendent Ramirez was a big man with a shock of silver hair and a permanently tanned complexion. TPS's version of George Hamilton. Say that to his face and it might be the last thing you utter with all your teeth.

"I'd like you to meet Frank and Marian Covingston."

The couple sitting in front of Ramirez's desk — big, like the office — were mismatched. The woman was slim, dressed in a dark suit; she studied Jack with a distasteful slant to her perfectly painted lips. The husband wasn't big but had a solid build. He wore jeans and a denim shirt with the sleeves rolled up over thick forearms. Jack guessed Frank had built his muscles through years of manual work and not in the gym.

Jack shook with both of them. Briefly with Marian — definitely the lawyer of the two — and firmly with Frank. Jack got the feeling Frank was not happy about being there.

"And you've met their son, Matthew."

Matthew was seated next to his mom and there was no doubt about him not wanting to be there. He didn't shake hands with Jack. He didn't bother to look up. He was still sporting a white splint across his broken nose.

"Pull up a chair, Jack, and we'll see if we can get this settled." Ramirez gave everyone a dazzling smile as he sat down.

"I'm good, sir."

Jack remained standing. Ramirez was a good guy, solid and supportive of his men and Jack trusted him not to intentionally fuck him, but if this meeting was headed in the direction Jack thought it was, then it was going to be brief unless he got an Association rep in here with him.

"There is nothing to settle, Superintendent Ramirez." Marian's voice matched her suit: well cut and stylish. Jack wondered what type of lawyer Marian was. "This officer — and I use the title with no respect intended — assaulted my son, causing bodily harm and if you do not discipline him accordingly we will be laying charges against him. It is only out of respect to your profession in general that we agreed to this meeting." She shot her husband a challenging look. "I wanted to proceed directly with the appropriate charges."

Yup, this is going to be brief.

"Mrs. Covingston, Officer Warren is a decorated veteran officer. He was honoured as police officer of the year last year."

That caught Frank's attention. Out of the corner of his eye, Jack saw the man studying him with new interest.

His wife, however, was not impressed. "Police officer of the year? For what? Assaulting teenagers?"

Ramirez placed his hands calmly on his desktop as he faced Matthew's mom. The wattage of his smile had been reduced from accommodating to placating. "Your son is hardly a teenager, Mrs. Covingston. And he has been charged with assaulting a police officer and resisting arrest."

"Of course he was resisting. *He* was assaulted by this . . . barbarian."

"I understand your concern, Mrs. Covingston. Matthew has no criminal record and a conviction of either of these charges could affect the rest of his life, especially career-wise. Now, I've spoken with the crown attorney and he has assured me that if Matthew pleads guilty to the assault police we'll drop the resisting arrest charge and he'll be given a conditional discharge. That way, if he stays out of trouble for a year — and I'm sure he'll have no problem doing so after this incident — the conviction will be erased and his criminal record will remain clear."

You should be selling used cars, boss.

But Marian wasn't buying. "No, Superintendent, you don't understand. This officer is the one who should be worried about arranging a plea bargain, not my son. Matthew was targeted and assaulted for no other reason than he was at hand and this thug wanted to intimidate some children and prove how tough he is."

Oh, for fuck's sake. Jack knew he should keep his mouth shut.

Knew it. Knew he would be drilling it into Manny's head if Manny was the one hauled up on the carpet. Absolutely knew it. But he couldn't keep his mouth shut.

"Did his version of the story include the part where he spat on me?"

"He did no such —"

"Marian, enough." Frank's voice was soft, gentle almost, yet it commanded attention.

"Frank —"

"No. You've said your piece. Now let me say mine."

Marian opened her mouth as if to present another argument, but Frank hushed her with a look. Jack wasn't sure he'd keep talking if that look was turned his way.

"Matthew, look at me." No response. *Matthew.*

The son reluctantly raised his eyes to his father's and Jack could see the effort it took for Matthew to maintain eye contact. Jack got the impression that Marian did most of the talking in the household but that when Frank did speak, people listened.

"You tell me right now, son, and look me in the eyes while you do. Did you spit on this officer?"

"Yes, sir." The admission was quiet, almost a whimper.

Frank nodded, stood up. "We're done here. Superintendent, I'm sorry we've wasted your time." He shook hands with Ramirez across the desk.

"Frank, we can't leave." Marian remained sitting, her hand on her son's shoulder to keep Matthew from following his father.

"We can and we are. Officer." Frank shook Jack's hand. His grip was strong, unyielding. "I'm sorry to have met under these circumstances. I was no angel growing up and had my run-ins with the law. Even had my head cracked by more than one cop. Sometimes I deserved the crack, sometimes I didn't. You don't strike me as the type of man who'd hit unless it was necessary."

"Thank you, sir."

"No, thank you. Like I said, I had my scraps with the law,

but what I never did, *never*, was spit on an officer. That's just downright disgusting and shows what kind of man you are. I've worked hard all my life, got my own landscaping company and I bust my ass so my son can have a job where he wears a suit and tie and doesn't come home with mud under his fingernails." Frank shook his head sadly. "Maybe a summer of hauling dirt and stone will do him some good."

Matthew blanched at the words but rose disconsolately to his feet. Jack thought Marian was going to hold her ground, but her resolve wavered then failed. She got up, levelled a disapproving glare at Jack and walked, back straight, to the door, defeated but not beaten. Jack did not envy Frank the shitstorm that was undoubtedly headed his way. The resigned look on his face said Frank knew it was coming too but also that it was not the first, nor would it be the last, he endured.

Frank stopped on his way to the door. "That happen at the house party?" He tapped a blunt finger against his eyebrow.

Jack shook his head. "Couple of days later."

"A knife?"

"Nope. Broken beer bottle. Guy didn't like the look of my face, I guess."

Frank nodded knowingly, one old scrapper to another. "This city is going down the shitter, fast. We need more officers like you."

"Why can't there be more parents like him?" Jack mused after the Covingston clan left.

Ramirez, a lifelong bachelor, dropped a heavy arm across his shoulders. "Because the smart ones don't have kids."

Jack stretched in the sun. The interview with the little shit and his parents had gone better than he had hoped. With a dad like that, there might be hope for Matthew.

Now to get the fuck out of Dodge. He keyed his mitre. "PC Armsman on the air? Armsman on the air in 51?"

Manny crackled back almost instantly. "Armsman, talk to me."

"Manny, I'm done at 53. Come and get me."

"10-4, Jack. On the way."

53 boasted underground parking, but that was for personal cars. The scout cars were relegated to a tiny strip of asphalt behind the station, with barely enough room to pull in and out of the slots. Whoever designed the building must not have been thinking about full-size Crown Vics when it came time to allot space for parking. Add in concrete planters every third slot and the overlap of day and evening shifts in the afternoons and you had a parking nightmare.

Jack headed for the street — no sense forcing Manny to navigate the lot — and spotted Brett sitting in the nearest scout car. He had his head down on his arms folded over the steering wheel, but there was no mistaking his mass filling the driver's seat.

The window was down, so Jack rapped gently on the roof. "Hey, Brett, you okay?"

Brett jerked erect, rocking the car with his sudden movement. He glanced at Jack, then quickly dropped his eyes. "Yeah, I'm fine," he said, wiping viciously at his eyes while talking down into his lap.

"You sure?" Brett's eyes were red rimmed and the dark smudges under them were more pronounced than before. It also looked as if Brett had forgotten to shave that morning. "No offence, man, but you look like shit."

Brett laughed, a hollow, sardonic croak. "Gee, thanks. Nice to see you, too." He produced a pack of cigarettes from his uniform jacket and lit up. The grey smoke drifting lifelessly about his head matched the pallor of his skin. "It's just a headache. Kept me up all night." Again that croak of a laugh. "Maybe I caught it from you."

"Since when do you smoke?"

Brett shrugged. "I stopped when we had the kids, but since the ex won't let me see them I figured why not. Got to have something to do when I can't sleep."

Brett was parked next to a planter and Jack settled against it. Crossing his arms, he studied his friend. "Have you seen a doctor about not sleeping? I can't remember you ever saying you had a decent sleep. Maybe you shouldn't be working nights. I know night shift fucks up a lot of guys and I certainly slept better when I wasn't doing nights."

Brett examined Jack in turn, as if he was considering how much to say. After a lengthy drag on his smoke, he confessed, "It's not just nights. I can't sleep. Period." He held up a forestalling hand. "I've already talked to my doctor and he thinks I need to get off the compressed work week, says the rotating shifts are fucking me up."

"I'm assuming there's a problem, though."

"With the police? Never." His mouth twisted as he ground his cigarette out on the car door. He flicked the butt away. "I sent a letter from my doctor explaining everything to the medical bureau, advising them I needed to go on straight days or something for a while." The set of his mouth hardened his face as he scowled at the memory.

"And . . . ?" Jack prompted.

"And this morning I got an e-mail from medical saying my situation does not justify shift restrictions." Brett lit another cigarette and savagely huffed out the first drag. "The fucking doctor down at medical made that decision without ever seeing me or asking me a single fucking question. Supportive, huh?"

Jack was shocked, not sure he had heard Brett right. "How can they make a decision without examining you?"

"They did, and it doesn't matter." What he said next was lost beneath the engine's rattling as it coughed to life. He dropped the car into reverse. "Listen, Jack, I gotta go."

"Give me a shout later and we'll hook up for coffee."

"Yeah, sure."

Jack watched his friend drive off and wondered how he really was doing. As he had pulled away, the rigidity had drained from Brett's face. What was left in its wake was a man who looked tired down to his soul. If Jack was a praying man, he would have offered up a plea for his friend, for if Jack had heard correctly, what Brett had said when the engine started was "Nothing matters anymore."

"Anything new to the description, Jenny?"

Her voice fought through a crackle of static. "No. Male, black, black hoodie, black pants."

"That narrows it down," Jack reflected as he scanned the pedestrians in the Queen and Sherbourne area. "Everyone is wearing black hoodies and pants."

"Moss Park?" Manny suggested and Jack nodded.

Moss Park, the third piece in the division's shithole trifecta with Regent Park and St. Jamestown, sported three high-rises along Shuter Street. Manny turned into the driveway that snaked up from Queen to wrap around the front of the apartment buildings.

Jenny was in the baseball field behind the Moss Park community centre with the victim of a purse snatch. The suspect, the oh-so-distinctive male, black, black hoodie, was last seen running toward the apartment buildings. That was more than five minutes ago. More than enough time for someone to vanish in the dense concrete landscape.

"5106 to radio," Jenny called, more static than words. "I'm taking the victim to the station for a statement."

"10-4, 5106," the dispatcher acknowledged. "You may want to get a new portable while you're there. The one you have isn't very clear."

"Big shock there."

"Only the best for Canada's largest municipal police force," Manny added. "Dude, don't you know we're on the cutting edge of transistor technology?"

Jack smirked. "Don't let Greene hear you talking like that; he'll do you for insubordination."

"Dude, don't even joke about that." Manny slowed for the speed bumps laid out haphazardly in the driveway that linked all three apartment buildings along the north side of the complex. "He chewed me out this morning for taking so long on B and E calls."

"You did explain that you're soco? That fingerprinting and photographing the scene takes time?"

"I did. He said as a Scenes of Crime Officer I should have the experience and knowledge to investigate a B and E faster than others." Manny yanked on the steering wheel in frustration.

"He's just looking for things to get on your back. He'll never formally document you," Jack assured him. "He knows he's talking bullshit and he'd look like a moron if he ever submitted the paperwork."

"But, dude," Manny beseeched. "He threatened to send me to Ident for a six-month lateral."

"Ouch." Jack could understand Manny's concern. Manny needed to be constantly moving, usually at a full sprint — how he had escaped being diagnosed as ADD when he was a kid, Jack would never know — and the meticulous, detailed work done by the Forensic Identification Services would drive him insane. Greene had certainly come up with a legitimate threat.

"Stand by for the hotshot," the dispatcher announced. *"Go ahead to 51."* There was a pause as the dispatcher was given the details; then she relayed them to the cars. *"Unknown trouble. 285 Shuter Street, apartment 712. Hysterical female screaming into the phone. Call taker can't get any details from her. Time, 1249."*

"Not another diaper domestic," Jack groaned. He snatched the mike. "5103, we're right outside 285. Throw us on the call."

"10-4, 5103. Apartment 712, hysterical female on the phone. No further details. Use caution. Is there anyone who can back up 5103 on the

unknown trouble call?" No answer. *"5103, no one to back you up at this time. 10-4?"*

"10-4, dispatch. We'll advise." Jack hung up the mike. No surprise on the backup, not when they only had seven people on the road. "I heard a story once that manpower wasn't always this short."

"Do tell."

"Apparently, there was a time, long long ago, when coppers were so plentiful that on night shift the sergeant would ask on parade who wanted T.O. because there weren't enough cars for everyone. If you didn't take the time off, you were walking until the evening shift came in at three."

"Dude, that's unreal."

Jack snorted. "Now we think it's a bonus if we put more than half a dozen out."

285 Shuter was the middle building of the three high-rises that made up Moss Park. It was shaped like a wide V and, like Regent Park, it was a mixture of decent people and shitheads. Manny parked the car a short distance from the building; the shitheads had a tendency to throw things off their balconies using the police car as a target. Jack kept a wary eye skyward. Sometimes the shitheads preferred the challenge of a small moving target.

Getting through the inner lobby doors proved to be no problem as the locks were broken, as usual. If the locks were ever fixed, they didn't stay fixed for long. After all, you can't run a successful crack house or whorehouse out of your apartment if your customers can't get in the building. As they waited for the elevator, they slipped on their gloves. Inside the elevator, they turned off their mitres; the radios lost reception in elevators and whined annoyingly. They'd turn them back on as soon as they were back in a hallway.

The elevator jerked to a halt at the sixth floor and they headed for the stairs. Fewer surprises that way. The seventh-floor hallway was clear. Jack really disliked the building's design: because the building was shaped like a V, he couldn't see the whole hallway at one time.

"Is 5103 on the air? 5103?"

"Hang on, Manny." Jack freed his mitre. "5103, go ahead, dispatch."

"Is 5103 on the air? 5103, call radio."

Jack grunted his annoyance and tried again. "5103, go ahead, radio."

"Is that you, 5103? All I'm getting is static. Try changing your location."

"For fuck's sake," he grumbled. "Piece of shit radio." He backtracked to the windows opposite the elevator doors. "5103, is this better?"

"Not by much." She sounded as frustrated as Jack felt. *"Further information on your call. The call taker is still on the line with the complainant, who is still hysterical, but the call taker heard something that sounded like 'cutting herself.' Unknown if anyone else in the apartment. 10-4?"*

"Got it, dispatch. Thanks. We're almost at the apartment." Jack joined Manny down the hall. "You hear that?"

Manny nodded, never taking his eyes off the hall and its multitude of doors. Just because the call had originated from a certain apartment didn't mean it couldn't move.

"Gun or stick?"

Manny considered his options. "I'll go gun," he decided and tugged his Glock from the holster.

Jack slipped his baton free, keeping it in the collapsed state, tucked up along his forearm. Out of sight, out of mind. Until he needed to use it.

A hysterical woman was one thing. She could be calling about anything. The diaper domestic from the other day proved that, but add in references to cutting herself and Jack would rather err on the side of caution. If the weapons weren't needed, they could be put away. He already had one souvenir from underestimating the seriousness of a situation and wasn't in a hurry to add to it.

Frantic shouting, almost shrieking, reverberated through the metal door. Jack tried the knob and found it unlocked. He looked at Manny, nodded and shoved open the door. It banged against the wall.

"Police!" Jack stepped into the apartment, Manny to his right, gun held in a double grip, pointed at the floor.

"Hurry! She's in the bathroom! Please help her!"

The bathroom was at the end of a short hall off the living room. Jack gave the living room and adjoining kitchen a quick glance. Empty.

"Hurry! She'll kill herself!" A woman, her face a mask of panic and concern, flung herself at the closed bathroom door, hammering her fists on it, leaving bloody smears across the wood. "Babe, open the door! Please!" She slumped against the door, her head cradled in her arms. Her phone slipped from her fingers and exploded on the floor.

Jack pointed to the single bedroom door as he knelt in front of the woman. Manny darted into the bedroom and returned seconds later, whispering "clear" as he holstered his gun.

In the sudden silence, Jack could hear a noise from the bathroom. A hissing but not quite. Heavier than that. It sounded familiar, but he couldn't place it. He turned his attention to the woman on the floor.

She was young, no more than a teenager, he thought, and very thin, almost to the point of malnourishment. Strawberry blonde hair hung limply around her face, a face ravaged by anguish. Whoever was in the bathroom meant a great deal to this young woman.

"Miss, who's in the bathroom?" Jack gripped her by the shoulders when she didn't answer. He shook her firmly but gently until her eyes focused on him. "Who's in the bathroom?"

"My girlfriend. She's cutting herself." Her voice was hoarse from screaming, weak from the abrupt loss of strength. "Please help her."

"We need you to move."

Jack lifted her to her feet, shocked at how little she weighed. He passed her to Manny, who deposited her on the bed. She curled up into a fetal position, sobbing quietly.

"She's already given up on her friend." Manny glanced at the floor as if he expected to see blood seeping ominously beneath the door.

The door was locked, but bathroom doors tended to be flimsy things and this one was no exception. A quick kick and it slammed open on a nightmare.

At first, Jack couldn't believe what he was seeing. No one could lose that much blood and still be alive. The woman was in the tub, crumpled near the faucet. Only by the fluttering of her eyelids and the ragged hitching of her chest could Jack tell she still lived.

My God, the blood.

The walls of the shower stall dripped crimson as if someone had flung cans of red paint on them. She appeared to have bathed in blood; no clean skin showed anywhere and she sat in a half inch of blood. She wore jeans and they were saturated. The smell of blood, sharp, metallic, hung heavy in the air and Jack's stomach rolled as he breathed it in.

But he had no time to vomit; that she was still alive was a miracle.

Jack lunged for the tub and Manny shouted a warning. "Watch out for the torch!"

So focused on the woman, Jack missed the propane torch on the floor, hissing out its blue flame into a puddle of blood. He snatched it up and thrust it blindly behind him for Manny to take. He had to get to the woman. He wasn't going to let someone else bleed to death. Not this time. His feet slipped in the slick blood and he crashed to his knees beside the tub.

Her throat. She must have cut her throat.

She was slumped next to the tap. As Jack reached for her, he slipped again. His stomach slammed the edge of the tub and his hands slapped the bottom of the tub by the woman's legs. Blood, warm and slick, splashed his face. Cursing, he pushed himself upright and jumped into the tub with her.

His hands went to her throat, searching desperately for the cut. Nothing. *What?* He wiped at her throat, baring it of blood as best he could, but still no cut, no wound.

Dimly, Jack heard Manny on the radio. He had to find the wound. He moved back, frantically scanning her naked upper body. She was a big woman, muscular like a man and he knew it would be hard to lift her, heavy as she was and on blood-slicked porcelain.

"Oh, my God," he breathed, not believing, not wanting to understand, what he saw.

She had cut off her breasts.

The left breast was completely gone and it passed through his mind that it was in the tub with him, that he could be kneeling on it. The right breast was a mangled flap of meat hanging from her chest by threads of flesh.

She cut off her breasts. The torch was for — He slammed that thought away. *No, please, God, no.*

"Manny! Get me a towel!"

Manny thrust a towel into his arms and Jack shoved it against the woman's chest. She arched her back, groaning feebly, but Jack bore down, pushing her hard against the tub. Gentleness would kill her. In seconds, blood was seeping around his fingers, the fluffy white towel quickly turning dark with her blood.

"More towels!"

Manny disappeared and was back in seconds, dumping an armload of towels by the tub. *He must have gone to the linen closet,* Jack thought as he heaped another towel on top of the soaked one. The second towel reddened almost immediately; the third still held most of its blue colour. The fourth, miraculously, thankfully, stayed dry. For now.

"Where's the fucking ambulance?"

Something smashed in the bathroom, loud and sudden, then Manny was tearing at Jack's radio. Jack asked no questions, just lifted his left arm out of the way. Manny yanked the mitre free.

"5103, we need a rush on that ambulance!" Static. "Fuck!"

Manny fled the bathroom. The woman's life depended on an archaic technological piece of shit.

"Hang on. Don't you die on me. Don't you fucking dare."

Jack knelt beside her, twisting to apply pressure. "Fuck it." He carefully shifted, felt blood squish from her jeans as he straddled her thighs. He leaned in, adding his body weight to the pile of towels. His face was inches from hers. With her short haircut, strong jaw and muscular physique — a detached part of his mind noted how large the quads were that he was sitting on — she could probably pass for a man.

Is that why she did this? To be a man?

"Hang on. Hang on. Help's coming, Sy. Hang on."

Shadows rippled at the edge of his vision and suddenly Jack was back in that alley and Sy was dying beneath his hands. His blood soaked impossibly into the asphalt and Jack knew the stain would remain forever. It would always be there to remind him of the night he failed, the night he let his friend die.

Not again, never again.

Then her hysterical girlfriend was in the doorway, clawing at her own cheeks, overrun by the horror in front of her.

"Manny! Get in here!" The last thing Jack needed was a panic-stricken girlfriend trying to get to her lover. "Manny!"

But Manny was there even before Jack's second yell was fully voiced. He wrapped his arms around the frail girl from behind. Talking soothingly into her ear, he plucked her free of the floor and carried her into the bedroom.

More screams but, thankfully, the screams of sirens.

"Hang on." The sirens rose to a fury before choking to silence. "They're here. They're here." The towel beneath his hands was still clean. He smiled. "I won't let you die."

"It doesn't look like you got any in your eyes," the paramedic declared, shining a light at Jack's eyes. "The blood seems to have hit you on the cheek and chin." She clicked off her flashlight and tucked it away. "Did you get any in your mouth?"

Jack shook his head.

"You sure? Did you spit at any time? No? Then you're good to go, although I would recommend getting a new uniform."

Jack nodded mutely. Every piece of his uniform had blood on it. His pants were soaked from mid-thigh down and when he had stripped off his leather gloves in the apartment they had hit the floor with a wet splat.

He was sitting on the rear bumper of an ambulance, exhausted. Wrung out. The victim had long since been rushed by emergency run to Sunnybrook Hospital, the nearest trauma centre. The last he had been told, she was going into surgery and her chances weren't looking good.

"You've had one hell of a week."

"Hm?" Jack tried to focus on the paramedic. Fuck, he was tired.

"First the guy killed by the truck, now this. They should be giving you some time off to de-stress."

Jack looked at the medic, really looked at her for the first time. "Oh, sorry. I didn't recognize you."

She was the pretty blonde who had shushed him while she and her partner were dealing with the truck driver at the Mr. Big and Tall.

"No problem," she said with a smile. "After this, I'd be surprised if you recognized yourself in the mirror. And I'm sorry about snapping at you the other day. I didn't realize until later that you didn't know about the other guy."

Jack waved off her apology. "No big deal. I've snapped at my share of people this week."

"You know, I'm serious about taking some time off. This is the shit that post-traumatic stress is made of."

Jack chuckled. She had no idea. "Not likely. We're too short as it is. Hell, I'll be lucky if this is the last call I have to do today, depending on how long the report takes."

"Yeah, we're in the same boat. Here." She handed him some wipes. "Clean up your hands and face so you don't end up ingesting any of her blood. Hope you have a towel at the station."

He nodded as he accepted the wipes. A shower — a very hot shower — sounded ideal. But . . .

"What about the girlfriend?"

The medic shook her head, setting her blonde ponytail bouncing in the sunlight. It looked so clean. Blood-free. In fact, the whole parking lot in front of the apartment building looked clean, the colours sharp, fresh. Which was good, considering that whenever Jack closed his eyes he saw red. So much red.

"She went to Sunnybrook as well." Manny plunked down next to him. "Shock or something."

"I guess we're heading there to talk to her?" Jack tried to stand up.

"Relax, dude. Someone else is doing it. We need to get you to the station to clean up."

"What happened to you?"

Manny had his jacket off and his right forearm had a wrapping of white gauze around it.

"Nothing. Don't worry about it."

Jack grabbed him by the shirt. "What is it?" he insisted.

"Just a little burn, dude. Don't worry about it."

"A burn? Aw, fuck. Did I do that when I threw the torch at you?"

"You didn't throw it *at* me, man. And besides, you had more important things to worry about. Buy me a coffee before we go in and we'll call it even."

"That's either going to be one big coffee or that's a lot of bandage for a really tiny burn."

Jack grabbed a plastic sheet from the ambulance to put over the car seat so he wouldn't contaminate it. As he crinkled onto the seat he asked Manny what he had told Sergeant Rose about his mitre.

"The truth," Manny admitted, firing up the cruiser. "I threw it on the floor because it didn't work. I mean, she was dying, man. I needed to get through to radio and the shitty thing wasn't working. That's why I grabbed yours. And it didn't work until I got next to the window."

Jack nodded in understanding. "Yeah, they're crap. Probably were already out of date when they were bought. Fucking cheap bastards." Jack leaned his head back. "What did Rose say?"

"She suggested I was mistaken and that it slipped from my hand sometime during the stressful situation."

"That's what I'd go with. If Greene finds out you deliberately broke it, he'll make sure you end up on the hook for the replacement cost." Jack hoisted the car's mike. "5103, call radio."

"Go ahead, 5103."

"Mark us heading to the station for this report. 10-4?"

"10-4. 5103 to the station. You guys okay?"

Jack smiled a weary smile. "Yeah, we're good, dispatch. Thanks for asking, but could you do us a favour? I know the chief wants a helicopter, but if you see him could you tell him it'd be nice if we had some radios that worked?"

A small number of stars peered down, their gaze cold and indifferent. Their companions hid behind clouds, invisible in the night sky, as if they cared not to view the wretchedness that was humanity and had drawn a veil to hide the sight.

What a fucking day.

Jack sipped the cold cider and eased as far into the hot tub as he could while keeping his left arm out of the water — no submerging a new tattoo for three weeks — letting the heat melt away the day's stress. It did little for the memories, though. If he closed his eyes, all he saw was blood. So much blood. He kept them open, focused on the uncaring stars, watching uninterestedly as they slid from sight behind the clouds. He sipped the cider again.

"Hey, hon. I didn't expect to find you still up." Karen slid the kitchen door shut and came down to the deck's lower level.

"Couldn't sleep, so I thought a soak might make me sleepy. Care to join me?" He splashed the water beside him. "Plenty of room for one more."

The hot tub was a recent addition to the back deck. Jack had extended the two-tier deck to encircle the round tub, so instead of climbing up to get into the tub all they had to do was step down.

Karen sat on the edge, dangling fingers in the bubbling water. "It's getting a little late for a dip."

Jack splashed the rationale aside. "No it's not. Come on in. You don't even have to bother with a bathing suit."

She smiled at the flirtatious suggestion. Their house sat on the outside of the street's curve, which gave the backyard a wedge shape. The house was slightly behind the neighbours', adding to the privacy established by the high wood fences. If Jack had learned one thing in his time as a cop, it was that good fences made good neighbours.

He pushed off from the seat and bobbed over to Karen, resting his chin on his folded arms. "Come on. I promise I won't look while you're undressing." He playfully covered his eyes, peeking out between the fingers.

Rather than answer, she pointed at the bottle of cider. "How many of those have you had?"

He shrugged, unconcerned. "Two or three." *Guess I'm not*

going to get a show. He drowned the bitter thought with another drink. *Bet Jenny would've stripped.* The idea startled him and also stirred something in his belly and lower. He chuckled and took another sip.

"You're drunk, Jack," Karen accused.

Again he shrugged. If the stars didn't care, then neither did he. "A little buzzed, maybe. No big deal."

"You have to go to work tomorrow." She didn't have to remind him that he was usually up at 3:30 on day shift to hit the station's gym before work and, as a result, was normally in bed by nine at the latest.

"I know," he said defensively. "I couldn't sleep." He waded back to his original seat and settled in, keeping his left arm high and dry. "After the day I had . . ." he muttered before draining the last of the cider. He set the empty down, reached for another, thought better of it. Karen was right: he was drunk and tomorrow would be hard enough as it was.

"What happened today?" Concern laced her voice.

He snorted softly, shaking his head. "Doesn't matter. I'll be in soon." He rested his head on a foam pillow and stared at the night sky.

"Jack, tell me," she pleaded.

He felt like an ass for shutting her out. "Sorry, Kare. It was just a really . . . tough day." He moved close to her, one hand resting on her thigh, the other cushioning his chin.

"Tell me." She tenderly stroked his hair.

"Manny and I responded to an unknown trouble call today. We had no idea what it was. . . ." He gathered his thoughts. How to get across the enormity of what he had seen? "Kare, this woman — young, in her twenties — had cut off her own breasts and tried to cauterize the wounds with a blowtorch."

Karen's hand stopped moving at his words. "Oh, my God," she breathed. "Why?"

"We didn't know at first. Could only guess." Jack's words

were hushed, as light as the steam rising from the water. "The roommate — girlfriend, actually — told us that our victim had problems with her sexuality or being a lesbian or something like that. It was hard to get a clear story from her."

"I wouldn't doubt it. Did she see her friend . . . cut herself?"

"No, thank God. She was outside the bathroom. Good thing, too; she's messed up enough as it is. Nineteen years old, living with a woman she met just three weeks ago." Jack shook his head at the injustice of life. "She left home at fourteen to get away from an abusive father and kept moving from one asshole to another."

"They abused her as well?"

Jack nodded. "Yeah. Then a few weeks ago she meets this woman and moves in with her."

"Please don't tell me she abused her, too." Karen had lived a sheltered childhood in Sudbury, a little town in northern Ontario and had seen little of life's ugliness since then. She was seeing it now, through his eyes.

"Doesn't sound like it," he assured her. "But who knows? She could be keeping that from us to protect her friend, but I doubt it."

"Did something happen today to . . ." Karen floundered, unable to find the words.

"To trigger the friend's self-mutilation?" Jack supplied, the cop in him tossing out the phrase he had typed repeatedly in the report. "We didn't find out until Jenny went to the hospital to speak with the roommate and we won't know for sure until the detectives can interview the victim. She was still in surgery and they'll have to wait until tomorrow, at the earliest."

"She'll live?"

"Yeah, but they weren't able to reattach the breasts. There was just too much damage. She'll have to undergo reconstructive surgery sometime later."

"That poor woman." Karen was silent for a moment. "How

could she do it without passing out? I mean, the pain must have been incredible."

"Oh, yeah. She's a big woman, muscular, and probably no stranger to pain, but the determination it must have taken." Again Jack shook his head. "I can't imagine the self-loathing she must feel."

"But why today? What happened?"

Jack sighed. How bad could things get? "She was raped."

"Jack, no." Karen was close to tears.

He could hear them in her voice. But she had to hear the rest; she had to know, to understand.

"Remember that Kayne guy I told you about? The one that was carving his initial into people's foreheads? It was him. From what we can gather from the roommate, Kayne ran into our victim, mistook her for a guy and beat the snot out of her. But when he found out she was a woman and not a guy, he decided to rape her instead of cutting her up." He laughed, sick and bitter. "Quite the gentleman, eh? So, that's what triggered it, we think. Maybe she thought if she'd been a guy or didn't have the breasts he wouldn't have raped her."

Jack felt better for having shared the tale and Karen had wanted to know why he was in the hot tub and drinking on a work night. Hell, it would have scared him if he'd been able to go to sleep sober.

The tub's jets clicked off, the timer run down and into the new silence Karen asked, "Why do you want to stay there?"

"Please, Kare, not that again. Not tonight."

But she would not be dissuaded. "Don't you see what it's doing to you? You never used to drink on a work night. Never needed to. And now you're trying to drink yourself to sleep. The scars, the tattoo, the sleep problems, your temper. That division is changing you. It's killing the man I married."

"Oh, don't be so dramatic," he protested, the first touches of anger flaring.

"It is. It's killing you."

"Do you know what else happened today?" he snapped. He didn't give her a chance to answer. "I saved a life today. That woman would have bled to death if we hadn't been there. I saved her!" He stood up, too frustrated with her deliberate blindness to stay still.

"Someone else would have answered the call if you weren't there," she countered, also standing up.

"But someone else didn't. We did." He held his hands out, as if beseeching her to understand. "I held towels against her chest to slow the bleeding until the ambulance arrived. Even then she almost died. Don't you see, Karen? I saved her life. That's why I stay there."

Karen's voice was cold. "You didn't save the one hit by the truck, Jack. You can't save everyone. But every day you're there you lose a piece of yourself." She went inside, leaving Jack in the cold.

"Fuck," he grumbled. He hit the button and the jets jumped to life, churning the water around him. He slid into the water and stared at the uncaring stars.

Tuesday, 27 March
0742 hours

"He's an asshole. A freaking asshole."

"We know, Jenny, we know." Jack handed her a cup of coffee and steam wafted free into the cold, damp air as she pried the lid off. She wrapped both hands around the Tim's cup and tentatively sipped the hot liquid.

Tuesday of day shift, day four of seven. They were over the hump, on the down side of the shift and should have been feeling a renewal of spirit as days off drew within reach, but good old call-me-Staff-Sergeant-Greene-or-I'll-do-you had ruined the day minutes into parade.

Sergeant Johanson had finished reading the assignments and was into the day's alerts — a teenager with a drug history missing from his group home who was no doubt catching up on his habit, Jenny's purse snatch suspect from yesterday who had struck twice again and still no decent description and the marker of a car involved in a drive-by shooting in 52 Division last night — when Jenny had checked her hair. The French braid had passed Greene's inspection, but she must have thought it was too loose. Jack had watched in fascination as she had freed her waist-length hair and rebraided it in less than a minute. As simple as that and Greene had spent the next three minutes chewing her out in front of the platoon.

"You're right, Jack; he is a prick. If he was a woman, I'd call him a cunt." Jenny sipped her coffee.

"Don't worry, Jenny. We all know he's an idiot." Manny brightened a touch, offering what consolation he could. "We're almost done. Just two more wake-ups to go." Manny was the type to cross the workday off once he got to the station.

Jack didn't close the book on the day until he wrote "Report Off Duty" in his memo book. He envied Manny's way of thinking.

And right now it seemed Jenny was firmly entrenched in Jack's view of the world. "As if embarrassing me wasn't enough, he documented me for having my hair down on parade."

"That's bullshit!" Manny blurted, spilling hot chocolate on his hand. He sucked on his hand, then waved it in the cold air. "He can't do that without cautioning you first." He turned to Jack, seeking reassurance. "Can he?"

Jack nodded solemnly. "He can. Technically, she wasn't prepared to go on the road during parade."

"Jack, we have to do something," Manny implored, trusting Jack to find a solution.

"I know, I know."

All week Jack had pondered the problem that was Staff Sergeant Greene. The solution Johanson had offered on Friday — fuck, had he been back in the division only five days? — was a tried and true method of passive resistance used by coppers everywhere. If everyone stopped putting in numbers for tickets, tags or 208s, it sent a clear message to the higher-ups that something was not right on the platoon. In professional sports, if the team kept losing, the coach got fired. In a division, the staff sergeant got transferred. The plan could backfire, though: management would have an excuse to transfer the perceived troublemakers. Passive resistance took a long time and Jack knew the platoon needed to make a statement soon.

He leaned against the scout car and tried not to feel his friends' weighty gazes. Everyone on the platoon was looking to him to fix the problem and he didn't have a fucking idea.

What a perfect start to a shitty day.

Snow so wet it was almost rain dropped from a grey and miserable sky. A day meant for staying indoors with a fire and a good woman in your arms. Not a day for driving, especially in big rear-wheel-drive cars whose asses tended to slide out at the slightest change in direction on wet roads. But on the plus side, the snow-rain had a dampening effect on the radio: the dispatcher had no calls to hand out.

The three of them were at the Waterfall, out of the drizzling slush. The water pipe was quiet for the time being, but the bridge's underside resounded with the morning's rush-hour traffic. The noise did little to help Jack's thinking.

"That was quite the scene you guys had yesterday," Jenny offered. "You've had one hell of a homecoming week, Jack."

He snorted. "A paramedic said the same thing to me yesterday. Did the victim say anything at the hospital? Last we heard, she wasn't talking."

Jenny sadly shook her head. "I didn't have much of a chance

to talk to her before they took her in for surgery and she wouldn't tell me anything. Not even her name. I had to get all her info from Sherry the roommate."

"Did the roommate know anything that could help us?"

Again a negative shake. "Just what I added to your report. So, unless the victim changes her mind, we've got squat."

A silence slipped over them once more as they all fell into their own thoughts. Jack couldn't fathom the hatred, the sheer loathing, the victim must have had for herself to take a butcher's knife to her breasts. And then try to cauterize the wounds with a blowtorch. Next time he ran into the CIT unit, he'd tell Aaron, the psych nurse, about her and see if he could shed some insight on it.

"I guess I shouldn't bitch so much about Greene; life could be a lot worse." Jenny held her cup aloft. "Here's to a speedy recovery and a better life for that poor girl."

They touched cups and drank, then Jenny hugged herself and shivered. From the cold or memories of yesterday, Jack didn't know and doubted she would like to say. Sometimes it was better to jam the bad memories behind the cop mask and deal with them later.

"I know I said I shouldn't bitch, but I'm still pissed off about Greene. I can't believe he documented me."

"You're going to fight it, right?" Manny asked.

"Damn right I am." She blew out a frustrated breath. "If Greene wants to treat us like children, why doesn't he just spank us and get it over with?"

Jack wagged a cautionary finger at Manny. "Don't start visualizing, grasshop —" A smile flickered over Jack's lips, then settled in and grew to a face-splitting grin.

Manny's eyes widened with elation. "You've got an idea, don't you? What is it?"

"Get everyone down here, Manny. We need to have a platoon meeting."

"I'm not doing it."

"What do you mean you're not doing it?" Six pairs of eyes stared at Borovski in silent accusation. It was Paul who spoke.

Boris wilted under the scrutiny but found the courage to stand his ground. "I don't want to do it." He searched for a friendly face, some sympathy, but found none. "It's stupid," he added lamely.

Six police cars and seven officers — Jack and Manny were once again the only two-man unit in the division — were grouped under the bridge. Karl Morris and Gerry "Double G" Goldman had joined the group. They were the entire head count for the early portion of day shift and Jack hadn't seen much of them this week. It was amazing how starting an hour earlier could offset you from the rest of the platoon for the whole day. But they were part of the shift and had braved the crappy weather and roads to join the meeting. The drizzling wet snow had turned to rain and the waterfall was gurgling to life.

Jack could understand Boris's reluctance. In his head, Jack's idea involved a shocking display of platoon unity. When he'd said it aloud to Jenny and Manny, it had sounded stupid and childish. But they had both jumped on it eagerly and Manny had texted the other cars to join them. Jack was surprised that Boris had showed up until Manny explained he had told Boris there was a box of Timbits to share.

Suckered in by the promise of free doughnuts. Could the guy be any more stereotypical?

"It's *because* it's stupid that it's the perfect thing to do," Jack explained. The other coppers nodded in agreement. "Come on. Even Morris and Goldman are in on it." The early shift officers would parade at six, as usual, then return to the station to join the "rebellion" at seven.

"You gotta do it, man," Morris chided. "If I can do it, so can you." Morris was a human scarecrow with a shock of red hair and long, gangly legs.

"Forget him, Sean." Sean was Borovski's first name. Like everyone at the Waterfall, Jenny was being careful not to use the detested nickname Boris. "If anyone should be bitching about this, it's me and I'm all for it."

Boris studied Jenny with his little piggy eyes. Jack could see the image developing behind the eyes, but even that visual wasn't enough to sway Boris. He hooked his thumbs behind his gun belt — his belly flab pushed out in the gaping expanse between belt and the bottom of his external vest carrier — and shook his multiple chins and jowls defiantly.

"I'm not doing it." He thrust a sausage of a finger at Jack. "And you can't make me." Apparently, even Boris regarded Jack as the platoon leader, but unfortunately the position was honorary and carried no actual authority.

"So you're just going to show up on parade tomorrow like normal?"

Boris's smile was greasy. "Yup. But the rest of you can go right ahead with your little demonstration."

You fat fuck. Jack burned with the desire to smash that grin off Boris's pudgy lips. He kept the tension from his voice. "We need the platoon to stand together. If it isn't all of us, then it means nothing."

Boris shrugged his meaty shoulders. "Like I care." He dismissed his fellow officers with a flick of his fat fingers and headed for his car.

"For fuck's sake, Boris," Jack snapped. "Be a team player for once in your life."

Boris had his car door open but slammed it shut. He stalked back to the group, the force of his steps sending ripples through his fat, from thighs to chins. For the second time, he shoved a finger in Jack's face. "I am a team player!" he shouted, spittle spraying from his lips. "Who keeps this platoon's numbers at the top of the division, huh? Me, that's who!"

Morris spoke. "And while you're doing radar, the rest of us

are covering the calls in your area."

There were murmurs of agreement.

Boris whirled on Morris. "Fuck you! Fuck all of you!"

Jack figured his team player comment had struck a buried nerve; Boris had never before shown such fervour. Unshed tears glistened in his eyes. For the first time, the angry, hurt child that was Sean Borovski was pushing free of the man that was Boris.

"Sean," Jack said softly, "we need you."

"Uh-huh. No way! And if you try to make me, I'm going straight to the staff sergeant."

"With what? What we're talking about here?"

Boris laughed and the child was smothered. "Don't forget I saw you beat that guy up in the stairwell. Oh, yeah. You thought I forgot about that? Well, I didn't and I'll tell Greene all about it. How'd you like to have some assault charges against you? Huh, tough guy?"

Boris stomped away, the hotdog-like rolls of fat on the back of his head quivering with each step.

So much for platoon unity.

Paul stopped Boris dead in his tracks with two words. "Amber Smith."

Boris slowly turned. "What?"

Paul was smiling, but the smile wasn't friendly. "You forget we arrested her a few weeks ago? And how your hands got a little too personal during the pat down?"

"That's a lie!" Boris blustered, but the colour had suddenly drained from his face.

Paul wasn't finished. "I imagine I could persuade Amber to lodge a complaint regarding sexual assault."

"Like they'd listen to some crack whore." The strength was gone from Boris's voice.

Jack thought Boris was close to whimpering.

"I imagine my recollection of the events might mesh closer

with her version than yours." Paul crossed his arms over his massive chest and waited.

"Professional Standards, dude. Those guys are nasty," Manny added, shoving the verbal knife in a little deeper.

Jenny took hold of the knife and buried it completely. "Forget Professional Standards, Boris. Sexual assault. That's Special Investigations territory."

Mention of the cop-crucifying civilian watchdog unit whipped the last resistance from Boris. Meekly, he plodded to the group. He studied the unyielding faces and knew he was beaten. He sighed. "What should I wear?"

Oak Street apartments — Regent Park's dirty little cousin. Technically not a part of the park, the three high-rises were separated from the government housing complex only by the four lanes of River Street and were therefore seen as an extension of it and its drug-infested reputation. Guilt by association.

Oak Street, looking more like a glorified driveway, ran east off River and looped back on itself, resembling a lower-case b that had smoked too much crack and fallen on its back. The three apartment buildings sat in a triangle around the loop. A single tree, looking as tired and ailing as the dogshit-choked grass, held court over the tiny island in the centre of the driveway.

The rain had petered out with the end of morning rush hour, but dark clouds hung heavy in the sky, threatening more rain. Manny eased the scout car to a stop in front of 220, the tires scrunching on deposits of winter road sand made muddy by the morning's rain. He was trotting toward the lobby doors before Jack was even out of the car.

"Slow down, Manny. It's just a crack house," Jack said, giving a verbal jerk on Manny's leash.

Manny waited impatiently by the door. "But if we hurry they might still be there."

Jack smiled, amused by his friend's enthusiasm. Four years in

51 might have hardened Manny as a cop, but they hadn't even dented his boyish spirit. He liked to tell people he got paid to play cops and robbers for real.

They were responding to a simple noise complaint, people yelling, possible sounds of a fight, but the apartment was well known to the residents and security as a crack house. Manny was hoping to grab a pinch to finish off the day. The lock on the inner lobby door was broken — were they ever not broken? — and they went in.

A scrawny mess of a human was sitting on a lobby bench reading the newspaper. Or examining the pictures. He looked up when the door opened and a flash of fear darted across his face. It was quickly gone, and he held his hands up in mock surrender. "I didn't do it," he declared, grinning and showing a set of badly stained teeth. His army jacket hung loosely on his emaciated frame, a sleeve flapping like a loose sail as he wiped his crooked nose.

"You sure?" Manny asked seriously. "Maybe we're looking for a guy matching your description." The man's smile faltered. "Relax, bud. We aren't here for you."

Jack gritted his teeth. *Fucking crackheads are everywhere. Probably coming from the apartment we're heading to or waiting to head up.*

He and Manny headed for the elevator. Manny's enthusiasm ended at taking the stairs to the seventeenth floor. Had Manny suggested it, Jack would have smacked him; they'd had a pretty heavy leg workout before shift.

Only one of the two elevators was working. They waited patiently.

"You think tomorrow's going to work?" Manny asked as he tugged his new leather gloves on. The ones soaked in the woman's blood had gone straight into the garbage.

"Depends what you mean by 'work.'" Jack flexed his fingers to smooth out a roll in the Kevlar lining of his gloves. "It'll get a reaction, that much I can tell you."

Manny suddenly smiled. "Hey, maybe it'll give Greene a heart attack."

"Our luck it'll give Johanson the heart attack and Greene'll do us all with manslaughter."

"You're not telling the sergeants?"

"Nope. Where the fuck is the elevator? If the sergeants don't know, they can't get in trouble for it." Jack thumbed the call button a few times. He knew it didn't do anything, but it felt better than doing nothing.

"You think Boris will do it? Here we go." Manny stepped forward as the floor indicator hit Ground, but the car headed for the basement without stopping.

"We may end up taking the stairs after all." Manny blanched at Jack's suggestion. "Boris better join in."

"Would Paul really go to the staff about . . ." Manny quickly looked around. The paper reader was listening intently. "About that search thing?"

"Of course not. But Boris thinks he would because it's something Boris would do. Finally."

A weary *ping* — more like a *pang* — announced the elevator's arrival and the doors wheezed open. An elderly lady stood huddled in the far corner, her small purse clutched protectively against her stomach. She relaxed her stance and the death grip on her purse when she saw she was going to be sharing the ride with two policemen. Jack and Manny nodded hello, then turned to face the doors for the long, slow trip to the seventeenth floor.

"Think we'll find anything?"

Jack shrugged. "It's a crack house. We could find nothing, or the fecal matter could hit the oscillating blades, as my training officer used to say."

Manny cocked an eyebrow at Jack before understanding blossomed on his face. He smiled and tented his gloved fingers in front of his face. "Ehhh-xcellent," he hissed.

Jack snorted. "That's got to be the worst Mr. Burns I've ever heard. But I'll tell you this, if we get a body, we're taking the stairs down."

There was a horrified gasp behind them and Jack quickly turned to the elderly woman. "No, not that," he reassured her. "I meant if we arrest somebody. Not a dead body."

She edged past them when the doors opened on her floor, not looking completely at ease with Jack's explanation. Manny waved goodbye.

A man's hoarse yelling and a woman's harpy-like screeching greeted them as the doors sagged open on their floor.

"Please, not a domestic," Jack groaned, but it sure as hell sounded like one.

Manny, ever the optimist, chimed in. "Maybe it won't be a domestic. Remember what we got last time for a call about a woman screaming?"

"What? Oh, right." Visions of a self-mutilated woman flashed through his head. "Okay, I'll take a domestic."

The apartment was at the end of the hall — naturally — and they were met halfway there by the complainant. His door was open and he was leaning against the frame watching the end of the hall. An unlit cigarette dangled from his lips.

"Thought I heard the elevator."

He appeared to be in his forties, but his raspy voice sounded twice that old. Jack figured the cigarette wouldn't be unlit for long.

"You heard the elevator over that?" Manny asked. The screeching could have drowned out a buzz saw.

"Oh, yeah. My vents rattle when the doors open." He snapped open a beat-up Harley-Davidson lighter and touched the flame to the cigarette. He flicked the lighter closed with an unconscious snap of his wrist and blew a lungful of blue smoke over his shoulder into his apartment. "You guys made good time."

"We were in the area." Jack hooked a thumb down the hall. "This been going on for a while?"

"Nope," Mr. Harley-Davidson said, spitting out a bit of tobacco. "The fight I called about ended a few minutes ago. Couple guys tore outta there like their asses were on fire. This one's new. Girl with a shitty green dye job went in not too long ago and started screaming like some wild she-bitch."

"The two that ran out," Jack wanted to know. "Were they running to get away from something or being chased out?"

Mr. H-D scrunched up his face in thought and the cigarette's tip bopped up, spewing a cloud of greasy smoke into his eyes. He didn't seem to notice. "Being chased, I'd say. Weren't carrying nothing either."

"One of them a skinny white guy in a big black army jacket?" Jack was thinking of the crackhead in the lobby.

Mr. H-D thought for a moment. "Nope. Does it matter?"

"Just someone we passed on the way in."

"Customers low on cash?" Manny suggested.

"Probably," Mr. H-D agreed. "The guy in there don't seem too friendly."

"But a lot of buyers?"

"Oh, yeah. Day and night. 'Round the clock. You guys be careful. And could you do me a favour? Don't be letting him know who called."

"Anonymous call," Jack assured him.

Manny added, "Happens all the time."

"Then I'll bid you fellas good day." Mr. H-D saluted, fingers to forehead and stepped into his apartment.

Manny checked the stairwell; then he and Jack took up positions on either side of the door. They could make out the words perfectly.

"I don't care who your man is, bitch," a male voice roared. "No money, no rock. Now get the fuck outta my face 'fore I kill you."

Who could ask for a better trafficking utterance? And a death threat. Well, a quasi-conditional threat but good enough.

Now, if only he's left his door unlocked. Jack turned the knob and the door clicked open. *Sometimes the gods of policing smile on us.* Manny's thinking must have been along similar lines; his grin just about split his face in two.

Manny tapped his gun butt and looked the question at Jack. Jack nodded and rested his hand on his Glock but didn't draw the pistol. Luck had been with them so far, but there was no need to push it. Someone inside could hear the safety clasps popping open now that the door was ajar. Walking into a crack house blind was bad enough. Giving the occupants a heads-up was just plain stupid. And stupid cops ended up dead cops.

Of course, technically, they weren't allowed to draw their guns anyway. Under the Police Services Act, police officers couldn't even unholster their guns unless faced with serious bodily harm or death to themselves or someone else. Obviously, whoever had made the rules for policing had never been a cop, let alone gone through a door not knowing what was on the other side.

Manny flung the door open hard, slamming it against the wall in the narrow entryway. Jack was through the door and drawing his gun before anyone inside knew what was happening. *Anyone* turned out to be two people: the green-haired girl Mr. Harley-Davidson had seen and one very angry black guy.

They were in the living room and the woman was on her knees, but not by choice. The male had her right wrist in his hand and was wrenching it at an awkward angle. His free hand was cocked as if he was getting ready to slap her head from her shoulders. And judging from her twig-like arms, that was a real possibility. But what caught Jack's eye was the handgun tucked into the waistband of the man's jeans.

"Police! Don't move!" Jack's Glock was up and targeted on the man's chest. "Move and you die. Your choice. I've got him, Manny. Check the apartment."

"I'm on it," Manny called, moving into the apartment.

"Let her go and put your hands over your head. Do it now,"

Jack ordered, never taking his eyes from the man.

With a contemptuous sneer, the man tossed her away as if she was a piece of trash. She scurried on her hands and knees as far as the room would let her and huddled against a wall. They stood, or cowered in her case, at the points of a triangle.

Jack thought they all looked like actors out of a bad remake of *The Good, the Bad and the Ugly. If she's the Ugly, then that makes this guy the Bad. All we need now is a soundtrack.*

And as in the movie, Bad's hand was ever so slowly drifting toward his gun.

"I said put your fucking hands up. Now." Jack's words were calm, strong.

Bad had a look in his eye that Jack didn't like, as if he was calculating the odds on drawing down on Jack before Manny finished clearing the apartment. It made sense; if Bad was going for a shootout, he had to do it before he was outnumbered.

"If you reach for that gun, you die." Jack's voice turned hard. "I got news for you, bud. I'm going home tonight. I don't care where you go. Jail, hospital or morgue. Makes no difference to me."

Bad smiled and Jack knew he was going to go for the gun.

"Apartment's clear," Manny announced from behind Jack, then ducked into the little walk-through kitchen to face Bad from a different direction.

The triangle had grown a fourth point and Bad had to deal with two guns.

"Hands up. Now."

Still Bad hesitated, his eyes flickering between cops.

There was a scramble of motion to Jack's right as the woman bolted from the room. Seconds later the stairwell door slammed open and the frantic clacking of her heels on concrete quickly faded.

Guess that makes Manny the Ugly now.

And still Bad hesitated. The sneer on his lips — why did that sneer look so familiar? — had reached his eyes. It was the look of a man who had nothing to lose and was willing to gamble it all.

"Think about it, man," Manny said, sounding much calmer than Jack felt. "Two cops, one bad guy, no witnesses. Who's to say you didn't go for that gun after all?"

The silence stretched out and no soundtrack was needed to build the tension. Hours were squeezed into heartbeats. Finally, Bad raised his hands above his head, then spat his disdain on the floor.

Jack heaved a relieved sigh; Manny had the last word. "Spitting aside, that's the first smart move you made today."

"I don't believe it. I don't fucking believe it." Jack deposited Bad in the caged back seat, then slammed shut the car door. "Charged with attempted murder on two cops, not to mention a shitload of gun and drug charges and an outstanding warrant for sexual assault and he gets bail? Can you explain that to me?" he beseeched.

Manny shrugged. "Welcome to the Canadian legal system," he offered and actually, that summed it up quite well.

Bad's sneer had seemed familiar because Jack had seen it over the barrel of a gun once before. Bad, or James Dwyer, had shot through a bedroom door at Jack and Detective Mason with an assault rifle last fall. Only bad ammunition had prevented someone, cop or criminal, from dying that day.

And here he was, out on bail and back in business, self-employed and doing rather well, considering the wad of cash Jack and Manny had found on him during the search.

"What does it take to get someone held in custody? I just don't get it."

"We deal in real life, dude, but lawyers work with technicalities and judges live in, well, I don't know what world they live in, but it sure ain't this one."

"Maybe we should have shot the fucker and been done with

it," Jack muttered as he climbed into the passenger seat. They were heading to the station with the body — the elevator had been surprisingly prompt and the stairs hadn't been necessary — while Morris and Goldman were up at the apartment. Sergeant Rose was on her way over to make sure they didn't fuck anything up.

"We could have taken the stairs. He could have tripped somewhere on the walk down," Manny proposed.

All it took was a single glance at Manny's stern expression — about as natural on his face as a smile was on Staff Greene's — and Jack burst out laughing. Manny joined him and both laughed out the tension left from the arrest.

"No, thanks," Jack managed at last, wiping away a tear. "Two investigations by the SIU are enough for my career, thank you. Let's get buddy here to the station." Jack picked up the mike. "5106, heading to the station with one."

"10-4, 5106. Time, 1537." The dispatcher paused, then came back at them. "5106, I know you have a prisoner on board, but could I get you to take a look at the parkette at the southeast corner of River and Oak on your way in? I've got a call on my screen that's about ten minutes old for a male abusing a pup. Could you just spin the area, see if he's still there?"

"10-4, dispatch. We're on our way."

Jack didn't have to check with Manny. Most cops were able to distance themselves from the tragedies they encountered every day, usually by developing thick calluses on their souls, but even the most hardened coppers had a weak spot, an Achilles' heel. For some it was children. For others it was animals. And dispatchers were no different.

"Thanks, '06. The male you're looking for is short with red hair, wearing a jacket. The dog may be a German shepherd. The complainant saw him kicking the dog. Last seen by the playground."

"10-4. We're right around the corner." Jack cradled the mike. "It sounds like that asshole again."

Manny nodded. "Joey Horner. Let's hope he's still there."

There was a convenience store at the corner of Oak and River and the little park was nestled in behind it, bordered by a townhouse complex on the east and Cornwall Street on the south. A small playground and benches shaded by trees made it a family-friendly spot in warmer weather, but only if the crack-heads and dealers weren't around.

The drug trade was quiet in the park today, but that could have been due to the scout cars parked around the corner. There was no one in the park and no dog.

"Damn. This is what? The third time we've missed this prick?"

Manny nodded. "Something like that. Where to?"

"Let's take a quick look down Cornwall, then check inside the store. Something tells me James here isn't all that anxious to get to the station."

"You sure it was him? The cop with the scar?" Jesse dragged a finger through his eyebrow to illustrate in case Lisa was too stupid or cracked out to know what he meant.

"Yeah, the one with the scar," she snapped. "Now get the fuck off my back, asshole!"

"That's him. That's fucking him." Jesse rubbed his hands together gleefully. The Grinch had nothing on him for sheer evil expressions.

"What about him?" Kayne was propped against the couch, his long legs sprawled out before him.

After nipping at Jesse, Lisa rested her head on Kayne's thigh, the faithful crack poodle. Kayne absently stroked her filthy green hair.

"He's the one I told you about." Jesse was too wound up to sit still, no matter how much grass he had just smoked. He paced the floor of the one-room apartment, flicking his fingers as thoughts came to him. "The cop who iced that dealer. The one everyone was afraid of."

That caught Kayne's interest. Jesse watched, irritated and worried, as Kayne tried to focus his eyes. Jesse studied Kayne closely. He still wore the same sleeveless sweatshirt — fuck, how it stank! — and his arms were still thick with muscle despite all the crack and weed he'd smoked since Jesse had met him. But how long would Kayne last before the crack burned the muscle from him? Not long, since he was smoking more than he ate.

Kayne's pet bitch was looking pretty bad. Her face was nothing but sunken eyes and hollow cheeks. Where Kayne's face was all sharp angles and tight skin, Lisa's was slack and sickly looking. How Kayne could stand to have her touch him, let alone fuck him, was beyond Jesse. That Kayne was keeping her to himself and not letting Jesse fuck her was fine by him. Jesse wouldn't even stick his dick in her mouth for fear of what he might catch.

"The cop's name is Warren. Jack fucking Warren."

"I don't give a fuck what his name is," Kayne laughed and his crack poodle cackled along with him. Suddenly, his eyes narrowed and he peered at Jesse suspiciously. "How come you know his name? What's he to you?"

Oh, fuck. "Nothing, man. Nothing." Jesse back-pedalled frantically. If Kayne figured out that Jesse was trying to use him to exact his own revenge — although Kayne wasn't the brightest, he had a predator's natural cunning and Jesse had to make sure not to dismiss it — then he would be in shit and sinking fast. At the least, Kayne would cast him aside and the free ride would be over. More likely, though, Jesse would end up bearing one of Kayne's marks for the rest of his life. And the length of that life would definitely be in question.

"So how come you know his name?" Kayne asked again, the shrewd look never leaving his eyes.

"His name was all over the place when he iced the dealer, that's all. I got nothing against him personally." Jesse fingered his broken nose unconsciously, the one Warren had smashed into Jesse's breakfast.

Jesse heaved a sigh when Kayne waved the thought of the cop aside. Jesse still had to push forward with his plan if he didn't want to start all over again once Kayne was straight. If he planted the idea while Kayne was baked, Kayne would need just a little nudging in the right direction later. Hell, he might even think the whole thing was his idea.

Jesse squatted between Kayne's legs. He balanced himself with a hand on Lisa's grungy head. Lisa didn't mind; the crack poodle had passed out.

"This is how we can set it up. . . ."

Wednesday, 28 March
0658 hours

Staff Sergeant Greene sat stiffly in his chair, but his thoughts were not on the parade sheet before him. He had arrived at work by ten to five and by five — half an hour early, as usual — he had been sitting in the staff sergeants' office, the memo books of his officers stacked neatly on the desk before him. Every day, regardless of the shift, Greene was at the station and behind the front desk thirty minutes early. The staff sergeants he relieved were overjoyed at first, thinking they could head home early, but they quickly learned otherwise; Greene was there in order to review his officers' work from the previous day.

He examined each book to ensure they were completed in accordance with the service's rules and regulations. The date had to be underlined, the twenty-four-hour clock had to be used, the daily activity stamp — he determined that the ink pad must be running dry as most of the stamps were faint and made a mental note to have it replaced — had to be properly and fully completed and, of course, every entry had to be in black ink.

Each day he selected one memo book at random and read through it entirely, from the day's date and "Commence Duty" line to "Report off Duty" and the officer's signature. Greene assured himself he was showing no bias in the selection, but surprisingly, his hand frequently landed on Constable Armsman's book. He was appalled at the sloppy note-taking skills some of the officers displayed and had offered numerous suggestions on how those skills could and should be improved.

Once the memo books had been inspected, he checked the Morning Report to learn what had occurred in his division since he had reported off duty the previous day. On the first day of each shift, he allotted himself extra time for this task as he went through the reports for each day he had been off duty. Finally, he spoke with the staff sergeant he was relieving in order to be up to date on what was happening inside the station and out on the roads. It was disgusting how lax some of the staff sergeants were, letting the sergeants handle the running of the platoons and station, but these supervisors had learned early on that Greene would only receive his briefing from the senior supervisor and not an underling.

Once he was fully informed and prepared to assume command of the station, Staff Sergeant Greene sat at the sergeant's desk to await the arrival of his inside people. Their haphazard approach to the shift's start time had ceased soon enough. It irked him somewhat that he could not seat himself at his desk to observe them, but the cramped, windowless office allocated for the staff sergeants had no view of the front desk area. The office's size and placement — tucked off to the side, it was used predominantly for passage from behind the front desk to the hallway leading to the lunchroom and he had put an abrupt end to that habit — had been one of many items he'd raised at his first management meeting. To date, there were no plans to relocate the office or install windows.

In his forty-two years on the job, Greene had never seen such shoddy discipline, on both station and personal levels. No wonder he had been transferred from his position at the Duty Desk at Headquarters to 51 Division. He knew, well in advance of his arrival, the reputation this division held: to those outside its boundaries, 51 was seen as a penalty box, a place where problem officers were sent for punishment. To the officers patrolling its streets, 51 was a testing ground where only the strong survived and to be able to "get the job done" with its limited resources and manpower was a badge of pride.

Both versions were true to an extent, but neither of them excused the slack discipline Greene had seen from the moment he had set foot in the station's cramped quarters but, in fact, was reason enough for tighter control. Both on an individual level and on a platoon level.

What had happened to the Service or, more correctly, the Force? When Greene had proudly joined the ranks of the Toronto Police, it had been a Force, not a Service, and there, he firmly believed, lay the root of the problem. Once the name and image had been changed to Toronto Police Service, the public's perception had changed as well. Wherever you went in the world, policing was about enforcing the laws and maintaining order, not "getting to know the community" or "establishing communication and understanding" between the police and those deviant, fringe sectors of society.

Back in his street-patrolling days, on foot, not by car, although he did admit the need for the faster response the cars allowed, the law was the law, regardless of your background, religion or whom you had sex with. As a male of average height, had he screamed for special treatment and consideration when the much larger officers who made up the majority of the rank and file back then shoved him about or teased him about his shortness? Hell, no. The greater the torment they threw at him, the greater his determination to succeed. He had carried himself with unyielding resolve and had triumphed over his adversaries, winning their respect if not their friendship.

"Slack, slack, slack," Greene muttered to himself as he collected the sergeant's clipboard in preparation for parading the late half of the day shift. Sergeant Johanson would normally join him as it was the sergeant's duty and not the staff sergeant's, to read out the day's assignments, but he was occupied releasing a prisoner from custody in order to cut down on the amount of overtime the arresting officers from the night shift would be claiming. Greene was amazed at how infrequently the staff sergeants of the other platoons actually attended the parades. No discipline whatsoever.

He trotted down the stairs to the basement, his polished shoes flashing brightly in the fluorescent lights. He paused at the base of the stairs to quickly study his reflection in the door's glass. His grey hair — iron grey, he liked to call it — was cut precisely to regulation, as it had been for more than the last four decades, his moustache was trimmed, waxed and symmetrically curled and his white shirt — he had praised the initiative to change the shirts of senior officers, staff sergeants and above to white from the black of the lower ranks — was pressed to within an inch of its life.

Every day Greene set a prime example for his platoon of how an officer should present himself. Or herself, he amended with reluctance. Allowing female officers was one of the initiatives he had not embraced wholeheartedly. Or at all.

But regardless of his example, in spite of his recommendations and assistance, the officers on his platoon failed to improve. They continued to perform as individuals, shunning the cohesive unity he desired them to adopt. In unity lay strength. If they worked the same, performed the same, then errors would diminish and, in time, disappear altogether. And unity began with appearance, hence the stand-up parades. And from those inspections came discipline and from discipline came cohesiveness.

But to this date, they had rebuked his efforts.

Don't they understand? he asked himself. If they all wrote their notes and prepared their reports the same, handled calls and situations in similar fashion, then they would work as a team and a well-functioning team was always stronger than a group of individuals.

Greene watched very little television, did not own one himself; he was of the firm opinion that television rotted the mind and stunted intelligence. Prior to his assumption of command of B platoon, a television had broadcasted its mind-numbing trash constantly behind the front desk. It sat dark and unwatched now. But on occasion he had observed some of the "entertainment" it had to offer and had once viewed an entire episode of what was referred to as a situational comedy. In this case, *M*A*S*H*.

The show had initially appealed to him, or at least had failed to immediately disgust him, as it was based in a military setting. One of the characters had spoken a line intended as a joke, but Greene believed it to be an absolute truth: individuality is fine as long as we all do it together.

There was a reason the military and police wore uniforms. When were the fools under his command going to realize they could achieve more working together? Greene had entertained hope when Constable Warren had returned to the platoon. He was senior — in Greene's younger days, seven years on the job meant you had just lost your rookie status — and seen as somewhat of a hero and Greene had hoped the platoon would cement under Warren's leadership, but so far there had been no improvement, especially in Constable Armsman. Greene smiled in anticipation of taking down that know-it-all pup a few pegs. Imagine, having the audacity to tell his staff sergeant that his approach to leadership was outdated.

Greene smiled as he mentally worded the documentation that would rid the division of the cancer that was William Armsman.

At precisely seven o'clock, Staff Sergeant Greene entered the parade room.

Jack and the other officers were lined up to the left of the parade room door. Morris and Goldman were there; even Boris was present, although not looking too happy. Manny, Jenny and Paul filled out the ranks.

If Greene wants unity, he's about to get an eyeful.

As if Jack's thought had summoned him, Greene strode into the room as the arms on the old clock above the door clunked to seven o'clock. If nothing else, the prick was punctual.

Greene strode to the podium, not sparing a glance for the officers lined up for inspection and completely oblivious to the hushed, expectant silence that hung in the air. Jack felt everyone in the line stiffen to attention as Greene slapped the clipboard on the podium, turned to face his officers . . . and froze.

The seven officers stood rigidly before him, hat brims and boots freshly polished, shirts crisp from the dry cleaners, socks pulled up, gun belts loaded up with the tools of the trade. And not much else. They all stood proudly at attention in their underwear. Boris's boxers hung almost to his knees, hiding his flabby thighs. Paul's muscular legs were on full display below a pair of tiny scarlet briefs. He had tucked his shirt up under his gun belt so his shirttails wouldn't obscure his undies. Not to be outdone, Jenny's panties were so high cut they disappeared under her belt and damn, her legs were amazing. Jenny had also tucked her shirt out of the way. Jack was wearing briefs that Karen had bought for him as a gag. They were decorated with crossed pistols and sheriff stars. Manny's snug boxer briefs were all Spider-Man.

Greene stared at them, dumbfounded.

You wanted unity, prick. Well, have an eyeful. "B platoon," Jack barked. "About-face!"

As one, the officers turned smartly — they had diligently practised the about-face before parade as none of them had marched since the college — and gave Greene their backsides.

Jack paused for a count of five then ordered another about-face. He hoped the underwear parade would shock or enrage Greene. When he faced the man, he was not disappointed.

Greene's eyes were wide in shock and his lips were pressed into a thin white line. The rest of his face was red and deepening to purple. Greene looked as if he was about to erupt. Or have a heart attack. While Jack didn't wish any ill luck on Greene, if he had a heart attack . . . Well, they'd cross that bridge if it happened.

Greene didn't have the big one, but it took him a full minute to regain a semblance of composure. "Wh . . . who's idea was this?" he sputtered.

As one, the seven officers stepped forward, even Boris.

Jack couldn't help it: he grinned. *Score one for the good guys.*

"I will see all of you on charges for this," Greene blustered, seeking safety in threats.

Do one of us, do us all and I'm sure the inspector will be interested in hearing why we felt we had to resort to such drastic measures.

The purple was not fading from Greene's face. He stormed out of the room, shoving past Johanson as the sergeant was stepping in.

Johanson stared after the fleeing staff sergeant, then turned to the platoon. "What hap — He broke into a huge grin. "Don't move. I'm getting my camera."

"Hey, Jack. Did you arrest a guy yesterday? Something about a gun in an apartment?" The station operator was holding the phone with her hand over the mouthpiece.

"Yeah, Manny and I did." Jack, fully clothed, was at the front desk grabbing car keys.

"Someone wants to talk to you."

Probably his lawyer bragging his client got bail again. "You sure they want me?"

The operator, a young woman who had been hit on by practically every cop in the station, both male and female, gave him a sour look. "Well, she didn't ask for you by name, but you're the only one I know with a scar through your eyebrow. Now, do you want to take the call or not?"

Building management, maybe? "Sure. Put it through to the report room, please."

In the report room, Jack propped his hip on the counter and snagged the phone on the first ring. "Warren, can I help you?"

There was a moment's pause and Jack was tempted to hang up. Then he heard a female voice. "Is this . . . is this the officer who was at Oak Street yesterday?" She sounded young. Young and nervous.

Definitely not management. "I was one of the officers, yes," he replied vaguely, not wanting to commit himself to anything until he knew who he was talking to.

Another pause. "Are you the one with the scar?"

Okay, enough of this. "Yes, I'm the one with the scar. Now, what do you want?" Not exactly the nicest phone etiquette, but Jack felt this call was nothing but trouble and he didn't need trouble. After Operation Underwear, Greene had retreated to his office and hadn't stuck his nose out since.

Now all we have to do is sit back and wait for his response. I wonder how long it will take.

The woman's voice dropped to a whisper. "I . . . I was in the apartment."

"And?" he asked, sounding unimpressed.

"I mean . . . I was there when you arrested him."

That caught Jack's attention. "You're the one with the green hair?" She had bolted from the apartment before they could stop her. But they had been a little busy at the time. Why would she be calling?

"That's me."

"And what can I do for you?" They had Dwyer dead on a slew of weapons and drugs charges and a statement from this woman saying she had been there to buy crack would be the final knot in the noose around his neck.

"I have information for you," she whispered and Jack could almost picture her checking over her shoulder as she spoke into the phone.

"That's great." Jack tucked the phone between ear and

shoulder and pulled out his memo book. "What can you tell me?"

"No." She was quiet for a moment. "Not on the phone. I want to meet you somewhere."

Jack's enthusiasm dwindled. *You mean you want money.* "Okay, where do you want to meet? Where are you now?"

Again a brief pause. "I'm at the Sherbourne subway. Do you know where that is?"

"I think I can find it," he replied sarcastically, but she didn't react to his tone.

"Good, that's good." Not an overly bright one. But then what crackhead was? "Meet me at . . ."

Jack thought he heard her talking to someone else. If she didn't get back on the phone soon, he was going to hang up.

"Are you still there?" she asked, sounding worried.

"Yup, waiting with bated breath."

"What? Oh, I see. Um, meet me at the Glen exit. By the foot bridge? No one will see me talking to you there. And don't bring anyone else."

This was starting to sound like grade-A crap or a really bad cop movie. "And why should I come alone?"

"Because . . . because you helped me once," she said quickly.

"I did?" Jack asked.

"Yeah. I used to work at Street City. You came once when someone threw bleach on someone."

That's why the green hair had seemed familiar. She had been the complainant at the first call he had gone to with Sy. *Guess she ain't working there anymore.*

"Okay, I'll meet you. Say, ten minutes?"

"Yeah, that's good. Come alone." She hung up.

Jack sat looking at the buzzing receiver for a few moments, debating whether to go or not. Chances were it was a pile of crap; no crackhead offered anything for free. He hung up the phone just at Manny breezed into the report room looking absolutely ecstatic. He didn't care if there was documentation down the road; they had finally won a battle in the war with Greene.

Manny plunked himself down at a computer and fired up the outdated machine. Despite the stack of Crown briefs for accident court he had in front of him, he was whistling happily.

"You going to be a while with those?" Jack asked, nodding at the paperwork.

"About an hour. That okay?"

"Yeah, no problem. I've got something to do anyway." Meeting up with a money-begging crackhead was better than sitting around waiting while Manny typed. Besides, he could do a coffee run on the way back. He gave his partner a condensed version of the phone conversation.

"Sure you don't want me to tag along? Sounds kind of hinky."

"I'll be careful, Dad. And it won't take long; as soon as she asks for money, I'm outta there."

"Cool, dude. Have fun."

"Buckets of it, I'm sure."

In the car, Jack signed on as a solo unit, letting the dispatcher know he would be picking up his escort later.

"10-4, 5103, escort at the station for paperwork."

"And could you mark me going to the Sherbourne subway station for a quick follow-up?"

"10-4, Sherbourne station."

Jack could hear her keyboard clacking as she entered the information.

"Any idea how long you'll be?"

"Can't see it taking too long, dispatch."

"Sounds good." There was a pause, then, *"Nice undies, by the way, 5103."*

Ten minutes later Jack pulled onto Howard Street, the little westbound-only road that marked St. Jamestown's northern border. He passed the high-rises to his left without really seeing them. Was it just two weeks ago he and Brett had come down here in answer to Manny's foot pursuit?

So much can happen in such a short time. He scratched the scar that was his memento from 53 Division. In two weeks, he had almost lost an eye, changed divisions, been promoted, so to speak, to platoon leader, seen a guy with his head crushed and held towels to a woman's chest after she gave herself a double mastectomy. And paraded in front of his staff sergeant in his underwear.

And let's not forget catching my wife trying to get pregnant behind my back, shall we?

Jack thought about that for a minute. *Would it be so bad if Karen got pregnant?* They wanted kids, were hoping and planning for kids. So what if it happened earlier than they expected? Would it really be that bad?

"Fucking right it would be," he told himself.

A child was one thing. If Karen was pregnant now, it wouldn't be a baby, it would be a lever. And Karen and her mom would use it to pry him out of 51, out of a job he loved, away from his friends and, eventually, away from policing altogether.

"You don't do that to someone you love," he muttered.

He and Karen had hardly spoken since he'd found the pregnancy test Sunday morning. The atmosphere at home was tense, to say the least, but what was there to say? She wanted a family and a husband who wasn't a cop. He couldn't think of doing anything else, anywhere else. He was a 51 copper to the core.

"Get your head in the game, Jack; you're here," he admonished himself.

Glen Road was a little stump that jutted off the north side of Howard. It sloped gently down and was lined with old houses and a squat apartment building on the east side. It was a dead end for cars but not pedestrians: there was an entry to the Sherbourne subway station and a concrete tunnel passing under Bloor Street and leading to a pedestrian bridge that spanned Rosedale Valley. Residents of Rosedale had an almost direct connection to the subway system. Would the people living in the affluent neighbourhood ride public transit? Jack doubted it.

He eased the car to a stop at the end of the street and saw his green-haired would-be snitch step out of the tunnel. A cold wind swirled the air around her and made her huddle deeper into her leather coat. Jack zipped up his coat as he walked toward her. She watched him approach with frightened eyes.

What's she so spooked about? Dwyer's in jail and shouldn't get out this time. Jack figured he knew exactly where this was headed. *I'm in no mood for a crackhead drama queen expecting to be paid for information.*

"You called?" he asked, stopping in front of her.

She nodded, then glanced around, sharp nervous twitches. "I don't want to talk out here. People might see."

Definitely a drama queen. "Well," Jack sighed, "why don't we head down there and you can tell me what you have." He gestured to the pedestrian tunnel. He could see that the bridge was boarded up but between the mouth of the tunnel and the temporary barricade was a platform, something like an observation deck. They could stand there and have what Jack expected to be a very brief conversation.

"Really?" She seemed surprised by the suggestion but quickly agreed and led the way down the tunnel. "I'm Lisa."

"When did you stop working at Street City?" he inquired, making conversation.

"What? Oh. Um, in the winter. They fired me for no reason." She glanced over her shoulder.

Jack was sure she wanted to see if he believed her. He didn't. "That sucks," he offered.

"Yeah, it does." Lisa nodded, her head hunched between her shoulders. Jack saw only a patch of spiky green hair sitting on top of her coat. She looked like a Chia Pet.

They reached the deck and Jack squinted as he stepped into the light. Before his eyes could adjust, there was a flash of movement to his right and he was knocked off his feet. He crashed into a metal railing that outlined the deck; Jack clung to it to keep from going down.

There were two men in front of him. One of them — a crackhead by the look of his gaunt face, crooked nose and the way his army coat hung off his wasted body — was keeping his distance and massaging his wrist. Jack figured he was the one who had knocked him down. That one, cringing in the background like some hunchbacked sidekick, wasn't the problem. The problem was front and centre and in Jack's face.

Where the sidekick cringed, this man quivered with intensity. He had one muscular arm wrapped around Lisa's chest and the other held something small and dark against her throat. The hood of his sleeveless sweatshirt was up and the morning sun behind him cast his face in shadows.

"Easy, man. Let's not do anything hasty." Jack cautiously rose to his feet, his left hand out beseechingly as his right slowly stole toward his gun.

"Uh-uh, copper. Hand away from the gun or I kill the bitch." The man holding Lisa pressed his hand against her throat and she squealed as a thin trickle of blood slipped out.

Jack still couldn't see what was in his hand.

Not again. Not again!

Suddenly, it was Sy held hostage in front of him. Gone was the morning sun and the sprawling valley. He was back in that laneway, that damned laneway, and Sy's blood was fountaining through the air, vivid red across a sea of black.

No, no, NO!

"What's wrong with him?"

"I thought you said he was some kind of badass motherfucker. He looks like shit to me."

Voices. Voices in the dark. And just as suddenly Jack was back in the light and it was Lisa, a crackhead named Lisa, who was in danger, not Sy. Sy was dead. Dead and gone. Lisa was not.

"Hey, copper. You fucking pig, wake up."

Jack banished the memories, the guilt and focused on the man in front of him. Sy's ghost faded away once again.

"If you don't want this bitch bleeding out, you'd better do the fuck as I say."

"Whatever you want, man. Let's just take it easy." Jack was in deep shit and sinking fast. He'd walked right into a trap that was hidden from sight. He hadn't told the dispatcher exactly where he would be. If he called for help, the subway station would instantly be swarming with cops, but how long would it take them to find him?

"Easy, my ass." The man in the hoodie whipped his head back and the hood fell free.

And Jack's gut sank. In shit? Fuck that, he was drowning in it. The man staring at him over Lisa's shoulder was Randall Kayne. What had Mason said about him? *Don't try to arrest him on your own. He's a badass and will hurt you.* The eyes beneath the Mohawk burned with an insane bloodlust and Jack remembered Mason saying Kayne might want to cement his reputation by carving up a cop.

I'm fucked.

"You're gonna follow me, pig. If you don't, she dies. If you try anything, she fucking dies. You get the fucking picture?"

"Loud and clear."

Kayne snapped at his sidekick. "Move the fucking board. Now."

The sidekick hurried to the barricade and shoved aside a loose board, opening the way onto the pedestrian bridge. He ducked through and out of sight.

Oh, no. Fuck, no.

"C'mon, piggy." Kayne carefully backed up to the wood fencing.

Sunlight fell on his hand and Jack could see that Kayne held a piece of slate to Lisa's throat. Some might doubt the effectiveness of a stone blade, but there were people out there who had run into Kayne and would bear testimony to the stone's edge for the rest of their lives.

Kayne stepped backward through the gap in the barricade and pulled Lisa in after him.

Jack knew going onto the bridge was wrong, and every nerve in his body screamed it. If he had his gun out, he could have chanced a shot; Kayne was close enough and his whole head was exposed. But to draw, sight and fire before he slashed open Lisa's throat? Jack was good with the Glock but not that good. He had no choice. He had to play along and hope Kayne made a mistake. Either that or let a crackhead die.

Jack knew he couldn't do that; his hands were already stained with Sy's blood.

He stepped through the barricade.

Kayne walked backward along the bridge until they were over Rosedale Valley Road. Would a driver look up and see them? Unlikely. A section of the railing on the east side of the bridge was boarded up, hiding them from westbound drivers and the rising sun would be in the eyes of those driving the other way. Had Kayne planned it that way? Did it matter?

When Jack had got out of the patrol car, the wind had carried a chill with it. On the bridge, with nothing around them, the wind's icy teeth tore at him.

"Now, copper, it's just you and me." Kayne flung Lisa away.

She slammed into the boards and screamed as they bent with her weight.

"Get lost, bitch," Kayne snarled.

Lisa leapt to her feet. As she ran past Jack, she uttered a pitiful "I'm sorry" and fled from the bridge.

"Fuck me," Jack whispered angrily. The whole fucking thing had been a set-up. If he hadn't been so fucking obsessed with the shit at home, he might have seen it coming. Anger boiled inside him.

"You gonna shoot me, copper?"

"I'm thinking about it," Jack admitted, his hand resting on his Glock.

Kayne tucked his stone knife inside his belly pocket and spread his empty hands wide. "You gonna shoot an unarmed man?" He spat and the wind whipped his spit away. "Hey, Jesse," he called over his shoulder, never taking his eyes off Jack. "I thought you said he was some fucking badass motherfucker. Toughest fucking guy on the streets."

Jesse, the sidekick, hadn't fled with Lisa. Jack realized he was waiting for the showdown. He reminded Jack of a hyena, waiting on the fringe for the larger predators to make the kill. Waiting for his chance to feast.

"I tell you, Kayne," Jesse the hyena called from a safe distance, "he's the one who iced that dealer. You do him, kill him and your rep is set. Forever."

"Is that what this is about?" Jack asked in disbelief. "Your reputation?" He pointed at Jesse. "And what the fuck is your problem? What have I ever done to you?"

"What have you —" Jesse sputtered, spittle flying from his lips. "You fucking asshole!"

Eyes blazing a maniacal fury, Jesse threw himself at Jack. Jack met the attack with a stiff left jab and Jesse's nose, broken once before and never set properly, shattered again. Jesse fell to his knees and Jack shoved him away with a foot to the chest.

Kayne attacked.

Caught with one foot raised, Jack went flying and landed heavily on the wood planking. He rolled to his knees as Kayne rushed in. Jack blocked a knee to his face with his forearms, then wrapped his arms around Kayne's legs. Jack twisted, heaved and Kayne toppled. Jack scrambled to get on top of the man in the hoodie, but Kayne was too fast. Both men rose to their feet.

Training screamed at Jack the cop to pull his baton or pepper spray, but Jack the cop was gone, buried beneath a primal rage that wanted to do nothing but hurt. All the shit, all the guilt and fear that he had fought and suppressed for the past six months, tore free of their chains and raged forward.

Jack lunged for Kayne and they grappled standing up. Kayne drove a knee into Jack's stomach, then aimed another at his groin. Jack twisted and the knee slammed into his thigh. Pain, dulled by adrenalin, exploded in his thigh, but he ignored it and slammed his forehead into Kayne's face. The head butt caught Kayne on the cheekbone and Jack followed up with a short elbow to the mouth.

Kayne fought back, hitting Jack repeatedly in the body and head, but Jack shrugged off the blows, never really feeling any of them. The rage inside him was too powerful to be stopped.

Jack slammed Kayne against the metal railing. Had the railing been only waist high, Kayne might have gone right over. But it was a good seven feet high and his head clanged off a metal post. He sagged in Jack's grip, but the rage inside Jack wanted more. More pain, more blood.

He drew his elbow back and drove it powerfully, unforgivingly, into Kayne's mouth. Skin split, teeth broke, Kayne became a dead weight in Jack's arms. Jack let him drop to the planks.

Chest heaving, Jack fought to slow his breathing. He looked to his right and there was Jesse, cowering, no doubt wanting to flee, but Jack was between him and the exit. No longer was Jesse a hyena: he was a little cowardly shit.

Jack pointed a finger at him. "Stay put."

He pulled out his handcuffs and bent to flip Kayne onto his stomach. Kayne's hand lashed out fast and Jack was too slow. The slate's razor edge slashed his neck and he felt a sudden burning across his throat. He staggered, his hands to his throat.

And in that instant, when he was positive he was dying,

that little voice from the back of his head spoke again. Calmly. Condemningly.

You couldn't save Sy. Now it's your turn to die. Karen was right all along.

Jack pulled his hands away from his neck, forced himself to look at them, to look and see only a small smear of blood.

"Almost got you, copper." Kayne laughed as he used the railing to pull himself up. He swung his stone knife in lazy arcs. "C'mon, pig. Let's finish it."

Jack glanced at the blood on his hands, the blood that told him how close he had come to dying and the rage flared anew. He threw himself at Kayne, who smiled in triumph and drove the piece of slate at Jack's stomach. Against flesh the slate was deadly, but it was practically useless against Kevlar. The stone hit Jack's vest, tore through the nylon carrier and jammed against the ballistic weave. The stone bit Kayne's hand, ripping open his palm's tender flesh.

Kayne screamed and dropped his weapon. Jack didn't notice. He grabbed Kayne's shirt, spun and flung him away. Kayne hit the wood that closed the gap in the railing and the flimsy barrier broke. He clutched madly at the wood still attached to the railing, but it could not bear his weight and tore free. His scream was cut short when he slammed into the street far below.

I hope he didn't land on anyone's car.

Jack's adrenalin was fading and his thigh was knotting up like a son of a bitch. He limped over to the gap, gripped the railing firmly and leaned over. Kayne was a crumpled mass on the asphalt.

Jack wiped his throat, then licked the blood from his fingers. He spat the blood at Kayne's corpse. He doubted he would hit the body, not with this wind, but he could always hope.

There was the sudden sound of running feet behind Jack and he realized he had turned his back on Jesse. Now he was leaning out into space with only one hand holding him safe.

You idiot, you fucking idiot.

But Jesse wasn't running at Jack. Jack watched as Jesse threw himself through the barricade and disappeared into the tunnel. Jack knew he should chase him, but he was just too tired. *Fuck it. I'll get him another day.*

He pulled his mitre out and keyed it. "5103 with a priority."
Karen is going to fucking love this.

Crap. Going home in the dark. Fucking lovely.

Jack pulled his old leather jacket around him as he plodded to his car. Old jacket, old car. Old but familiar and right now he could use some simple comforts; it had been one hell of a long day.

First there was the on-scene investigation of Kayne's death. Both Sergeant Rose and the detectives tore strips off Jack for getting suckered into such an obvious trap. Then a lengthy wait at North York General Hospital only to find out what he already knew: he was beaten and bruised, but nothing was broken. The cut on his throat wasn't severe enough to require stitching. Then off to the station to be isolated in an empty office and just when he was about to go nuts from boredom the Association-appointed lawyer showed up and Jack got to repeat the whole messy story.

Right now all he wanted to do was go home and crawl into bed. With his head pulled down into his collar for warmth and his thoughts far from the parking lot, he didn't see Sergeant Rose until he almost walked into her. He stopped just short of plowing into her, but the way he felt he probably would have been the one to go sprawling.

"Sorry, Sarge. Didn't see you."

"No harm, Warren," she told him with a tight smile. "I've been hit by bigger guys than you." The sergeant was wearing her own beat-up jacket and had her car keys in hand.

"You're still not here 'cause of me, are you?"

"Yeah, but don't worry about it," she reassured him again. "Someone had to run interference with the brass and SIU for you."

"Thanks, Sarge, I appreciate that." Jack grimaced. "Another SIU investigation. Lucky me."

"Yeah, you've had one hell of a week, haven't you?" Rose looked quickly about, but they were the only people in the poorly lit parking lot. "Listen, Jack. I'm really not supposed to be talking to you about this, but I think you should know: no one on our end is looking at you as the bad guy in this. We'll leave that up to the pricks in the SIU."

"Thanks. That's good to hear."

No doubt the civilian investigators would work the evidence and statements any way they could to bring criminal charges against Jack. But that was shit to be dealt with on a later day.

"Listen, Sarge. I'm bagged and just want to get home; if I'm lucky, I can put off the fight with my wife until tomorrow."

"You're a good man, Warren," the big sergeant said, laying a comforting hand on his shoulder. "If your wife doesn't appreciate that, call me and I'll fucking tell her."

Jack smiled, picturing Karen and Sergeant Rose having a heart-to-heart. "Thanks, Sarge. I may just take you up on that. Good night."

Jack had taken only a few steps when Rose called out to him. He waited, shivering inside his jacket — as much from exhaustion as the cold — as she plodded over to him.

"Fuck, sorry, Jack. I almost forgot to tell you." She frowned as if she were having second thoughts; then she shook her head and plunged in. "You know Brett Douglas up in 53, right?"

Jack nodded. "Yeah. We worked together at times. He's a good guy. What about him?" Judging from Sergeant Rose's grim face, whatever had happened wasn't good. "Don't tell me he got involved in something, too. The last thing he needs is to have the SIU raking him over the coals."

"He's dead, Jack."

The blunt words hit him like a sledgehammer. His knees suddenly buckled and he would have hit the pavement if Rose hadn't grabbed him and leaned him against his car.

"What happened?" Brett dead? Jack had talked to him just the other day.

"He took his Glock home with him after work today and shot himself." Again Rose was brutally blunt, as she should be; there was only one way to deliver shit news and that was quickly and directly. Explanations and answers could be given later.

Shot himself? "An accident?" Jack asked hopefully, but he knew the answer.

Rose shook her head. "No, it wasn't an accident."

"Shit," Jack muttered. "I knew he wasn't feeling good, was going through some trouble, but not this. Fuck."

"I'm sorry to tell you after the day you've had, but I figured you'd want to hear it sooner than later and from someone you know."

"Yeah," Jack mumbled, nodding absently. "It sucks, but thanks again, Sarge."

"You okay to drive?" she asked, genuinely concerned. "I can have a scout car take you home."

Jack laughed bitterly. "No, thanks. I think I've had enough of the Toronto police for one day."

Rose understood. "Go home, Jack, and get some sleep. You don't have to come in tomorrow, so take advantage of it."

Another sour laugh. "Yeah, I guess I'm off until the SIU decide how they're going to fuck me."

"They may want to, but they can't," she assured him.

Jack wanted to believe her, but he wouldn't consider himself safe until there was an official ruling. Preferably etched in steel.

He settled into his old Taurus and cranked the engine. Like Jack, the engine just wanted to sleep and it refused to wake up. "Ah, c'mon, please," he beseeched the old beast and it finally coughed to life. He offered silent thanks to the car gods.

The dashboard clock told him it was 9:15. Well past his day shift bedtime. But then again he was officially off duty during the investigation. Right now he was Injured on Duty; if the SIU had their way, he'd probably end up suspended, pending charges.

"Like I give a fuck right now," he told the tired cop in the rear-view mirror and the cop agreed with him. Fuck it.

He raised a hand and gave Rose a tired wave as she drove past. Her tail lights flashed before she turned onto Regent Street and as soon as her car was out of sight, Jack broke down.

"Damn it, Brett!" he cried. "Why didn't you call me? Why did you have to . . ."

He slumped in the seat and grief washed over him, a drowning tide of pain for a friend gone forever. For minutes he sat crying and in time the rawness searing his soul faded as he buried it beneath his cop mask.

"Sorry, Brett," he said, his voice thick and sore from crying. "I just can't handle this right now."

He palmed his tears away, the heel of one hand grazing the bandage on his throat. Jack angled the mirror to check his throat. The slash had scabbed, but the scab was ugly; the doctor had slapped a bandage on it. There was so much gauze wrapped around his neck it looked like he was wearing an ascot, for fuck's sake.

To take the bandage off or leave it on? What would freak Karen out the least? Or did it really matter? She was going to use his day as fuel for her argument to leave 51, to leave policing. Never mind that he had stopped a brutal, sadistic criminal. Or — here's a thought! — maybe Jack wasn't in the mood for a fight because he had killed someone today. Did anybody think about that?

Manny had. He had made it his personal mission to see that Jack didn't go hungry or thirsty all day and when he wasn't fetching food he was Jack's doorman and bouncer, screening anybody who wanted to speak to Jack. Jenny had stopped in as well, at both the hospital and the station. The support of those two got Jack through the day. He only hoped Karen would be as sensitive.

Yeah, right.

Jack sat in his car, reluctant to head home. It wasn't right. Sy had been right all those months ago when he told Jack that a supportive, understanding spouse was a copper's greatest strength. So why was Jack thinking about taking Jenny up on her offer to crash on her couch if he needed a sympathetic ear?

"Fuck it, Jack, just head home and get the fight over with." He yawned, then scrubbed his face to wake up. "But first some caffeine."

He paused at the parking lot's exit, considering where to get his hit of caffeine. "I think I deserve some of the good stuff and maybe a cookie to go with it."

Jack turned south on Regent and west on Shuter, heading for the Second Cup at Church and Wellesley. An Earl Grey with honey and one of the oversized oatmeal cookies sounded just about perfect.

The sky was that oppressive grey-black only a late-winter night could fashion. Even the streetlights along Shuter seemed tired and dull. At least it wasn't snowing. God, he couldn't wait for summer.

Even though he was off duty, he scanned the streets as he drove. It was a habit he had developed when he transferred to 51 and it drove Karen nuts when she was in the car. He glanced at the Moss Park baseball field and hammered the brakes.

"What the fuck?"

Horns blared behind him and he swung to the curb, then slammed the car into park. He couldn't believe it, just could not believe it. Jack got out of the car and headed for the baseball diamond.

The diamond sported bleachers and in front of the metal

stands some asshole was tormenting a dog. The dog, a young German shepherd by the looks of it, was tied to the stands. The asshole was standing just out of reach, jumping in and out, teasing the dog. At least that's what Jack hoped he was doing. If the owner was doing anything worse, someone was headed for the hospital.

As Jack reached the curb, his worst thoughts were confirmed. The owner, a red-headed shrimp, darted in and landed a heavy kick to the dog's ribs. The dog yelped, then snapped back, barely missing the owner. Cackling with laughter, the owner feinted a kick, then slapped the dog on the head. The dog screamed — Jack didn't know dogs could scream — and flopped to its side. It was up in an instant, snarling teeth flashing, but the rope snapped tight and its lunge was jerked short.

"Hey!" Jack roared as he got nearer. "What the fuck are you doing?"

The man stopped his scampering and turned to face Jack. The dog strained at the rope, snarling in defiance.

"None of your fucking business, asshole," the man growled. Or tried to. His voice was as intimidating as his five-foot-nothing frame. His clown-curly red hair and disfigured nose didn't help.

It was the hair that clicked in Jack's memory. "Horner. You're the fucking asshole we've been looking for all week." Jack headed straight for the dog. There was no way he was going to let this piece of shit keep the poor dog.

"Yeah? Tough shit." The little twerp leaped at Jack, his left hand — the one he had slapped the dog with — swinging wildly at Jack's head.

Jack got his arm up to block the blow and pain lanced through his forearm. He grabbed Horner by the jacket and pulled him into a crushing head butt. The little man crumpled to the ground, blood from his newly broken nose gushing over his mouth and chin. He was on his knees and Jack knocked him onto his back with a nudge of his knee. Then he stomped on the guy's left arm, pinning it to the ground. Horner had been palming a metal pipe tucked up his coat sleeve. Jack grabbed the pipe and tossed it away. He left the tough guy curled up on the ground, crying over his shattered nose.

"Hey, buddy, you okay?" Jack spoke softly, crouching as he neared the dog. It was a German shepherd and young, no more than six months old. Its ribs were painfully visible. "It's okay, it's okay," he murmured, slowly inching closer to the dog.

The dog backed up, growling softly in its throat, but Jack kept on talking quietly and calmly. The real test would be when he moved inside the reach of the rope.

The dog's fur was matted with dirt and blood clotted the fur around the right ear. He — Jack could tell it was a male when the dog began pacing in front of him, uncertain of this new human — was in rough shape and in need of some loving care.

"C'mere, buddy. I won't hurt you. No one's going to hurt you anymore." Slowly, patiently, Jack coaxed the dog closer.

After a few minutes, the pup reached out to sniff his hand. Jack held perfectly still and let the dog come to him.

The dog growled and lunged. Jack threw himself out of the way, but he wasn't the dog's target. Horner had been sneaking up on Jack, his retrieved metal pipe held high over his head for a skull-bashing blow. The dog smashed into his chest. Horner fell backward, just out of reach of the dog's claws.

Jack's anger, on a tight leash most of the day, exploded again. Sanity was washed away in a sea of red and all that was left was a rage, primal and pure and it wanted nothing more than to beat this little piece of shit to death.

Jack threw himself at Horner and drove a knee into his ribs as he landed on him. Horner howled in pain, and Jack grabbed him by the throat with one hand and squeezed. He cocked his other arm, ready to smash Horner's face into bloody pulp. A small part of his brain screamed at him to stop; the last thing he needed was to be arrested for assault.

Jack froze, his body quivering with the desire, the need, to pummel Horner into the ground. The red haze clouding his vision slowly receded and Jack dragged Horner by the throat over to the dog and dumped him just out of fang reach. With the dog's bared muzzle inches from Horner's face, Jack eased off on his throat, then crushed a knee on his chest.

Jack lowered his face so he was as close to Horner as the dog was. "If I ever see you with a dog again, I'll fucking feed your balls to him, got that?" Horner didn't answer. "Got that?" Jack yelled.

The dog barked and Horner flinched, then nodded frantically.

"This dog is leaving with me and if you're smart — which I doubt — you'll stay down until we're gone." Jack stood.

"Who are you?" Horner asked as Jack untied the dog's rope.

Jack glared at him. "You don't want to know who I am or what I am capable of."

Horner cringed back as the growl in Jack's eyes was echoed by the dog. "But . . . but what about my nose?" he cried.

"Consider it street justice."

Jack headed for his car, walking slowly as the dog limped along beside him, favouring his right front leg.

"I hate to take you to the Humane Society, buddy, but any-where is better than with that asshole."

They reached the curb and the dog sat down as they waited for traffic. The dog nuzzled Jack's thigh and looked up with big brown eyes. And that's when Jack fell in love.

"Well, my friend, if Karen can have a baby behind my back, then I can bring home a dog. What do you say?"

Jack's new friend thumped his tail in agreement.

Here's a sneak preview of the next book in Brent Pilkey's series:

"A masterful piece about street crime."
— *New York Journal of Books* on *Savage Rage*

BRENT PILKEY

author of LETHAL RAGE

a mystery

SECRET RAGE

Wednesday, 18 July
2332 hours

The heat hung lifeless in the night air, a soggy mass refusing to relinquish its oppressive grip on the city. Star Logan stood on her usual corner at Church Street and Gerrard Street East, praying for a cool breeze. The passing cars left the air oily with exhaust fumes and she stared enviously at the people comfortable in their air-conditioned havens.

She glanced at her watch. Not even midnight. Too early and too slow a night to call it quits. But damn, it was hot. Even in a halter and miniskirt, it was hot.

"Hey, Star. How you doing, girl?"

Star looked up and smiled. "I'm doing okay, Casey, but not much business tonight."

Casey Joanes, a veteran of the downtown Toronto streets, smiled back. "I hear that, sweetness. Hang in there a little longer. The bars'll be closing soon and there's always some poor white boy who needs to get laid."

Star laughed. Casey could always cheer her up, was always there to help. Star had met her almost a year ago, after taking her first working steps on the streets. The tall black working girl had taken the young blonde runaway under her wing and taught her how to survive. They worked the corner together, watching each other's back, enduring a life neither of them had chosen.

Star was checking the cars coming north on Church and spotted the cop car. "Casey, cops on the way. Better take off."

"Thanks, sweetness." Casey sauntered away, never glancing over her shoulder at the approaching cruiser. Star admired her nerve, doubting she herself could be so cool under the same circumstances, but Casey had taught her early on about the cops. If there was a warrant out for you or if you were breaking bail conditions, the last thing you wanted to do when the cops were around was give them the old nervous glance, no matter how casually you walked away. Might as well hold up a sign saying, "Wanted. Come and Arrest Me."

Star kept an eye on the cop car. The street lights kept reflecting off the windshield, stopping her from getting a look at the cops inside. It didn't take long to learn faces, to know which cops were only passing by for a free look and which ones were apt to check you out. She was clean right now, no wants, no bail conditions, so she didn't have to hide.

As the cop car drew closer, she turned and slowly walked up the sidewalk, swaying her hips provocatively. She had a good ass and knew it. The longer she could keep the cops' attention on her ass, the more time it gave Casey to duck out of sight.

From the corner of her eye she saw the cruiser slide up to the curb and stop. Oh well, time for name, date of birth and address.

"Excuse me, miss. Could I talk to you for a moment?"

The cop in the passenger seat had to be a rookie. He was young, probably not much older than Star herself, and she couldn't remember the last time a cop had said "Excuse me, miss" to her.

She took her time walking over to the car, a bemused smile on her lips as she watched the rookie try not to look at her legs below her short — very short — miniskirt. She squatted by the door and let her eyes slide shut as she luxuriated in the cold air spilling out of the open window.

"Hey, Star, how's business?"

Oh, shit. She forcibly fixed the smile on her face before opening her eyes.

The driver slouched in his seat, a hungry leer on his fat face. He was a slob in uniform whose gut had grown out to touch the steering wheel. He was a regular in the area, always cruising by the girls, asking for free flashes, and he could be quite the shit if he didn't get what he wanted. It was hard to do business with a police car sitting at your corner.

It could be worse, though. Star had never heard of him demanding free hand or blow jobs. She figured he had a small dick and didn't want the girls laughing at him behind his back. At least, no more than they did already.

"Business ain't too good, Sean." That was another thing. He insisted on the girls calling him by name. Star had asked Casey about that once and the older sex worker had laughed and replied, "So he knows what it's like to have a woman say his name, sweetness."

"You gotta show more skin, baby doll, if you want the tricks."

"I'm not likely to get any business with you sitting here." The clammy heat was making her irritable and she almost added *Boris* but pulled it back in time. Other, less lecherous cops had told the girls in the area that Boris was Sean's nickname but warned them against using it to his face; he hated it and was likely to go apeshit all over them.

Boris brayed an ugly laugh. "Hey, Star, show the rookie why you're called Star."

"That's all right, miss. You don't have to." The young cop shifted uncomfortably in his seat, his eyes darting nervously between her face and his hands entwined in his lap. She felt sorry for him, having to ride with a pig like Boris, but also wondered how he figured he was going to make it as a cop if he didn't have the balls to look a prostitute in the eyes.

Boris whacked the rookie in the shoulder. "Of course she has to. You ain't a fag, are you, Artie?" He hawked and spat on the car floor between his legs — Star was amazed he could still hit the floor past his belly — then wiped the spittle from his lips with a meaty hand. He glared at Star. "C'mon, Star. Show him. Or I might have to drink my coffee here. And every night after — I'm working in 52 now, baby doll, so you're in my division. You're going to be seeing a lot more of me." He had ugly little eyes. The kind of eyes that told Star if he was a trick he could be cruel.

She glanced at the rookie once more to see if he had the backbone to speak up, but he sat silently, a small boy playing at being a policeman. Disgusted by the pair of them, she stood up and turned her back to them. She obediently hiked her skirt up to her waist to reveal the shooting star tattooed on her left cheek.

"Now that's an ass! Nice thong! See ya, Star." Boris peeled away from the curb.

"Asshole." She adjusted her skirt and watched as the police car made a fast right without stopping for the red. She imagined she could hear the fat slob braying like a donkey as cars braked to avoid the cruiser.

That's it. I'm going home.

She slung her small purse over her shoulder and, cursing the fool who had made stiletto heels — it had to be a man — headed home. She and Casey shared an apartment up on Maitland, a quick walk from their corner. She wondered if Casey had seen Boris's cruiser as a warning and decided to pack it in for the night. If she was home they could share some wine and the weed Star had taken as payment for a quick hand job.

She had made it less than a block when an old Honda eased up beside her. She glanced at the car and thought about ignoring the open passenger window but decided against it. It had been a slow night and she could use the cash one more trick would bring. She fluffed her shoulder-length blond hair and strolled over.

"Hi. Looking for a date?" Leaning into the open window, she gave the driver an eyeful of cleavage while she checked him out.

The first rule of survival Casey had taught Star was never — never! — get into a john's car without examining the situation first. Look for weapons, look for people hiding in the back seat, learn to read people and if anything didn't feel right, walk away. Fuck the money and walk away. Tricks are like streetcars, Casey said. Another one will be along in a few minutes.

Star had gotten good at reading johns and had only a few bad dates in her time. Nothing serious. One look at this guy and she knew his story. He was young, her age, and he wore a shapeless T-shirt, but his forearms were thick with muscle. His hair was a dull brown and it looked like he had cut it himself, hacked short and uneven. Not bad looking but his jaw was too heavy for her liking. Not that it mattered; she wasn't going to be jerking off his chin.

She figured him for a jock, maybe a university kid who couldn't get a date for the night or had one but she didn't put out. *Young and with a bad case of blue balls.* She'd be on her way home in five minutes.

The guy opened his mouth to answer her but choked on his words. Star smiled. Probably his first time with a working girl. She opened the door and slid into the passenger seat.

"How much you got, honey?"

"A hundred," he managed, his voice barely above a whisper. He glanced at her and then away. His hands anxiously gripped the steering wheel.

"Well, hon, a hundred'll get you the best blow job you've ever had." She put a hand on his thigh and he jumped. "Relax, hon. You interested?" He swallowed and jerked his head in a frantic nod. "Then turn up the AC, hon, and let's get going."

Star had a hotel room where she normally took her tricks but this one looked like he'd come before she got his zipper down so she opted to stay in the car. Rolling up the window to take full advantage of the AC, she directed him to a laneway off Gerrard and had him park close to the street but out of sight.

"Business before pleasure, hon. You'll enjoy it more if we get the money out of the way first."

Rule number two: always get the money first.

He reached into his jeans with a trembling hand and pulled out two crumpled fifties. The bills disappeared professionally into Star's purse. He was back to gripping the wheel and staring out the windshield. Poor guy. Some cocktease of a bitch had probably stuck him for dinner and a movie and left him hanging.

"What's your name?" She hardly ever asked a john his name but this one was so pathetically nervous she felt sorry for him.

"T — ah, Tim. Why?" He looked startled she had asked but at least he was looking at her.

Star smiled. If he didn't want to use his real name, Tim was fine by her. "I like you, Tim. I want to give you a little extra." Whether it was the long, slow night or a bad feeling left over from Boris's visit, she couldn't say, but she wanted this john to really enjoy himself and maybe she could have a bit of fun herself.

She popped the clasp on her halter and let it slip down her arms. Her nipples puckered in the car's cold air. She shook her breasts at him and smiled. "Do you like them?"

He could only stare and nod. Despite the cold air blowing through the vents, sweat beaded his brow.

Star snuggled into him. She could feel the muscles in his arm where her breasts pressed up against it. She slid her hand across his chest and he flinched. Hard muscle, not huge like a body-builder but definitely a jock. Her hand slid lower. She could feel his stomach muscles quivering under her touch.

"Relax, hon. Lie back and let Star take care of you." Her fingers expertly popped the button on his jeans and inched the zipper down. "You got something in there for me, Tim? Something big and hard?"

His elbow smashed into her jaw, rocking her back in the seat. Pain exploded in her mouth and she tasted blood. The thought that Casey would be very disappointed in her judgement flashed through her mind before the john rammed his fist into her nose. She felt and heard her nose break. All thoughts of Casey vanished in a wild surge of panic.

Oh my God, he's going to kill me!

She opened her mouth to scream but he was on her, a powerful hand clamping shut her throat, cutting off her voice and air. He dragged her close, close enough to kiss.

"You're a fucking whore," he snarled at her and she could hear the hate in his words as he spat his anger in her face.

She went for his eyes, gouging flesh. He roared and shoved her away. Her head smacked against the passenger window, shattering stars across her vision. Dazed, half-blinded by pain, she groped for the door handle. If she could get out she could run, reach the street and people. Safety was there. All she had to do was open the door.

Her fingers found the handle. Pulled. The door jerked open just as strong fingers dug into her hair, dragging her back. She tried to turn, to go for his eyes again, but he smashed her head against the dash. Again. And again.

He flung her back into the seat, her consciousness all but gone.

"Fucking whore."

She barely heard his words through the drumming in her ears. And the pain, so much pain. Better yet to just let go, sink into the darkness, away from the pain. Escape. But a part of her wouldn't let her escape, the part that stayed free while johns used her body, distanced her from the daily filth, forced her to stay awake. To survive.

She knew if she continued to fight back she would die so she sagged in the seat, feigning an unconsciousness that was so tantalizingly close. She lay there as rough hands pushed at her skirt. She did nothing as they ripped her underwear. She survived as fresh pain tore through her.

Dimly, she heard someone crying.